Visit the author's website at:

www.joannebodin.com

Orchid
of the
Night

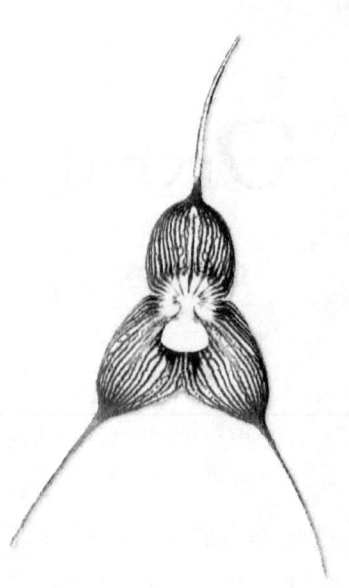

Orchid

of the

Night

J. S. BODIN

Orchid of the Night

ISBN: 978-1-940769-64-6

Also available on Kindle

Publisher: Mercury HeartLink

Printed in the United States of America

Front cover image: *Dracula vampira* orchid

photo copyright ©Gary Meyer

Mercury HeartLink
www.heartlink.com

Orchid of the Night

Part One

Part Two

ACKNOWLEDGMENTS

Although this book is a work of fiction, it is inspired by real events. Names and places have been changed in order to preserve anonymity. I could not have written this book without the help of the following people. First, I would like to thank Steve Fisher, Sherry Robinson, Deborah E. Lieberman, Jane N. Cole, Kenneth Cole, Keith Mead, Judi Mead, Susan M. Brych, Mable Orndorff, Eddie L. Plunkett, Clark Haskins, Vicki Haskins, Kathy Mancini, Barbara Lipchitz, and Les Lipchitz, all dedicated members of the New Mexico Orchid Guild. I would also like to thank Gary Meyer of Hawk Hill Orchids for his detailed consultant work, journaling vignettes, and expertise on the *Dracula vampira* orchid. A special thanks to Peter Grahame and Henry Seale for wonderful meals and discussions that inspired my research into the gay liberation movement.

I would also like to thank my two children, Aaron and Stacy, for their unwavering love and understanding, and my ex-husband Stuart Tolchin and his wife, Irene Aguilera, for their incredible support and friendship. A huge thank you to Don Morgan and Jeanne Shannon, dear members of my writing community, for their encouragement and support. Thank you to Roberta Murata for her unwavering friendship, her editorial skills, and for being my literary critic. Thank you to Jules Nyquist for her inspirational writing classes where I learned so much about the use of literary conventions. Thank you to Shirley Blackwell and Gail Turnmire for their brainstorming sessions. Thank you to Andi Penner and Susan Paquet for taking the time to comb through the manuscript and to give me invaluable feedback. I want to particularly thank the late Bob Gassaway for his expertise on police work and forensics, and for his countless hours of "tea and talk," at our hang-out in Albuquerque. Thank you to Steve Brewer, mystery writer and mentor. Thank you to South West Writers of Albuquerque, New Mexico. None of this could have happened if I hadn't joined your organization where I had access to classes, workshops, and an entire community of writers. Thank you to Gary Doberman, whose expertise and advise has allowed me to pursue my dream of writing as a profession. A special thanks to my editor, Joan Rogers, without whom this book would never have come to fruition. Her incredible knowledge base, her attention to detail, her flexibility with scheduling, and her insightful editorial comments were invaluable. A special thank you to my publisher, Stewart Warren of Mercury Heart Link for finding a home for *Orchid of the Night*.

And finally, thank you to my partner of twenty-six years, Rona Fisher, whose love and encouragement has allowed me to fulfill my dreams.

To my two wonderful children,
Aaron and Stacy,
and to my partner Rona.

Orchid
of the
Night

BETWEEN WORLDS

between the worlds are shadows

where shimmering rivers run clear on the surface

and skies paint the desert with brilliant colors at sunset

it is in the shadows that reality and illusion merge into one

silhouetted under the surface we float downstream

where humanity and the natural order of things find balance

each day we greet the dawn with our

morning cup of dark roast coffee

and our blind adherence to routine

but the shadows are all around

they form the spaces between leaves of trees

cast patterns along our desert landscape where

reflections of white billowy clouds hover above our reality

and in the darkness of night they turn our world upside down

where we have no restrictions no boundaries no control

shadowdream

a place where night crawlers cling to tendrils of illusion

wait for the first rays of sunlight

yet images linger

signs are all around to point the way back

a flicker of candlelight

a baby's cry

the smell of hot chocolate

the sound of a barking dog

a crow flying south

a rain shower

only some can find their way back

only some can hover between the worlds

where night and day merge into one

and where the shadowdream becomes their reality

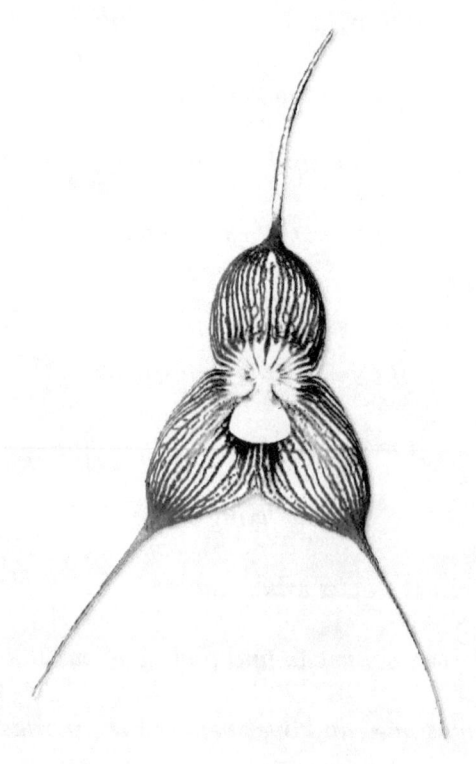

4   J. S. Bodin

PROLOGUE

Officer Andy Gomez fell to his knees. Uncontrollable heaves racked his entire being, his vomit landing on the moldy, soggy carpet beneath him. He tried to avert his eyes from the dead body lying naked, face down. A double-bed mattress, half-covered with a moldy sheet, was all that separated the body from the mire and slush of the water-soaked carpet below. When he arrived at the scene, it all unfolded like a dream, in slow-motion. First the putrid smell, right out of a sewer. Then the sliding glass back door unlocked, opening into a room beyond description. The sound of running water. The slow, uncertain resonance of his feet walking on the soggy carpet, deeper into the mire of mold and mist. The bathroom. Water spewing from a broken pipe behind the toilet. The half-dead dog at the foot of the bed. He clenched his stomach, picked up the animal, and made his way outside, taking in deep breaths of Tempe air. A salmon glow hinted of sunset over the Arizona desert. As he looked down at the small dog, now beginning to show signs of life, the scene of the dead body in the bedroom flashed before his eyes. He thought, *Poor bastard. What did he do to deserve this?*

Part One

"*In a world where death is the hunter... there is no time for regrets or doubts. There is only time for decisions.*"

—Carlos Castaneda, *Journey to Ixtlan*

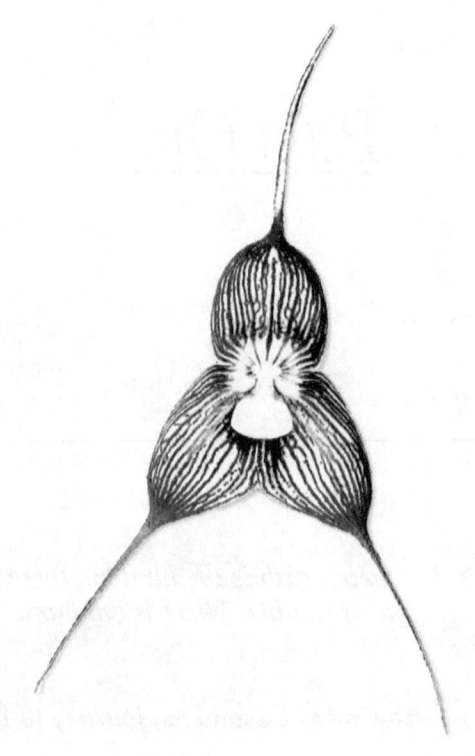

CHAPTER ONE

Maui

The faint smell of charred remains lingers in early-morning mist, sending Kyle into the depths of despair. Smells do that to him. Like the smell of rotten eggs, or coconut suntan lotion, or tangy aftershave, or salty air, or mold. He hates early morning. His Aunt Molly tells him he's just like his mother, a night owl. Why can't things be either light, or dark? Nothing in between. Early morning is worse than twilight, when sunlight fades into hues of brilliant color off the Maui shoreline. There's no color in early morning, only a gray mist that holds the smell of death mingled with the odor of burnt palm branches and salt air. The fire had engulfed the three greenhouses, along with the main house. Gasoline was the culprit. Some say the arsonist knew Kyle and his Aunt Molly. Others say it's a random act of violence. Kyle wonders if the smell is just in his mind. How can he still smell the burnt flesh of his Aunt Molly? It has been almost three days since the fire.

Smells aren't the only things that swirl around in his head like sharp pinprick openings into meandering recesses of memory. As hard as he tries to redirect his thoughts, he can't seem to dig his way out of ghoulish dreams of childhood. The shadowlands, where creatures of the night comfort him, ease his longings, and direct him to places imagined only in nightmares—that's where he belongs. He's just like his mother, a creature of the night. It doesn't take a full moon to arouse him, only the sweet pungent odor of plumeria, strongest in the evening hours, and he sinks into nocturnal realms, goes on the prowl, covers his signature carrot-orange hair with a black hoodie, blends into the underbelly of Maui night life where he's slammed against the brick wall of dissociation. The secrecy, the underworld of the nightlife of gay bars and the street scene where he finds others who, like himself, wallow in forbidden realms.

ଔ   ଔ   ଔ   ଔ

Kyle's small metal trailer sat at the back of the property near the charred remains of the main house. The trailer, untouched by the fire, a place to crash if he got home too late after hanging out at the gay bars. Aunt Molly had been a sound sleeper. As long as he'd stumbled into the house before she woke up, his late-night antics had gone undetected. But none of that mattered now. Maybe it was for the best. How long could he have kept up his charade? It had been Molly who raised him as her own son after his mother died. She'd made sure he'd gone to school every day, telling him to buck up and ignore the bullies who teased him: "Girly girl, sissy, Reddylocks." Hawaiian boys let their thick black hair grow down past their shoulders. The girls loved it that way. So Kyle let his wavy, thick red locks grow down past his shoulders too, but not for the girls. On the playground he used to stand out like a beacon of red light in a sea of black.

If it hadn't been for his Aunt Molly, he would have ended up in the foster care system. Molly would tell people, "Orchids are my children—that is, until Kyle came into my life." With the same red-orange hair and freckled skin, they looked like mother and son. His mother, who had silky black hair, used to joke with Molly that they came from two different fathers. Like night and day, the sisters' lives took divergent paths from the time they were children. Molly tried to keep her sister away from the booze and uppers that whipped her around from the time she was a teenager into fits of hysteria, depression, and finally into the nightlife of Maui's underworld.

A knock on the door pulled Kyle out of his half-awake stupor. "You up yet? I've got hot coffee and fresh muffins. Open up."

Kyle rolled over in bed. "Hold on. The door's locked."

It was Sara Santos. She lived less than a mile down the

road on a sugar plantation that had been in her family for generations. Sara was like a second mother to him. She was the one who helped Molly through the grieving process after the loss of her sister. It was Sara who sat up nights with Kyle when he had nightmares about the "boogie man" who lurked in the shadows of his mother's bedroom the night she was murdered.

The Marlboros take up most of the top shelf of the freezer, holding a prominent place above the frozen bottle of vodka. On the second shelf, a box of Eggo frozen waffles and Oscar Meyer wieners. The bottom shelf holds a paper bag full of frozen soup bones for Rover, the black lab. But it isn't what is in the freezer that catches Kyle's attention that night, even though he's hungry. He hasn't eaten since breakfast. When his mother is in her bedroom with one of her "callers," he has strict instructions never to leave his bedroom until she gives him three knocks on his door. Usually it is so late that he's already fallen asleep, but this night is different. He knows his seventh birthday will come with the sunrise. He can't sleep. All he thinks about is the new train set he will get. His mother has promised him the set if he is a good boy. If he doesn't leave his room at night. If he doesn't cry at school when he's bullied because of his red hair and freckles. If he does his chores for the dog. He wants so badly to go into the kitchen to find something to eat, but he knows there is no edible food inside the refrigerator. His mother has thrown out the sour milk, the moldy white bread, the moldy bologna and peanut butter. She says she'll take him into town for his birthday and buy him a hamburger and fries at Joe's Hamburger Hut. And he knows he can't eat what is in the freezer without making noise while he puts the wieners or Eggos into the toaster oven.

His bedroom is right next to the kitchen. He hasn't gotten used to the harsh sounds coming from the freezer, as the ice maker clunks out cubes at irregular intervals throughout the night. But the sounds are a small source of comfort as he lies in his bed trying not to hear the sounds coming from her bedroom. Usually it is muffled cries or yells. She tells him that it is just her way of having fun with her callers. That adults like to make those kinds of sounds in bedrooms. But, just like the ice maker, her sounds irritate him to the point that he has to hide inside his closet and shut the door in order to fall asleep.

This night is no different. He decides to curl up on the sleeping bag on the floor of his closet. He keeps the door open a crack so there is a tiny ray of light. Her sounds seem louder than usual. And her caller's sounds are also getting loud. He hears her cry out, "No, please don't hurt me again." Then the caller yells, "You slut, you deserve it." There are some new sounds coming from his mother. Sounds that he's never heard, like when he brushes his teeth and has to gargle. He opens the door to the closet and slowly opens his bedroom door. A shadow of the caller whizzes by him. Then he hears the front door slam. He calls out for his mother. No answer. He tiptoes toward her bedroom. There are candles by the bed, and in the flickering *light he sees something red next to her naked body on the floor. He walks over to her. Rover has already started licking the blood from her neck. Her eyes have a vacant look. There is blood everywhere, and the lingering smell of tangy aftershave. He goes back into his bedroom closet, shuts the door this time, and in the darkness he disappears, soaring above the volcanoes and palm trees into white billowy clouds, and sinking into the soft white sands along the shore of Maui's crystal-clear ocean.*

Sara pounded on Kyle's trailer door again. He rolled out of bed, stumbled to the door. "You look like shit. Here, have some fresh coffee." She entered the trailer with a ceramic mug in each hand and a cloth bag draped over her right shoulder.

He took the coffee mug from her hand and stared into the swirling steam, then set the mug on the table. Sarah put the cloth bag on the table next to the mug. "Pineapple muffins. Made them early this morning. Have one."

He absently reached into the bag, took out a muffin, and pulled up a chair next to the table. The aromas of freshly brewed coffee and freshly baked pineapple muffins filled the small trailer. Kyle closed his eyes and lifted the hot mug to his lower lip.

On the beach with his mother, running through the lush undergrowth of palm branches toward a stretch of white sand. Metal pail and shovel hooked on his shorts with a gold chain clanking against the metal. His mother follows behind him.

"Kyle, be careful. Don't trip. Wait for me; I'm coming." He reaches the clearing and looks out at the pure-white sand and crystal-blue ocean. Surfers on distant waves punctuate the blue with specks of red, orange, and purple. He takes off his sandals and runs barefoot in the warm sand toward the water. His mother puts out an orange towel with blue fishes embroidered around green seaweed, lies face down on the towel, and takes off her shirt. "Kyle, come over here. Put some suntan lotion on my back."

He smiles, turns around, and runs through the crystal white sand toward her. She's sipping hot cinnamon-flavored Kona coffee from a large Styrofoam cup. He picks up a tube of coconut suntan lotion and squirts the sticky liquid on his mother's silky back, then along the backs of her legs. Then he rubs his hands together and cups them in front of his nose, smells the scent of coconut, looks out toward the water, and squints to keep out the sharp light from the sun's rays.

His mother turns over and says, "Now the front." Kyle dribbles the lotion along her bare breasts, her stomach, and down toward her bikini bottom. Tiny hands work the lotion along her smooth skin like he was back in kindergarten, finger-painting. He leans over her mouth and gives her a kiss, letting the aroma of the cinnamon coffee fill his nostrils. Her eyes slowly open and she squints into the bright sunlight, reaches for her sunglasses, and says, "Now you."

Kyle sits next to her while she rubs the gooey lotion all over his thin body. She takes his face into her hands and smears lotion along his forehead, his cheeks, and puts a dab on his nose. Lotion covers his milky-white freckled skin like a thin layer of whipped cream. "There, my little man. You're good to go."

He jumps up and runs to the water, letting the frothy liquid run along his toes and up his calves. He yells out, "Mom, can you see me?"

"Of course, darling. Don't go out too far."

Sara reached over and took the coffee mug from his lips. "You been smoking that pot again?" She sniffed around his trailer. "You've got to wake up, get alert. Officer Miles called me this morning. He wants to talk to you later."

Kyle squirmed in his chair. "The police?"

"Said they called you but your phone's dead." Sara gathered up the bag of muffins. "Why don't you come to my place? It'll be better there. Your place is a mess. And it, well, it...." She lowered her head. "You know what I mean." He looked up at her. She was looking out toward the burnt palm branches. He knew exactly what she meant.

"I'll be over later, thanks."

After Sarah left, Kyle crawled back into bed and covered his head with the sheet. He wished she wouldn't treat him like a child. He was tired of being mothered. Sara's good intentions made it even harder. As he started to drift off, he had an image of his aunt lying in a heap of ashes, indistinguishable from the rest of the charred vegetation. *How can this be happening? Who would want to destroy Molly's property? Who would want to kill her?* Everyone knew how hard her life had been. First the murder of her sister, then a few months later the untimely death of her husband, his Uncle Russ. When she refused to leave the house after Russ died, Sara Santos had organized the neighbors to bring food over to the house every day. It took months for Molly to come out of the depression. But when she did, she became even more active in the orchid community. She said it was her way of leaving a legacy for her husband. She hosted lavish events in front of the main house for the Garden Society of Maui, inviting members and their families. She hired a caterer to make the more traditional Hawaiian foods, but she insisted on making two of Russ' favorites —macadamia nut-crusted coconut shrimp, and Hawaiian sweet potato pie. She hired hula dancers for entertainment, and her greenhouses were open for her guests to buy plants. The tribute to her late husband was just the beginning. Every year Molly held a special greenhouse tour and fundraiser, inviting the Garden Society's families and friends. Again, she hired a caterer and had entertainment. Money from the sales of her orchid plants went into a special scholarship fund in her late husband's name. The yearly scholarship would go toward a child's college education.

Officer Miles seemed to be the harbinger of bad news. He was the one who had brought Kyle and his dog Rover over to Molly's the morning after his mother was murdered. The police found her lying naked in a pool of blood with her throat slashed ear to ear. Kyle was found in his bedroom closet. When Molly took him inside her place, his eyes had a vacant stare. Officer Miles told her that he hadn't uttered a word since they found him. They tried to get him to tell what he saw, but he just stared ahead. They called it a catatonic state induced by trauma.

Molly tried to muster a smile as she said, "Kyle, do you know what today is? It's your seventh birthday. I have something special for you in the kitchen." She thanked Officer Miles and led Kyle into the kitchen, poured a glass of cold milk, and set it on the table next to a plate of freshly baked chocolate chip cookies. But Kyle didn't respond at all. He stared straight ahead with that vacant look in his eyes. This wasn't the Kyle she remembered. Ever since he started talking in complete sentences at age two, he would chatter about everything he saw, everything he was thinking. It was actually annoying to most people, but Molly knew how bright Kyle was. He got it from her side of the family, most likely, although it could also have been from his father…if only her sister knew who Kyle's father was. By the time he was five, he'd memorized almost all of the scientific names of the orchids in the greenhouse. Uncle Russ would go through the various plants, pull out the tags, and have Kyle spell the names until he knew them by heart. Once, during an AOS judged show, Kyle was the star attraction. He walked around with his uncle and read the tags for each entered plant. The local TV station even featured him on the morning news as the "orchid boy genius." By the time he was six, he was making up stories about the orchid adventures he'd gone on with his uncle in search of rare orchid species in far-off lands. Kyle had learned to live in his own fantasy world. Molly knew how difficult it was for him when her sister brought home her "callers." She even offered to keep Kyle with her, maybe get custody. But her sister made it clear that if Molly tried to take Kyle away from her, she'd leave Maui and never let her sister see Kyle again.

A few months later, the dreaded early-morning knock on the door. The same officer came to tell Molly that Russ didn't make it after his small motor boat capsized in the Amazon River during an orchid expedition. Molly's face went blank as she said, "I'm not surprised. It was just a matter of time. If it wasn't yellow fever or malaria, it would have been something else. What happened?"

Officer Miles stammered, "F-fell overboard. They tried to fish him out before the gator got him, but... I'm so sorry."

Molly knew how dangerous Russ' orchid expeditions had

been. There were so many dangerous trips. Some, he'd come home with malaria, with ant bites that were infected, with intestinal parasites. She'd known all of this when she married him. He called it "orchidelirium." Said he couldn't help himself. To help justify his reasoning, he would read to her from one of his many orchid books, hoping that she'd understand his obsession. His deep, commanding voice echoed in the small study while he read. "Orchidelirium was the name given to the Victorian era of flower madness when collecting and discovering orchids became the rage. Wealthy orchid fanatics of the 19th century sent explorers and collectors to almost every part of the world in search of new varieties of orchids, often resulting in the theft of exceptional orchids, black markets, and other illegal orchid activities."

Molly's lips quivered. "Are they flying the body home?"

"They said it will take a few weeks."

Molly knew what that meant. *That is, if there was anything left of the body after the gator had his fill.*

Sara knocked on the door of Kyle's trailer. "Kyle, open up. The police are on their way to my place now." Sara hadn't made it even halfway home when she saw the police heading toward her house.

Still in a daze, Kyle lumbered out of bed, grabbed his inhaler, and opened the door. Sara stood outside on the step while Kyle put on some sandals and a clean Hawaiian shirt.

They left together and walked along the dirt road to Sarah's sugarcane plantation. Morning light flickered through the thick vegetation that lined the same road Kyle had walked hundreds of times before. But this time was different. He noticed every shadow, heard every sound, and smelled every smell. He couldn't keep up with Sara so he called out to her, "You go on ahead. My asthma is acting up." He stopped to take a couple of puffs of medicine. He hated having asthma, especially because the doctor said it was probably all psychological. It started when he went to live with his aunt after his mother's murder. He'd wake up in the middle of the night wheezing, barely catching his breath, sometimes needing to be taken to the emergency room. As soon as he got his inhaler he felt more secure. He had his "magic puffer," as Molly called it, to use in the middle of the night when he'd wake up in a sweat, gasping for air. His inhaler had become like a security blanket. He never went anywhere without it.

When they arrived at Sara's place, he saw a police car parked in front of the huge wrought-iron gate that opened to the plantation. Sara walked ahead to let them in. A young Hawaiian girl came out of the house with a tray of cold papaya juice. They sat outside on the patio. Officer Miles turned toward Kyle. "My, how you've grown. You probably don't remember who I am, but I remember when you were just a kid."

Kyle looked up.

"Yep. You were about seven when I...well, when I came to your aunt Molly's door for the first time. In fact, now that I recall, it was on your seventh birthday."

Kyle squirmed in the chair. "I'm sorry. I don't remember much from then."

"I understand. You were pretty traumatized. You and your aunt have really had a streak of bad luck."

Kyle didn't answer.

"So, anyway, I need to ask you some questions. I hope you don't mind. I know how hard this is for you." Kyle looked up at the officer, then pulled out his inhaler and took a puff of the medicine.

"So, where were you the night of the fire?"

Kyle tried to stay focused. "I was...well, I was with a friend."

"You'll need to give me a name." Officer Miles grinned. "Look, don't worry. It's okay. Just tell me the name so we can check out your alibi. It's standard procedure."

Kyle knew if he just stayed calm they'd prove his innocence, but instead he blurted out, "Look, I feel like shit. It's my fault that she's dead. I should have been there to save her."

Sara spoke. "No it's not. You couldn't have known."

Officer Miles reached for Kyle's shoulder. "Son, this is not your fault. Just let me help you now. Who were you with the night of the fire?" He winked at Sara. "Son, I'm sure she won't mind if you give her name. That way we can rule you out as a suspect."

Kyle tried to hide his shock. *She? Of course. The perfect alibi.* His eyes darted back and forth, then he blurted out, "Lilly. I was at her place." *Lilly always covers my ass.*

"Lilly Salmon, the judge's daughter?"

"Yeah, that's her."

"Good-looking girl. Know her dad pretty well. I'll talk to her tomorrow."

Kyle picked up the papaya drink and gulped it down. He couldn't possibly tell the truth. How could he tell them he'd been with Lilly's father that night...that he'd been the judge's "twink" since he was fifteen? First the streets, then gay bars, eventually building up to high-end clientele. The judge had become his sole provider, paying Kyle enough that he dropped everyone else. Well, almost everyone else. He still had Danny. His first. It started behind Molly's greenhouses in a grove of coconut palms where they'd go to smoke weed. They were both thirteen. They'd been buddies since second grade, but after a few years they started fooling around like boys do, and one thing led to another. Danny was the dominant, Kyle pretty much the submissive. Once in a while they'd switch, but Kyle liked to serve. Danny tried to keep Kyle on a short leash. As they got older Danny said he didn't trust him anymore, that

Kyle was acting weird, distant. Danny had no idea Kyle was fucking the judge. Besides, the judge was way out of Danny's league. To pacify Danny, Kyle would give him gifts —gifts that he'd gotten from the judge. Danny loved gifts.

Wandering the dark streets of Maui's nightlife, black hoodie covering his red hair, Kyle heads toward his most lucrative pick-up spot in front of the Butterfly Lounge, hoping he'll make a few bucks giving blow jobs. He needs cash for pot. A car pulls alongside, a window rolls down, a voice says, "Kyle."

Not one of his regulars. He gets in and sits on the soft brown leather seat. "Judge Salmon, what are you doing here?"

The judge's face flushes. "Me? What are you doing here?" The judge coughs, then starts up the car. They drive a few miles in silence; then the car pulls into an underground parking lot. The judge unlocks the doors and motions for him to get out. They walk to an elevator and go to the eleventh floor. They walk down a carpeted hallway to room 1106. The judge takes out a card key and opens the door. They go inside. Kyle looks around the room, clearly a suite, with a panoramic view of the ocean. He takes a seat on a white leather couch. The judge walks over to a full service bar and pours himself a glass of brandy. Kyle looks out of the window, sees flickering lights from off-shore boats; the rest is darkness.

The judge takes out a carton of milk from the refrigerator. "Here, have some."

Kyle pours himself a glass. He asks the judge what he wants. Says, "So, you like them young?"

The judge walks over to the white leather couch and sits down. He says, "This is so awkward."

Kyle says, "Is this where you like to take your twinks?"

The judge smiles. Kyle reaches for the zipper on the judge's black trousers—probably a designer label. The judge says, "Promise you'll never tell Lilly about this." Kyle nods, then unzips the pants and puts his warm mouth over the half-erect cock. After their encounter, Kyle doesn't do the streets again. He's found himself a sugar daddy who wants to protect him from the harsh street scene. The judge gives him a gold bracelet.

Officer Miles reached inside his jacket pocket, pulled out a gold chain bracelet in a plastic bag, and held it in front of Kyle. "Know anything about this? We found it at the crime scene next to an empty can of gasoline." Before Kyle could answer, the officer's cell phone rang. He answered it and said, "I've got to go. Sorry. I'll come back later." He didn't notice that Kyle's face had drained of color. Kyle knew exactly who set the fire—and it wasn't meant for his aunt, it was meant for him. *This can't be happening. That shit, Danny. He's gone ballistic. Why's he doing this?* Then Kyle remembered the look in Danny's eyes when he told him he didn't want to hang out with him anymore. It was the same look Danny had when he talked about his stepfather—vacant, almost evil. It had been a few weeks after Kyle started up with the judge and Kyle's whole life had suddenly changed. Now he could quit the street scene. The judge had offered to take care of him. He'd moved up in the world, and Danny had become a liability.

ଔ   ଔ   ଔ   ଔ

It was now late afternoon. Lilly waited inside Kona's Cafebrew for Kyle. When he arrived, Kyle walked over to her table, sat down, reached into his backpack, and took out a paper bag. "Here. Locally grown, no pesticides." Lilly took the bag of pot and slipped it into her purse.

"Look, I need an alibi for the night of the fire. The police are going to talk to you tomorrow."

"Me?"

"It's just a matter of time until they put two and two together."

"What do you mean?"

"Cops found a gold bracelet in the rubble of the fire, exactly like the one Danny wears."

Lilly's face turned white. "Shit. He loved that bracelet. Never took it off. Do you really think he set the fire?"

"Don't know yet, but I can't stay in Maui. Danny's getting crazier every day. Has that look in his eyes —you know, the one he got when he tortured those animals before he buried them near our fort."

"But why would he want to kill you? Maybe it was just an accident during one of his drugged-out drunken rages."

Kyle looked down at the table. Lilly. She had no idea about some of the things Danny sucked him into when they were younger. He answered, "I know it's him. I've seen him following me around—like he's stalking me or something. He hates that I've moved on, won't fuck him anymore."

"Maybe you should tell this to the police."

"No. There's no actual proof yet, and frankly, I don't want them snooping around in my life. I'll leave Maui. You're off to college soon. And now that Molly is gone, I have no one. It's the only way. I know Danny. Once he gets something into his head, he doesn't stop. He's been jealous of me for years. Probably wants me all to himself. But that'll never happen." Kyle looked around the room. There were only a few people left. No one he knew. He fidgeted in his chair while Lilly got up to order coffee for both of them.

Danny and Kyle meet at the secret fort behind Molly's greenhouses. This time Danny has a fresh cast covering his left arm, shoulder to wrist. He tells Kyle his stepfather broke his arm during one of his drunken rages. Kyle reaches out to touch the cast. Danny flinches. "Don't touch me," he says, then bursts into tears. Kyle asks if he can sign the white cast, be the first one. *Danny nods. Kyle takes a pen from his backpack and writes "Reddylocks." Danny smiles. Kyle takes a toke from the joint he's just rolled and offers it to Danny. He asks Danny what he will tell the teachers and the kids at school.*

Danny says, "I'll tell them I fell off my bike and broke my arm."

Kyle asks, "Who took you to the doctor to get the cast?"

Danny answers, "I did. I rode my bike to the hospital, and they believed me about how I broke my arm." Danny sits on the dirt inside the fort and just stares ahead. Kyle knows something is up. Danny never sits quietly unless he's hatching one of his crazy schemes. Danny blurts out, "I want to kill him."

Kyle squirms. "What?"

Danny says, "You heard me—I want to kill him."

Kyle asks, "How?"

Danny's eyes dart back and forth while he thinks. Then he says, "I don't know—you're the genius. Help me out here."

Kyle paces back and forth over the dry palm branches outside the fort. "Does your stepfather ever hike Haleakala?"

Danny says, "Yeah, every Sunday morning. How'd you know?"

Kyle smiles. "It's something you once told me he said.

That he keeps fit so he can keep you in line by beating the crap out of you."

Danny takes another hit of pot. "So what?"

Kyle says, "Maybe you can hitchhike to the top one Sunday before he gets there... then you can, well, you know...."

Danny's eyes open wide. "You mean, push him off the edge?"

Kyle sees that wild look in Danny's eyes. He's afraid Danny took what he said seriously. "Oh, c'mon Danny. I was only kidding."

ભ ભ ભ ભ

Every Sunday at dawn Danny's stepfather, Mr. Leavenworth, drives halfway up Haleakala, parks his car, and hikes to the top. He likes to watch the sunrise. Then he hikes back down to his car. One Sunday, Danny gets up early and puts on his black jeans and black hoodie. He covers his eyes with huge sunglasses so no one can recognize him even though it's pitch black outside. He waits over an hour until someone stops to pick him up. It's beginning to get light now, almost dawn, almost the time his stepfather would be at the top of Haleakala. Danny hides behind a boulder watching, waiting. Then Mr. Leavenworth appears out of nowhere. Danny waits while his stepfather looks at what will be his last sunrise. There are a few other people there too, but Mr. Leavenworth manages to find a secluded spot. Danny knows about this spot, because when he was younger he went once with his stepfather. It was one of the few good memories he had of their time together. After his mother died, his stepfather turned into an alcoholic and took everything out on ten-year-old Danny.

A slow mist begins to engulf the summit, blocking the view of the sunrise. Danny slithers out from behind the boulder, looks around to make sure no one is watching, then walks straight toward his stepfather, who still stands motionless at the edge. With both hands outstretched, Danny pushes him over the edge. Mr. Leavenworth never saw Danny coming. Within a few seconds it is over. Danny walks down the mountain along the road, as if nothing has happened. He's left his bike tied up in front of a convenience store at the bottom. He unlocks it and rides home. He calls Kyle and tells him, "It's done."

The next day the police knock on Danny's door to tell him the news of his stepfather's death. It's all over the local news. "Tragic hiking accident at the top of Mount Haleakala." Danny plays it to the hilt, collapsing onto the floor in sobs, saying that now he has nobody. The policeman takes him to the substation where a social worker meets him and takes him to a temporary foster home in Maui.

Kyle's eyes scanned the coffee shop again. Paranoia was beginning to set in. Lilly had no idea about his involvement in Mr. Leavenworth's murder. No idea that it was her father who had given Kyle the gold bracelet in the first place. Or that Kyle was the one who gave the bracelet to Danny. Or that Kyle was her father's twink.

Lilly took Kyle's hand in hers. "Don't worry. I'll say you were with me the night of the...." She stopped short. "Wait, that's the night my mom fell and broke her leg. She called me but I was too far away, visiting a friend on the Big Island, so I called Dad and he said to call an ambulance."

Kyle remembered that night perfectly. He and the judge had been watching TV at the judge's suite when the judge's private phone rang. It was Lilly, frantic, saying that she couldn't get help for her mother. The judge told Kyle to stay at the suite, that he'd meet the ambulance at the hospital to be with his wife. He told Kyle to leave in the morning. It was already past midnight and Kyle had smoked so much weed that he was half asleep anyway.

Kyle squeezed Lilly's hand and pretended that he didn't know about her mother's fall that night. "So, you never really went to the hospital that night then, right?"

"No. I was on the Big Island. Stayed there a couple of days with Laurie. She got into Caltech too. We're going to room together."

"Well, I already told Officer Miles I was with you at your apartment. He thinks we're, well, fucking. Would that work?"

"Fucking?" Lilly laughs. "Sure. That's fine."

Kyle felt sorry for Lilly. And he felt like a shit for how he'd had to lie to her all the years he'd been with her father. She had been his best female friend. He had let her hang out with him and Danny after school behind the greenhouses on Molly's property. They had all built a kind of clubhouse out of palm branches where no one could find them. Misfits. All three, for various reasons. Lilly was beautiful and brilliant. She had skipped a grade in elementary school, so she was a year younger than Kyle, and quite developed by age thirteen when they first met in junior high. She knew how volatile Danny was, and warned Kyle over and over that Danny was "a loose cannon about to explode." Lilly hated the girl cliques that formed in junior high school, so she was relieved to be with the boys. The three of them would talk about their respective specialties. Lilly's was quantum physics. Danny's was chemical toxins and pesticides. Kyle's was orchids. Through their high school years, "the three fuckateers," as they called themselves, had helped each other through the teasing, bullying, and name-calling. They had covered for each other when they skipped school, or had gotten caught doing drugs. Lilly took Danny under her wing after his stepfather's death. She'd visited him in the foster home, but even she had to pull away from him because she couldn't deal with his emotional outbursts. He had been put on medication after his stepfather's death, but she knew each time he stopped taking it by the way he would act. Eventually, Danny dropped out of high school just before graduation. When Lilly graduated from high school, she took some time off to help out her mother, who had multiple sclerosis. Kyle took over Molly's greenhouse business full time. Danny worked odd jobs and disappeared from their lives. And since Lilly was about to leave for Caltech, Kyle figured he'd never have to confront her with the truth about her father, the judge.

Lilly reached out to comfort Kyle. "Don't worry. It'll be fine. Let me talk to the cops. I'll tell them all about us." She squeezed his hand and winked. "By the way, what were you doing the night of the fire?"

Kyle's body stiffened. A whirlpool of images filled his head. He couldn't tell Lilly the truth— that he had been with her father that night. Lilly idolized her father. Judge Salmon was a respected member of the community. He'd been appointed to the Second Circuit court only a few years ago. He bragged that he'd gotten his law degree from the University of Hawaii when he was still in his early twenties. A prodigy, like Kyle. Both too smart for their own good. Kyle couldn't believe that the judge was in charge of family court. *My God. If they only knew his secret life.* But the judge made it clear that in his world of work he had only the best interests of the children at heart. In fact, his rationale for taking care of Kyle was to save him from the streets. At least, that's what he told Kyle. And who was Kyle to complain? The judge had become a father figure to him, and hardly asked for sex after the beginning of their relationship.

And he was certainly a step up from the street scene, and from hanging out with Danny.

Kyle cleared his throat and answered Lilly. "I was doing tricks outside the Butterfly Lounge."

Lilly lowered her voice. "You shit. You told me you'd stopped that crap. You know you could end up dead one day."

ন্ধ ন্ধ ন্ধ ন্ধ

The brilliance of Maui's salmon-colored sunset reflected cascading color against the white metal sides of Kyle's trailer. He cocooned himself under a blanket and let himself descend into darkness—the place he felt most at home, in his world of deep purple-black shadows.

He's leaning over a still pool of clear water. Sees his reflection: a pimply face, red hair. A tear drops, ripples form, water's smooth surface reconfigures as he gazes upon himself now, Adonis-like, chiseled face, long flowing blond hair. Ripples form, water's smooth surface swirls with agitation, turns dark purple, murky black. His skin now bulges with distortion, blood-red color snakes into the shadowy mix. His face elongates, transforms into the orchid of the night—Dracula vampira hangs upside-down, bat-like, but Kyle cannot avert his gaze.

He awoke from the dream to the salty smell of early morning. Ocean mist wrapped around Kyle's body in a chrysalis of protection from the nightmares that plagued his subconscious. He worried he'd be back on the suspect list for the fire if he just disappeared. But first things first. He'd need a new identity before he left Maui. And he knew just the place he could get one. That night he covered his head with his black hoodie and went to his old teenage haunt, the Butterfly Lounge. He took a wad of cash with him, enough to cover a forged social security card, a passport, and an Arizona driver's license. The judge had once talked about a place near Tempe, Arizona where gay boys were safe from the street scene, where they could seek sanctuary without fear of being sent home to families who shunned them for being gay. He couldn't remember the name of the place, just that it sounded like some strange Indian name. The judge said he wanted to go there one day, maybe call it a business trip, or something. Kyle knew it was a long shot, but that was all he had to go on. He'd take his chances. It took a few days for his new identity documents to be processed. Kyle managed to stay focused, calm.

The handwritten letter on Kyle's kitchen table explained everything. That his Aunt Molly told him she'd changed her will when his uncle died. That she'd left her entire estate to Kyle. Who the lawyer was to call about the will. That Kyle didn't want the estate and that he was leaving it, or what was left of it, to the Garden Society of Maui in his aunt's memory. That the pain of her death was too much for him and he needed to leave Maui for a while. That his aunt's land was worth enough money so the Garden Society of Maui could rebuild or do whatever they wanted with it. And that he would contact them when he had settled, but he didn't know exactly where he would go yet. Of course, he knew he would never tell them where he was, or that he was about to disappear from the face of the earth.

Rays of early-morning light filtered through branches of tall coconut palm trees on the edge of his aunt's burnt-out property, making fan-like patterns along the charred underbrush. He carried his suitcase in one hand and picked up a canvas bag with the other, then closed the unlocked door to his trailer. *They'll all be shocked when they find the letter. It'll probably be Sara who discovers it when she comes over to bring my cup of hot coffee.* He got in his Jeep and headed toward the Maui airport. Maybe it was better this way. His life of lies had become a liability. There was no way he could keep up the facade. *A fresh start will be good. I can be whoever I want. Shit, I might even go to college, become a lawyer, maybe a judge. No. I can travel, like Uncle Russ. Go orchid hunting. Live in other countries. Become an ex-pat. Shit. Get away from that psycho Danny.*

At the airport he parked his Jeep, leaving the keys in the ignition to throw off the police a little longer. Even though he'd been taken off the suspect list for the fire, his paranoia kicked in, and the sooner he was off the island, the better. His flight wouldn't leave for an hour, so he took his carry-on bag and walked over to the food court to get a strong cup of coffee. He sat down at the table and reached into his canvas bag. One last feel to make sure the plants were safe. They were the only orchid plants that had survived the fire: his uncle's prize-winning vampira orchids, snugly packed in sphagnum moss. The small plants were older than Kyle. His uncle had collected them from the rainforests of Ecuador before Kyle was born. Kyle muttered to himself, *Dracula vampira, orchid of the night. How fitting.* The plants would be the only living thing Kyle had left from his life on Maui.

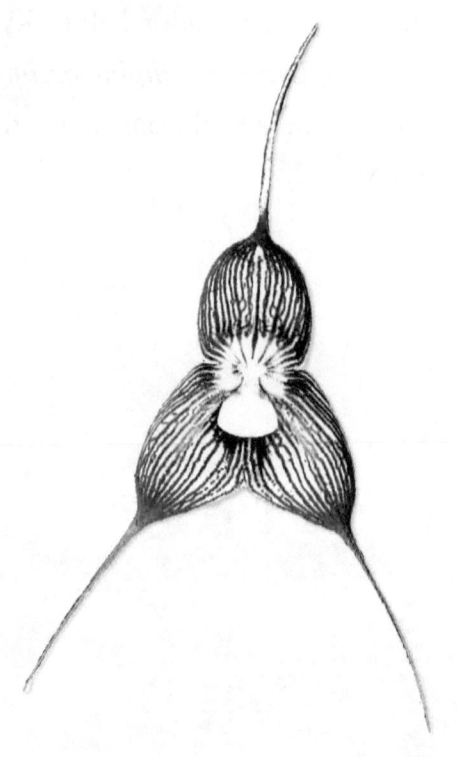

CHAPTER TWO

Tempe, Arizona

He floats effortlessly when street lights glow brighter than his nightmares. In the moonlight he glides over their sleeping cities and seething volcanoes. Below, lights flicker to remind him of the world he must return to before the first rays of dawn. A world where darkness comforts him. Dracula vampira, orchid of the night. He plummets from the safety of the mossy basket. Heart-shaped purple-black flower hanging alone, facing downward, but able to soar anywhere in effortless abandon. Now, the first rays of dawn, and he slowly glides toward the flickering lights of the city. Lands on the ground as gently as a snowflake. Shadowdream, a kaleidoscope of images, colors, smells, sensations, that lift him from the murky waters of his soul.

The Sky Harbor Airport in Phoenix was almost empty, except

for a few stragglers who wouldn't be with their families for Christmas Eve. Kyle felt completely alone, just like he had felt when his mother was murdered. They had called him catatonic when the officer brought him to Aunt Molly's the next morning. Catatonic, frozen with fear, unable to talk, unable to remember what he'd seen. Kyle headed toward the baggage claim area. He picked up his suitcase, then took a taxi to the nearest motel so he could figure out what to do next. He was exhausted from the trip. He'd rent a car and drive to Tempe tomorrow, after some sleep. He needed to find a place to live so he could get a bank account and apply for a credit card. The cash he'd brought with him wouldn't last forever. Kyle paid the taxi driver, got out of the cab, and walked into the lobby of the motel. He pulled out his new driver's license. The photo looked strange to him. So did the name, Tom Tanner —his new identity. Kyle had decided to shave off his hair before he left Maui so there would be no trace of red anywhere—only a military-style bald head. His shaven head made him look even younger than twenty-two. But that was his new identity, which included the purposeful demise of the red-haired Irish O'Sullivan gene from his grandmother. At first he'd dyed his hair black, but it made his light complexion look too pale, almost anemic. So he decided to shave off the final remnant of painful childhood memories. Besides, his uncle Russ had the bald military look, and it seemed apropos since he took his uncle's last name, Tanner. Kyle looked up at the clerk behind the desk. "Any place to eat that's open Christmas Eve?"

The motel clerk, an older woman with a cigarette hanging out of her mouth, pointed across the street. "Dingo's is usually open."

Kyle took his luggage into his room first, then walked into the cool night air toward Dingo's. There were hardly any cars on the road. It seemed as if the world had come to a screeching halt, just like his life. A new city and a new identity. He opened the door and went inside, expecting to see the local drunks and loners sitting at the bar. But no one was there. He sat down on a bar stool and said in a loud voice, "Anyone here?" No answer. He said again, "Anyone here?" Then he heard some rustling and quick footsteps. A scruffy, heavy-set bearded man appeared through the back doorway. "Yeah. Didn't expect anyone Christmas Eve."

Kyle adjusted himself on the wobbly bar stool, then said, "Sorry to bother you. I just arrived on a late flight. I'm starved."

The man propped up his jeans with a belt that held up his pants beneath his bulging belly. "Want me to make a fresh pot of coffee?"

Kyle nodded. "Great." He picked up a menu.

"Sorry, but I already closed up the kitchen. Don't know why I stay open on Christmas Eve. Guess I figure since I'm alone, maybe someone else who's alone might need company in here." He pointed to a glass case on the counter. "Think I got a few pies left from earlier."

Kyle leaned over and looked more closely. All they had left was cherry pie. That would have to do. "I'll take two slices."

"Want some whipped cream?"

"Sure."

The man opened the case, put two slices of pie on a large plate, and squirted whipped cream on top of each piece. Then he went over to the freshly brewed coffee and poured a cup for Kyle. "Where you from?"

Kyle paused. He wasn't prepared for the question. Should he tell the truth? He didn't have to. He could say anything he wanted. He felt a surge of adrenalin, just like when he was a kid at school and he managed to stop the bullying by reciting orchid adventures from his uncle's journal. He'd memorized most of the stories, and the one about his uncle getting kidnapped by diamond smugglers was the favorite. When he said his uncle managed to escape with a stash of diamonds, he had the kids hooked. He told them maybe one day he'd tell where the diamonds were hidden. Suddenly, Reddylocks became someone the kids treated with respect. *Yes. Lying was definitely better than telling the truth*. Kyle took a sip of coffee and said, "Bora Bora. I'm from Bora Bora."

The man grunted. "Never heard of it."

"It's one of the French Polynesian Leeward Islands."

"Long way from Phoenix. What brings you here?"

Kyle didn't want to talk anymore. He was exhausted. He answered, "Work."

The man eventually stopped asking questions and got up to leave. "Just put $10 on the counter when you go." He poured more coffee into Kyle's cup and walked through the back door of the bar.

Kyle had already started the first piece of cherry pie. It wasn't bad. In fact, it was just what he needed. The red jellied cherries slid down his throat with ease as he wolfed down the pie. He took another sip of the hot coffee then sat back in his chair, took a deep breath, and for the first time since he'd left Hawaii, he felt the full impact of what he'd done. He was completely alone— an anonymous blot on the desert landscape of Arizona. He could be anyone he wanted. And when his fork plunged into the second piece of cherry pie, he realized what he was eating. *Cherry pie. My God!* He hadn't eaten cherry pie since he was thirteen. He took another bite of the pie. It tasted rather good. He sat alone at the counter licking the gooey sweetness from his fork. Cherry pie turned out to be his best —and only —friend, on this lonely Christmas Eve in Phoenix, Arizona.

When he was thirteen, it all came back to him in a slice of cherry pie. He was at Kona's Cafebrew on Maui eating a piece of cherry pie when it happened. A flood of memories, gruesome memories of the murder scene, of the shadowy figure he'd seen from behind the bedroom door, of his mother's open eyes staring into space. The color and consistency of the cherry pie must have set off the memory with deep reds, the color of blood.

CR   CR   CR   CR

The Adobe Palms Hotel and Grille touted award-winning American and international cuisine, with elegant ambiance and dining opportunities for Tempe's downtown business community and visitors alike. Penelope Witherspoon had worked there for the past seventeen years, and it didn't look like she was going anywhere else soon. Her raspy voice and hometown friendly manner gave her a permanent following of late-night businessmen who sucked up her attention like little boys around their mommy. But Pen, as she preferred to be called, knew how to play it. She brushed up to them, making sure she was close enough that they could grab her ass and smell her cheap perfume. Then she used her sexy raspy voice. "Hun, what's it tonight? Same old, or perhaps, something new?" She raised her eyebrows, looked right into their eyes, and puckered up her lips. More than a few times she noticed a slight movement in the laps of her male customers after the lip pucker. Penelope Witherspoon had become a legend at the Adobe Palms Grill. She even appeared in the local paper once when she was honored for saving a man's life with the Heimlich maneuver. The article in the paper had been cut out, framed, and hung on the wall in a prominent corner next to the cash register.

The corner table next to a huge fish tank had a reserved sign on it. Pen put out the sign for Tom a week after she first laid eyes on him. He'd walked into the Grille for dinner one day, a few hours after his shift at the hotel. His clean-shaven angular face and sturdy frame, along with the red concierge uniform, gave him a certain presence that she couldn't resist. And when she brushed close to him after he ordered the steak and fries, he never once reached up to grab her ass. Even her pucker-up lip-trick didn't seem to arouse him. No. Tom was a real gentleman. He treated her like a lady with "please," and "thank you, ma'am." But when he ordered the steak and fries, looked up at her with his deep-blue eyes and said, "Can't wait to dive into this. I'm famished," Pen found herself pulled into a vortex of unknown proportion where night and day merged into one. After a week, she asked Tom if he wanted to come over to her place, where she'd personally make him steak and fries.

Pen's apartment was small, but Tom figured it was worth having a place to go besides his rental house on the outskirts of town, barely affordable with his salary as a concierge at the Adobe Palms Hotel. He pulled out his inhaler and took a whiff of medicine. He was allergic to Pen's cat. He set the inhaler down on a table while Pen made them a cup of coffee. He couldn't believe he was letting himself get so close to someone. Especially a woman—a woman who looked old enough to be his mother. It had been two months since he'd arrived in Tempe and he already had a new life. He was even beginning to feel like Tom Tanner. Memories of his life on Maui were fading. Even the warm, dry climate in Tempe seemed to appeal to him. His asthma was definitely better in a drier climate. Now all he had to do was remember his new identity so that he didn't slip back into Kyle O'Sullivan in moments of weakness.

Pen walked over to him and put her arm around his shoulders. "Tom, I'm sorry. Maybe if I vacuum before you come over, there won't be so much cat hair."

"It's all right. I'll be fine."

"Maybe we could go to your place sometime." Pen waited for a response, but instead there was only a smirk, a cough, and an excuse. Tom was the master of excuses. He'd been doing it so long that he'd sometimes forget which was the lie and which was the truth. He found that as the lies got bigger, lying got easier. It was turning out not to be that difficult to be Tom Tanner, after all. He just needed to keep his cool before he said anything.

After his mother's murder, when he went catatonic, he began to live inside his head in his world of imagination. He wondered if he had multiple personalities, because depending on what was happening, he could change in a split second to adapt to the situation. One moment he was Aunt Molly's adopted child, a bit unruly but devoted nonetheless. Another moment he was Danny's fuck-buddy and accomplice in a murder. And in yet another, the judge's twink at the same time he was Lilly's confidant and best friend. Shit, he could be anything to anyone. He'd learned how to navigate those dark recesses of his soul so well that he felt no emotion at all when he lied. He knew about moral compasses and all of that psychological jargon. His moral compass was on stand-by. Maybe one day it would kick in, but for now it was serving him quite well to feel numb while he figured out how to live his life as Tom Tanner.

Pen walked over to the kitchen table and sat down. She had only a couple of hours until her shift at the Grill began. "Want any more coffee?"

"Sure. Thanks." Tom sat down next to her. He was beginning to feel more comfortable around Pen. She reminded him of Sara Santos. Both women liked to mother him. Pen told him she was thirty-five, fourteen years older than him. But that didn't seem to bother her. In fact, she said she liked younger men. Especially younger men with blue eyes. Tom wondered how many men she'd had before him. She certainly looked like she'd been around. Her weathered skin and raspy voice made her seem even older than her years. She really could be his mother.

"Do we at least have time for a story?" Pen used her little-girl voice in hopes of stretching out a few more minutes before she had to leave for the evening shift at the Grille. Ships in the night. That's how she termed their newly formed relationship. A few hours a week—that's all Tom committed to. Tom had told Pen from the beginning that he wasn't interested in her for her body. That seemed to satisfy her. He was the first man who respected her for herself. Less was more. At least that's how she rationalized the situation. Tom's intellect, charm, and looks were enough. Just the fact that he spent time with her was also enough. No one had ever treated her so well. And so far, he never laid a hand on her in anger, or talked mean to her, or insulted her. But Pen figured it was better than nothing, convincing herself less was really more. With a name like Penelope Witherspoon, one would think she'd have ended up at Harvard or Cambridge, been a doctor or lawyer from a high-profile East Coast family. But she never finished high school, barely read above a fifth-grade level, and had waitressed for the better part of her thirty-five years.

Tom walked over to the window where the sun seemed to linger on the horizon, reluctant to descend into darkness. He lifted his arms, took a deep breath, stretched his body, then turned to face Pen. "I'll tell you about the time my Uncle Russ went to Ecuador to search for the dracula orchid."

Pen squealed with excitement. "Dracula orchid? No way." She flopped down on the couch and lit up a cigarette.

Tom opened the window. "You have to smoke now?"

Pen waved her hand over the swirling stream of cigarette smoke. "Just half. I'll only smoke half the cigarette."

Tom had been allergic to cigarette smoke since he was a child. And smoke reminded him of the fire and his aunt's death, and of his mother—who had smoked Marlboros, the same brand as Pen. He walked over to the kitchen table, sat down, reached into his briefcase, and pulled out a tattered leather journal held together with black duct tape. He opened the journal to a page with fine-lined writing in small script, almost of calligraphy quality. He kept the journal in a briefcase, like people keep a Bible nearby. It was a way to connect with his Uncle Russ and Aunt Molly. A way to remind him of the few good memories he had left from his life on Maui. Tom closed the journal. "Shit. I know all this stuff by heart. It's more fun if I tell you. It's like I'm really there." He closed his eyes and began to recite.

August 3, 1974 Expedition to Quito

I was put in touch with a German mining engineer in Quito by the name of Hans, who had a huge knowledge of the orchids of Ecuador. We talked about my desire to find the black Masdevallia chimaera that Lehmann, another German mining engineer, had collected near Quito a century ago. He sent this plant to Kraenzlin, and like all these other fantastic large hairy Masdevallias, he decided it was a color form of chimaera. It was apparently lost after that point, except for one collection in the mid-'60s. Hans told me about a guy called Malor, who happened to be in Quito, and who ended up being very helpful.

Despite my expectation that the local orchid collectors would be reluctant to give away the treasure map, Malor was very specific about where he found these black chimaeras and told me he is working with a surgeon-turned-botanist who did not think these were chimaeras—in fact, he thought all of these Masdevallias with the mushroom lip were a genus unto themselves—and to expect some radical changes to the taxonomy soon. Malor's plants were found on the south side of Pichincha, the giant active volcano that dominates the western Quito skyline, and I could get there by taking Chiriboga road toward the little town of Lloa (apparently the source of the trail that hikers would use to reach one of Pichincha's two summits, the active one). He drew me a map of how to find this Chiriboga road, and offered regrets that he couldn't join me, as he was heading home to Cuenca.

After we shook hands and turned to go our separate ways, he called back to me to offer one more bit of geographical trivia. Apparently the route I would be taking was the first valley to fill with lava, should Pichincha decide to blow.

I left at dawn the next morning in my rented Toyota 4x4. Apparently this road had reasonable traffic, but usually if an area was good for orchids, it was bad for cars. I found my way to the southwestern edges of Quito, but got horribly lost in a maze of unnamed streets that randomly changed from cobblestone to dirt and back, in neighborhoods that were poor— but did not appear to be as dangerous as some. Every few blocks I had to ask for directions, usually several times, because either my accent was not understood, or I was understood, but the person I was speaking to didn't really know how to describe the route. By 8:30 or so, I was finally at some sort of a threshold between urban Quito and wild Pichincha.

Hans told me to always look for recently colonized embankments—areas where there had been slides, recent road cuts, etc. These should be rich in orchids. I wanted to stop and explore these more, but since my goal was the black chimaera, and it was at the very end of the road, across a river, and up a trail, I decided to go full speed ahead toward Lloa. It took over an hour to get there, and despite my efforts to stay focused I did get distracted a few times by some extraordinary blasts of orange on the roadside. The first time it was a colony of Pleurothallis truncata, a wonderful relative of Masdevallias that has little orange balls on a string that dangle down the center of heart-shaped leaves.

I bemusedly thought of the well-placed pearl necklace on one of the women that rather obviously caught Malor's eye yesterday. The next blast of orange I initially thought was the same thing, but then I realized these blooms were much larger. Masdevallia sodiroi! Hundreds of them, poking up through *the grass like Chinese lanterns. I can see why this taxonomy surgeon Malor was talking about doubts we should be calling everything a Masdevallia – these were not like any Masdevallia I had seen. A few good chunks of both plants found their way into the trunk of the Toyota.*

Pen interrupted Tom's recitation. "I need to get ready for work. Could we finish this another time?"

Still engrossed in the story, Tom opened his eyes and watched Pen disappear into the bathroom. He wondered if she was paying attention. Some of his uncle's entries were more simplified, less technical. Maybe he should have told her one of those.

Pen came out of the bathroom, dressed for work. She walked over to the kitchen table and sat down. "My God. What a story. Did he ever find the dracula orchid?"

"Well, you'll just have to wait until the next installment, won't you?"

Pen averted her eyes. "I guess so. But maybe next time you could tell me one without so many weird words. I had trouble following."

Tom hardly heard her comment. He seemed mesmerized by the light streaming through the window from the setting sun. It shone directly on the bowl of oranges that sat on the kitchen table. He managed to answer. "He really found that orchid. In fact, I have a few of them at my house."

Pen turned around abruptly. "No shit. Can I see them sometime?"

Tom watched her go into the other room to change. He began to realize how limited Pen's life had been, and why she sometimes she got so excited, like a little child eating cotton candy for the first time. The orange glow of the fading sunlight along the table and over the bowl of oranges continued to captivate him. He let his mind wander into childhood memories at his mother's kitchen table in Maui.

It's one of those second-hand metal tables, probably one that's made its way from a hospital cafeteria to the Goodwill store. Kyle uses two old Yellow Pages phone books stacked on his wooden chair so he can comfortably reach the top to eat. Often he's the only one eating, since his mother feeds him just before her caller arrives. Then she goes into her bedroom to get ready. Kyle learns to keep himself company, with the help of his toy soldiers that he lines up on the table opposite him. With each bite of his peanut butter and jelly sandwich, he sets a small crumb in front of each soldier until all twelve have their fair share of his meager dinner. He lets his mind soar above the stained angular yellow walls of the kitchen into his escape route, the kaleidoscope world of imagination. Dragons and castles, distant lands filled with chocolate rivers and marshmallow mountains, secret caves with dark passages that aren't a bit scary. And for that brief moment in time, Kyle feels that warm tingly feeling of pure comfort, like nothing can harm him.

Then comes the dry crust of the bread —the part he won't even leave for his toy soldiers. The part that sometimes has spots of black mold that he's learned to pick off before he starts to eat. He finishes his milk, takes his plate and glass to the sink, collects his toys, and walks quietly into his bedroom, where he's allowed to watch an hour of TV before putting himself to bed. All the while, his mother is in her bedroom with her caller. Kyle knows he can't open his door until she knocks three times on his door to let him know she wants to come in to say good night.

Pen came into the kitchen finding Tom half-slumped over the table. "You okay?"

Tom sat up. "Just had a thought." He picked up one of the oranges in the bowl and held it up to the fading light. "Pen," he whispered. "Think I'll let my hair grow out."

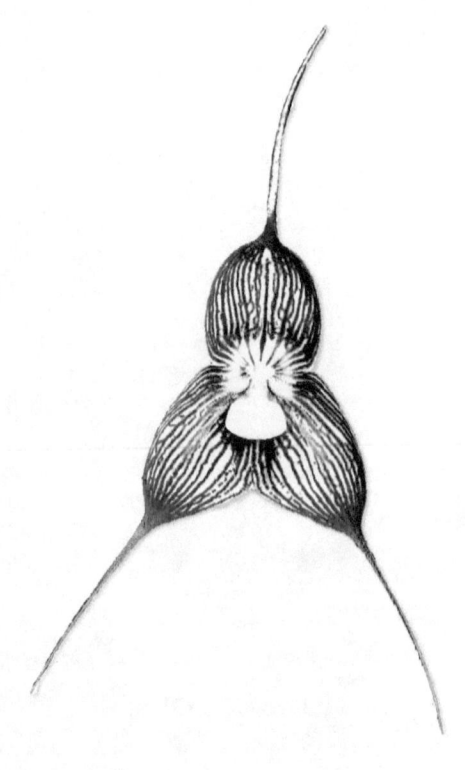

CHAPTER THREE

Phoenix Orchid Guild

Tom was at work at the Adobe Palms putting a heavy suitcase into one of the rooms, when he got a glimpse of himself in the dresser mirror. His hair had grown out in only a few weeks. Red curls began to pop out from beneath his red concierge hat. He realized he didn't look as dignified now. The military cut certainly made him look more sophisticated. He saw remnants of his childhood, the baby-faced youth with pimples, but he now had enough stubble for a beard. He'd never let himself grow a beard before. He hardly recognized himself anymore.

The fourteen- year age difference between him and Pen made Tom feel uncomfortable. Pen never mentioned their age difference. She'd already told him she liked younger men. But Tom didn't know what he liked. He just knew he was in some kind of relationship with her—not sexual, but still something that felt good. He told Pen he was going away for the weekend to check out the Phoenix Orchid Guild. It was the first time he'd gone anywhere outside of Tempe since he'd arrived in Arizona on Christmas Eve. Besides, Pen was beginning to grow on him. In fact, he found that he wanted to spend time with her—more than a few hours a week. He liked hanging out at her place after his shift at the Adobe Palms Hotel. He liked the way she made his favorite foods—steak and fries and lemon meringue pie. If she needed to leave for the Grille before he got to her apartment, she'd leave the meal prepared for him in the refrigerator with a note that said something like, "Enjoy. See you when our ships dock next time." Sometimes he'd stay until she returned from her shift so that she would wake him up by crawling in bed beside him.

The drive to Phoenix didn't take long. He decided to leave his new dog, Rover, in the house with a fresh bowl of water and dry food. Rover was a terrier mix Tom had rescued from the Humane Society a few weeks after he'd found his house in Tempe. Named after the black lab he'd grown up with at Maui, the second Rover didn't take long to become Tom's constant companion, just like the first Rover. The lab, Rover, had kept him company when his mother would disappear in her room with her gentlemen callers. But after the fire, Rover's body was never found. Tom was sure he died on the property, waiting for him to come home that terrible night.

He arrived well before the meeting started, so he parked his car in the parking lot and waited. Soon people began arriving. Some were carrying boxes with blooming orchid plants. Some had plates of food covered with foil. Most of the people were older than him, perhaps in their forties and fifties. He got out of the car and walked into the meeting room of the local church. People were mingling around a table with a display of plants for sale, and were setting up another table with a food buffet. Tom felt unexpectedly comfortable.

One of the members came up to him and introduced himself. "Never seen you here before. I'm Jim." He reached out to shake Tom's hand.

"Tom."

"Where you from?"

Tom paused before he answered. His mind began the sorting game he'd made up when he was a kid. *Which lie should I use now? Maybe I should make up a new one.* He really couldn't use Bora Bora again. This crowd was way too sophisticated for that. He thought for a moment; then the entire scenario unfolded like a scene out of a movie. He'd already told them at the Adobe Palms Hotel that he was from the Bay Area and needed a drier climate for his asthma. So he said, "I'm from California."

Jim nodded. "Used to live there when I was a kid. What part?"

Now Tom was into the lie. Words seemed to flow out of

his mouth with ease. "San Francisco. Had a huge greenhouse there, but it burned down. Some sort of electrical glitch."

"Oh my God. How terrible."

"Yes. Killed all the orchids, except a few miniatures in a glass case."

"Did you have insurance?"

"Thankfully."

"So what brought you to Arizona?"

Tom took a small breath before he answered. "Needed a change. Also lost my sister in the fire."

"I'm so sorry." Jim quickly turned toward the food table. "Uh, so glad you found our orchid society. Look forward to seeing some of your miniatures." He walked away.

Tom felt relieved. *How easy is this? I can say anything and they'll believe me.* He walked over to the sales table and picked up one of the plants. They were oncidiums with long spikes, some already in bloom. He knew he didn't want to buy one, but he acted like he was interested. An older woman came up to him and said, "It'll be a beauty when all the spikes are in bloom. I have about ten in my greenhouse that are blooming now."

"The dancing lady. Gorgeous flowers. Unfortunately, I lost all of mine in the fire."

The woman backed up. "The fire?"

Tom went into more detail, mentioning how he'd lost his greenhouse and his sister in the fire. The woman, still with a look of horror on her face, said, "I'm so sorry. Do you plan on staying in Arizona?"

Tom smiled. "As long as I can. I love the warm climate."

The meeting took almost three hours. Guests and new members were encouraged to stand up and introduce themselves. Tom briefly introduced himself and mentioned his move to Tempe because of the recent disaster in California. During the break, people came up to console him. He felt comfortable in his new identity. He felt comfortable being around orchids again. He joined the Phoenix Orchid Guild, and over the next few months he attended a couple of their meetings, bringing miniature orchids for show and tell. He told them he was an expert in miniatures. He ordered miniatures through the mail in spike or bloom, just before each monthly meeting, and removed the commercial tag, replacing it with his own. His perceived expertise in miniatures gave him the feeling of belonging. He was even asked to speak at one of the meetings on how he grew miniature orchids in a terrarium, except he didn't have a terrarium. All he cared about was his vampira orchids from Maui. The miniatures would either survive in the climate-controlled room he'd set up for the vampiras, or not. His life was moving along smoothly for once.

℘ ℘ ℘ ℘

Summers in Arizona were hot. Tom wasn't used to dry heat like this, but heat without rain was definitely preferable. After the July meeting of the Orchid Guild, Tom decided to hang out in Phoenix until later that night, so the short drive back to Tempe wouldn't be so hot. He went into downtown Phoenix and looked for a place to get a cold beer. He drove into the center of town and leisurely cruised up and down a street with bars. The name Caveman stood out—probably a gay bar. Tom hesitated, then continued driving. Should he go inside? No one would know him, with his new identity. *What's the big deal?* He turned the car around, parked in a well-lit lot behind the bar, and walked inside. He was immediately asked for his ID, just like the Butterfly Lounge in Maui. They were all the same. Men sat on stools talking with each other. Loud music. Men dancing. He sat at the bar and ordered a beer. A man at least twice his age came over and asked if he could sit next to him. Tom squirmed on the bar stool, then answered, "Sure."

The man ordered a beer for himself. "New here?"

Tom looked up from his glass. The man reminded him of the judge. Both with thick brown hair graying around the temples, in their forties, both with dark brown eyes. Bedroom eyes, as he used to tell the judge. There was something about dark eyes that Tom couldn't resist. The man reached up and touched Tom's hair. "Quite an unusual color. You Irish?"

Tom blurted out. "Yeah, Irish."

"So, are you the pot of gold at the end of my rainbow?" Tom blushed. That was probably the best pick-up line he'd ever heard. He took a sip of beer. "So, what's your story?"

The man said, "You really want to know?"

Tom figured he might as well enjoy the evening. It had been awhile since he'd done the bar scene. The man reached in his pocket and pulled out a card. Tom took the card and tried to read in the dim light. He saw a few words, "Legal Aid," then a name, Bill Jacobson.

Bill asked, "So, what's your story?"

Tom wasn't quite sure what to say now. The beer was beginning to relax him. He looked into Bill's deep brown eyes. "Came here from California a few months ago."

"California. What part?"

Tom hesitated. "Bay Area."

"That's where I'm from too. Moved to Phoenix to work for Legal Aid."

Tom wanted to know more about Bill, but he knew he wasn't ready for the life it might bring him. He'd left that far behind. The temptation felt overwhelming, like an addiction he'd finally broken. His new identity didn't include nightly escapades to gay bars. He stood up and headed toward the door. Bill followed him. "Hey, you never told me your last name. How can I reach you?"

"Tom Mann." Tom had no idea where that came from, but he didn't care. There was no way he could tell the truth. He didn't need to start up with anyone. He had Pen to keep him company—and besides, his new identity as Tom Tanner was still evolving. He wasn't sure if he wanted to start up the gay lifestyle again. He was lucky he found Pen. She made things so simple for him. But the Caveman had a certain familiarity, an allure that he found hard to resist. He felt like he was being pulled between two worlds where he needed to assume two different identities. Just like when he was at Maui. But going to the Caveman was not the same as hanging out in front of the Butterfly Lounge, turning tricks. No. This was definitely different. Maybe he'd come back in a few months, after he sorted out his relationship with Pen. He didn't want to screw things up now.

The drive back to Tempe was uneventful. It hadn't really cooled off. Tom opened the window and the hot night air blew over his face while he drove along the stretch of freeway, tires on pavement making a slow drone while he began to process what had just happened. He'd walked away from Bill, from the bar, from the temptation. He turned on the radio to a jazz station. He'd never really listened to jazz, but the Adobe Palms Hotel had jazz bands in the evenings, and he found himself mesmerized by the music. Maybe it was the unpredictable rhythms, the free-form riffs, the improvisation. He felt the same way about his life. He was improvising all the time, never knowing when he would need to lie—but the more he did it, the more he was drawn to it. Call it improvisation or call it lying; Tom figured it didn't matter.

છ છ છ છ

It was a relief to see Pen again. He went to her place after his shift at the Adobe Palms and knocked on the door, but there was no answer. He knocked again, then heard her raspy voice. "Hold on, I'm coming." She opened the door and smiled. "I should probably give you a key to my place."

The cat was curled up on her bed. The windows were open and a gentle breeze blew through her apartment, bringing the scent of trumpet honeysuckle. It grew wild around her building, especially in the summer. Its trumpet-like orange flowers attracted hummingbirds, so Pen had feeders outside the kitchen window. It drove the cat insane all summer, but Pen said it was worth it. Said the birds reminded her of her childhood when her mother did the same thing. Tom asked her to tell him more about her mother, but Pen managed to change the subject. He didn't push her. He knew what it was like to keep secrets and to avoid talking about the past.

Pen was wearing a sheer white nightgown, enough to cover her thin but shapely body. He walked over to her, reached out his hand, and touched her shoulder. Pen stiffened. They had now been seeing each other almost six months and never even kissed. Tom moved his hand over her shoulders. He felt goose bumps form on her smooth skin. He slipped her nightgown over her head. She was now standing naked in front of him. Their eyes met. He slowly undressed while she watched. They lay down on her bed and he let her run her hand along his chest and along his shoulders. She leaned over to kiss his lips. Then, she moved her hand further down until she reached his penis. Soon, he felt her warm, moist mouth covering it, moving up and down, up and down. He let himself relax into lovemaking with a woman, his first time. So different from Danny, and from the judge, and from the quickies on the street when he was a teenager. Much more gentle. Like when his mother put suntan lotion on his body at the beach. Pen moved her body on top of him and put him inside of her. She moved slowly at first, then faster, then in a simultaneous burst of pleasure, she collapsed on top of him.

That night Tom couldn't sleep. All he could think about was how different sex with a woman was. Pen had already left for her shift at the Grille. Tom wanted to see her. He put on some slacks and a nice shirt and drove over to the Grille to surprise her. The corner table was empty. He waited for her to see him and when she did, he saw the look of surprise and excitement on her face. She took out her pad of paper and said, "What can I get you, sir?"

He smiled. "Maybe more of what I just had."

She blushed.

"Wonder why I'm so famished?"

She walked closer and brushed up against him. "Gee, can't imagine why."

Just then a voice from the kitchen called out, "Pen, we need help in the kitchen for a few minutes."

"Okay, coming in a second." She handed Tom a menu. "Be right back. Don't get in any trouble while I'm gone."

Tom looked at the menu, then up at the 25-gallon fish tank where two large golden koi swam in meandering motions around the patterns of frothy iridescent sprays of bubbles. He felt relaxed, even happy. The peacefulness of the underwater world of the fish tank soothed him. *Maybe I'll get a couple of koi for my place.* Pen returned from the kitchen. Tom looked up with his piercing blue eyes, smiled, then pointed at the menu to the steak and fries that he ordered every time. Pen inched closer and closer until her hips touched his back. "Honey, maybe try something different tonight? How about some grilled mahi mahi with brown sugar sauce? Chef gets it direct from Hawaii. It's his specialty."

Without warning, Tom's back stiffened. Pen jerked away from his body. "Did I say something wrong?"

Tom lowered his eyes. "No, it's okay. Just give me the steak and fries."

Pen wrote down the order and walked out of the room. Tom began to feel light-headed. The forbidden food, mahi mahi. He felt nauseated, as the smell of burnt mahi mahi permeated his thoughts. The day before the fire, Molly had a bucket of freshly caught mahi mahi in her sink, on ice, ready to be grilled on her outside barbeque for the yearly greenhouse tour and fundraiser the next day. There would have been over one hundred members and friends of the Garden Society of Maui in attendance. The smell of grilled fish always used to make him smile, but he knew he could never eat fish again—especially not mahi mahi.

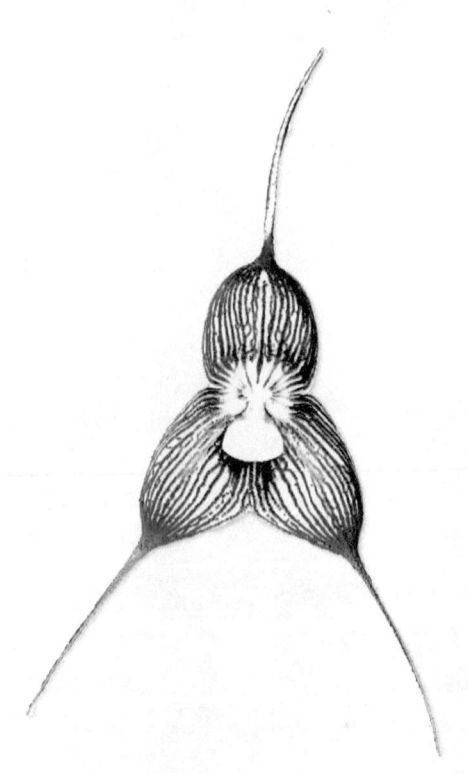

CHAPTER FOUR

Ixtlan

A desert landscape with miles of blue sky. Strange rock forma-tions in the distance. Burning embers, naked men sitting around a fire. Sounds of distant drumming. Smell of burning incense. The letter X flashes over and over in front of his eyes. Now he's in a car driving along a bumpy dirt road in the desert. The judge is at the wheel. They head toward a strange rock formation, round the corner and see a clump of saguaro cactus. Then a compound of wooden houses surrounded by a barbed wire fence. The judge says, "Welcome to Ixtlan."

Tom woke from the dream. He dressed for work, had a quick cup of coffee, and drove to the Adobe Palms Hotel. He couldn't get the image of the strange word out of his mind. After work he went to Pen's place. He told her about the dream. She laughed and said, "Honey, if I told you some of my weird dreams, yours would look pretty lame."

Tom ignored her comment. Why would he expect someone like her to understand him? He'd always lived in his world of shadows, at least since his mother's murder. But since he'd been in Tempe he hadn't had any nightmares, only strange dreams. He told Pen he was exhausted and needed to go home to get a good night's sleep. She got that pouty look on her face and said, "But you promised to tell me another orchid adventure."

"Next time. I promise. In fact, I'll tell you two." Tom wondered if he and Pen would have anything to talk about if he ran out of stories from his uncle's journal. The word *Ixtlan* kept him so preoccupied that he couldn't concentrate on anything else. How could he find out if it was a real place?

At home, he still couldn't sleep. He paced around his house, made some coffee, and sat at the kitchen table to think. But his restlessness took over. He'd drive to Phoenix and go to the Caveman to hang out. He put on his clothes, made sure Rover had enough food, and got in his car. It was early enough that the bar scene would just be ramping up.

When he arrived it was still light outside. He went inside and saw Bill sitting alone at the bar. Tom tried to avoid him, but the moment Bill saw Tom he got up and came over. "Well, well. Haven't seen you here for a while."

Tom ordered a beer. "Been busy."

"Doing what?"

"Just busy, that's all."

Bill ordered a beer for himself. "So, do you still have my card?"

Tom looked away. "Yeah."

Bill took a gulp of beer and said, "So, want to get out of here with me?"

Tom turned toward him and took a sip of beer. "I don't know what I want. Haven't been sleeping much lately."

"Well, I know just the cure for what ails you." Bill reached for Tom's waist and swooped him up, heading toward the back door. They began to kiss in the parking lot, Bill's tongue rolling around in Tom's mouth, now wet with desire. Bill moved his hand down the front of Tom's shirt, then down toward his crotch, and rubbed the jeans covering his bulging cock. Immersed in the throes of passion, Tom's mind went blank, as his body succumbed to Bill's touch. Then, without warning, he exploded in pulsations of ecstasy as he collapsed into Bill's arms. A deep cloak of purple-black darkness pierced into his very being. Bill led him toward his car and opened the passenger's door as Tom slumped down on the seat. Bill smiled. "Well, well. Looks like it's been a while for you."

Tom sat up. "Look, Bill. This isn't what you think."

Bill smiled. "What is it, then?"

Tom tried to compose himself. "I've been having this

strange dream about a place called Ixtlan. It's driving me crazy. I can't get it out of my head. Maybe I am going crazy."

Bill's back stiffened. "Ixtlan? You don't know about Ixtlan?"

"What?"

"My God. A dream about a place you've never heard of? Looks like this is your lucky day. Ixtlan's a sort of hippie-dippy New Age community outside of Tempe where gays can seek sanctuary."

Tom's heart skipped a beat. *This must be the place the judge talked about*, he thought. He looked at Bill, and in a quivering voice said, "Do you know how to get there?"

"No. But I know someone who does. Follow me." They got out of the car and headed back inside the bar. Bill pointed to a younger man dancing in the center of the room. They walked over to him and Bill tapped the young man on the shoulder. "Teddy, can we talk to you for a minute?" The man and his partner were embraced in the throes of sexual excitement, as they danced to the music of Beyonce. They both turned around. Bill said, "Teddy, meet my new friend, Tom. He wants to know about Ixtlan. I told him you'd been there recently."

Teddy looked at Tom and said, "How'd you hear about it?"

Tom looked at Bill but didn't answer.

Teddy smiled. "Okay. Sure. It's near the Papago camp grounds. I can give you a phone number to call for directions if you want." He pulled out his cell phone. Tom took out his cell phone and punched in the number. "Thanks."

Bill whipped Tom onto the dance floor. "Now, it's my turn." He brought Tom close to his body and let Tom feels his erection. Tom felt light-headed and the slow music helped him let his guard down. He felt Bill turning him on again. When the music stopped, Bill led him toward the back door and outside into the parking lot. It was a peaceful summer evening with stars now covering the sky. The night air was scented with jasmine and honeysuckle. Bill pulled Tom toward him and kissed his lips. Tom pushed Bill back abruptly and said, "Sorry, I can't do this."

Bill stopped and gently caressed Tom's red hair. "Sure you can. Just relax." He opened the passenger's door of his car, and Tom got in. Bill slid in the driver's side.

In a split second, Tom reached over to open the door on his side. "No, I can't. I've gotta go." He got out of Bill's car and headed toward his own. He didn't look back, but heard Bill yell, "You slut. You fuckin' tease."

Tom got in his car and drove around Phoenix for a while to make sure Bill didn't try to follow him. It was just before midnight when he returned home. That night Tom slept like a baby. No dreams. No nightmares. Nothing. Just perfect calm.

The next weekend Tom told Pen he was taking Rover and driving to Phoenix for an orchid event. Pen did her usual scowl and headed to her purse for a cigarette. She'd already told him that she wasn't working that weekend and hoped to spend some time with him. But alone was what she'd been used to before she met him. She once asked him if she could go with him to the meetings in Phoenix and he told her he needed his space, time to do his own thing, that he couldn't be in a relationship with someone who knew his every move. *Secretive.* She called him secretive—asked if he trusted her. Tom hated to hurt Pen, but he knew what he had to do. It wasn't a matter of his trusting her, it was a matter of her trusting him. He wasn't ready to split open his life and let her in. How could he tell her it was all a lie? No, he'd learned to keep a distance from everyone, even Pen.

When Tom called the number Teddy had given him at the Caveman in Phoenix, the person who answered sounded cautious at first. But when Tom mentioned Teddy's name, the directions to Ixtlan were immediately given over the phone. "Great to have a new face visit us. Especially a friend of Teddy's."

Tom and Rover got into the car. The first turnoff wasn't that far, even with the sketchy directions. It was an unmarked road, identifiable only by the broken fence post and upside-down rusted metal mailbox hanging from a hinge, probably left unattended on purpose to maintain their privacy. The dirt road seemed endless, just like the phone directions indicated, but the bumps and ruts were more than the Chevy could take. The car had been purchased with cash at a used car dealership the day Tom had arrived in Tempe, but he hadn't planned on the ruts and ridges of a washboard road trip like this one. Rover was beginning to moan. Tom stopped the car and let Rover out to pee. He took a deep breath of desert air and filled his lungs with the sweet aroma of desert wildflowers in bloom. The desert was in pristine form, no wind or even a gentle breeze. Only stillness. Tom walked toward a small mound of rocks shimmering with light from the overhead sun. He sat on the largest, flattest boulder, took off his shirt, leaned back, and basked in the desert heat. Rover came over, found some shade under a large waxy bush with yellow flowers, and lay down. There was an intoxicating camphor smell that seemed to be coming from the bush when Rover rubbed his body against it. With his eyes closed, Tom drifted into a memory from his childhood on Maui.

With Aunt Molly at the airport waiting for Uncle Russ' plane to arrive from somewhere far away. He'd been on another orchid adventure trip. Molly sits next to Kyle on the wooden bench outside the airport. Hawaiian women carry leis of fresh flowers to adorn each debarking passenger when the plane lands. Molly tells Kyle the tradition of Hawaiian lei. She says that a lei should be a welcome celebration of one person's affection to another. It is considered rude to remove a lei from your neck in the presence of the person who gave it to you. The plane lands. People walk down the steps toward the ground and a line of women greet the passengers one by one, putting a lei over each person's head. Uncle Russ gets a lei with white flowers that smell sweet. He walks over to Kyle and Molly and reaches out to hug them both. The lei is crushed in the middle of the hug and the smell becomes intoxicating. Molly says, "Plumeria, my love. It's magical, isn't it? A cure for loneliness." She gives Russ a big kiss. It is only a few days since Kyle's mother was murdered, and Kyle hasn't spoken a word. He looks up at his uncle Russ and says, "Plumeria," and they both smile.

Tom's face felt hot from the rays of the sun. He sat up and realized he was probably sunburned. Irish genes didn't do well in strong sunlight. He walked to the car and took a drink from his water bottle, then poured some water into a plastic bowl for Rover. He put his shirt back on, got in the car, and pulled down the mirror on the visor above the steering wheel. By now his face was beet-red, so he splashed some cold water on his head and started up the engine. The road continued to be rough, so he drove slowly. It seemed he'd never find this place. Then, off in the distance, he saw signs of life: a grove of saguaro cactus, some small wooden buildings surrounded by a barbed-wire fence, and a few cars parked near a larger building.

As he approached, three dogs ran toward his car. Rover started barking. The quiet desert erupted in a frenzy of animal sounds that brought a young man out of the main house to greet him. Suddenly, Tom felt light-headed. He realized he was stuck out in the middle of nowhere.

Tom turned off the engine just as the man yelled, "Namaste, Yogi, Zen, go back inside." The dogs headed toward the main house. Tom opened the driver's door and Rover jumped over his lap to join them. The man greeted Tom, saying, "Don't worry about the dogs. They just sound vicious. Watchdogs, that's all." He pointed toward the house. "Come in. I'll show you around. I'm Jeffrey, by the way. So, you must be Tom, Teddy's friend." Tom nodded. They walked toward the main house. The entire compound was surrounded by barbed wire.

Tom asked, "What is this place?"

"Used to be a POW camp for German prisoners. Now it's a sanctuary for gays. Go figure."

They entered the house and Jeffrey offered Tom some iced tea. They sat down at a wooden picnic table, a throwback to his childhood on Maui. There was a red and white plastic checkered tablecloth on the table with red plastic plates, and plastic glasses piled up on one side. Jeffrey said, "We're about to have lunch. Want to join us?" Tom was beginning to feel better. The trip from Tempe wasn't that long, but the ruts in the road made him nauseated. He looked around the room. It looked so run-down, almost like the place his mother used to take him to when she needed special medicine to feel better.

He has to walk fast from the bus stop until they come to her friend's place. The houses are old wooden structures with screened porches. Kyle gets to play with a litter of kittens in a box under a wooden picnic table in the screen porch. His mother goes into another room and leaves him there alone. When she comes out she wipes her nose with a Kleenex. Then she puts a small plastic bag filled with something white, like sugar, in her purse after she pays for her medicine. Kyle isn't sure why she needs the medicine, or why his mother doesn't get it from Dr. Luther in Maui. When they leave, his mother seems a lot happier and she has lots more energy. She even stops to get him a chocolate ice cream cone before they get back on the bus to go home.

Tom began to sneeze, then cough. He pulled the inhaler out of his pocket and took a whiff. Jeffrey said, "Maybe the incense is a bit too strong today." Just then an older man joined them. He had a striking appearance, probably because of his height. He must have been at least six feet four inches. His shiny brown hair, slightly graying around the temples, was positioned at the back of his head in a ponytail. Around his forehead, he wore a colorful headband made of feathers, and instead of jeans or pants he had on a flowered cotton skirt tucked over a white linen blouse. "My name's Dillon. Welcome." Tom tried to contain his sense of awe while Dillon sat across from him at the table.

Dillon smiled. "So, what brings you to Ixtlan?"

Tom noticed Dillon's deep brown eyes and perfectly groomed eyebrows. "Well, it's a long story."

"Then why don't we hear it over lunch?" He pointed to Jeffrey. "Let's have some fresh salad."

Jeffrey went into the kitchen in the next room and brought out a huge wooden bowl filled with salad. He served Tom and Dillon first, then sat down on the wooden bench and served himself. Tom couldn't help commenting on the array of colorful vegetables. "Do you grow your own food?"

Dillon answered. "We grow most of our food. We're pretty self-sufficient. Took us a few years. After we eat, I'll show you around."

They finished the salad with some freshly baked sourdough bread; then Dillon took Tom on a tour of the compound. One of the buildings looked like a warehouse, with a tin roof that was reflecting overhead sunlight, almost blinding Tom, who wasn't used to the bright Arizona afternoon sun. Dillon pointed toward a series of smaller wooden structures. "You see that cluster of buildings? My father bought them after the war."

Tom stopped walking. "The war?"

"World War II. This place was originally used as a POW camp for German prisoners."

Tom felt like he was floating above himself, looking down at his body, but not connected to it. *Just like in my dream. The barbed-wire fences. How could I have known?*

Dillon continued walking. "Yes. My father homesteaded here for a few years after the war, and after the camp was cleared out. There were over 2000 POWs here—mostly German, a few Japanese. There were over 250 buildings. Now this is all that's left."

Tom tried to keep pace with Dillon, who must have been twice his age. "What happened to the rest?"

"They were disassembled and the wood was sold dirt cheap, or given away."

Tom was dumbfounded. "How did your father even know about this place?"

Dillon paused to adjust his headband. Sweat was beginning to form on his forehead. "Dad—or Amsted, as he was called—moved to San Francisco for a while after the war. He was never actually deployed to fight, since he had polio as a kid. His whole left side was affected, and his left arm was shorter than his right. They gave him a desk job at the POW camp during the war, but when it ended, he knew he needed to move somewhere else. He was a gay kid who would have been miserable staying in Arizona. So he moved to San Francisco, where I was born. Too bad he was only around for a few years."

"What do you mean?"

"Dad died of AIDS when I was fourteen. After that, I was raised by a community of gay men who were engineers, like my dad." Dillon opened the door to a large structure. "This is the mess hall, or the common area. We still use the original water tower left over from the POW days." He pointed out the window. Tom saw an old wooden water tower near the building. Inside the mess hall a group of men sorted freshly picked vegetables on a long table. Some of the men were wearing long cotton skirts. Some had on headbands with wreaths of feathers, or flowers. Some had lipstick on their lips and rouge on their cheeks. A few had long braided hair with ribbons woven into the braids. Only a couple of the men looked more conventional in their blue jeans. None of them were wearing shirts. Dillon walked over to a stage area, raised both his hands, and shouted, "Blessed be. We have a visitor." The commotion stopped and all eyes turned toward Tom. "This is Tom, a friend of Teddy's from Phoenix."

In unison, there was a chorus of "Welcome to Ixtlan."

Tom felt his face flush. It was hot in the mess hall. That was probably why the men had no shirts on. Dillon motioned for the men to get back to what they were doing, and took Tom into a kitchen area where he opened an industrial-sized refrigerator. He took out a bottle of cold water, handed it to Tom, and then took one for himself. "So, what do you think?"

Tom gulped a long drink of water. "I think I'm in shock. I can't believe this is happening. Tell me more about how you ended up here."

They sat down at the end of one of the long wooden tables while the activity continued around them. Dillon began to tell more of his story. He was born in San Francisco, where his father was living "a sordid life" in the Castro district. After frequenting the gay bars and witnessing the homophobia, beatings, and killings of gays, he decided to move into a big house with a few of his gay friends. By then, he'd gotten his engineering degree and was making money, as were the other four roommates. Then Dillon was born.

Tom interrupted. "I'm confused. Your dad was gay, right?"

Dillon smiled. "Where have you been, boy? It was the early'60s in California. Free love, marijuana, LSD, communes, Bette Midler performing in bath houses, a plethora of Dionysian pleasures—enough to throw anyone into a hedonistic lifestyle."

Tom's eyes widened. "Guess where I lived we never really talked about that stuff."

Dillon stood up to stretch. "Where you lived. And where was that?"

Tom felt the hairs on the back of his neck stand up.

Suddenly the conversation had shifted to him. To his past. He paused, then said, "I grew up on Maui."

"Oh, that must explain it." Dillon winked.

Tom wasn't sure what that wink meant, or even if he should have told Dillon the truth. So far everything he'd told anyone since he left Hawaii had been a lie. But somehow he felt safe telling the truth to Dillon. He felt like he was in a surreal dream where past and present merged into one. Where the blurred lines between reality and fiction tangled his thoughts and forced him to let down his guard. After all, how could he have known a simple comment from the judge about a sanctuary for gay men in Arizona would lead him here?

Dillon continued, "So, do you want to hear more?"

Tom pulled out his inhaler and took a puff of the medicine. "Sure. Go on."

"Oh, I see you have asthma. Well, some of our other boys have it, or had it when they arrived here."

"Had it?"

"Gone now. Well, except for Danny. He's got other complications."

Tom looked up with a start. *Danny*. The name sent chills up his spine. He took another whiff of the inhaler.

"You all right? Want to go back to the house?"

Tom composed himself. *It couldn't be the same Danny.* "No, I'll be fine in a minute. Go on with your story."

"Dad told me that my mother was one of the many fag hags that hung around their place. One day the drugs took over, and well—one thing led to another. It was mostly her call, but Dad went along with it, and in a few weeks she announced she was pregnant. After I was born, she left."

Tom's eyes were glued to Dillon's. He felt like he was seeing through a window into the soul of history. History that was made over twenty years before he was born. History that he knew nothing about. His secret life in Hawaii wasn't that different from what Dillon's father had in San Francisco. But there were no fag hags hanging around him at the Butterfly Lounge. It was probably too seedy and dangerous. It had never occurred to him that there were other boys just like him, in other parts of the world. He was too wrapped up in his own life on Maui, isolated in his world of demons and lies.

Dillon continued. "I was raised mostly by Dad and his partner, Louie. And with the other men in the house, it became like one big family. When I was ten, Dad and Louie took me to see their land in Arizona. They had money and engineering skill. We ended up living there and refurbishing the structures, one by one, until they were livable. Those were probably the best memories of my father. When he died, Louie took me back to San Francisco, where I graduated high school and went to college."

Tom interrupted, "Sorry about your dad. My mom died the day before my seventh birthday."

"Then you know what it's like, don't you? Was she sick?" Tom began to tell the story of his mother's murder. The words flowed off his tongue in rapid succession with gruesome details of disjointed images. The blood, Rover licking it up around her naked body, his Aunt Molly, then the fire. Then, like someone muted the dial on a radio, there was only silence in his head.

He's out of his body, back inside the closet in his bedroom after the murder. A policeman opens the door and reaches out his hand. Kyle sits frozen with fear. The policeman lifts him up and carries him to Aunt Molly's house. There are chocolate chip cookies on the table. He can't smell them or taste them, but he is eating one. He takes a sip of milk. He sees the policeman's lips moving. Then his Aunt Molly's lips move. They must be talking to each other, but all he hears is the rhythmic sound from the beating of his own heart.

"You okay? Tom, what's wrong? Here, have some water." Dillon's gentle voice broke the silence.

Tom blinked. He took a sip of water.

"Where'd you go, man?"

Tom blinked a few more times. "They called it a catatonic state brought on by extreme trauma. I stopped speaking for weeks after that."

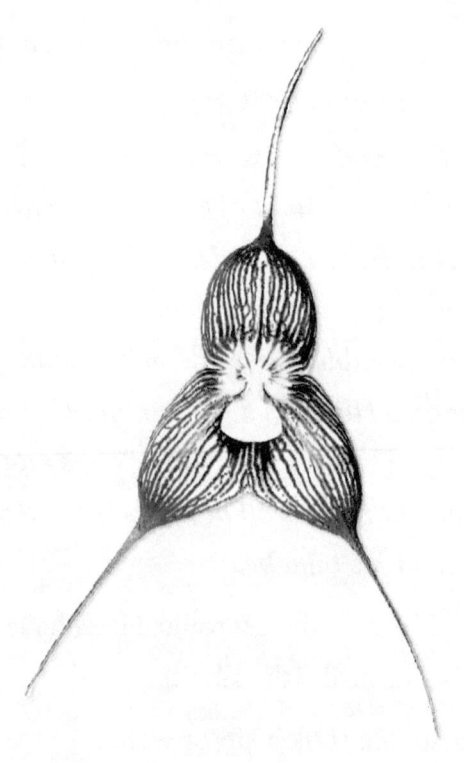

CHAPTER FIVE

The Gold Bracelet

It was late when Tom returned to Tempe. He fed Rover and flopped on his bed, too exhausted to get undressed. Bizarre images collided in strange dreams that had him tossing and turning until the bed sheets laid in a heap on the floor.

Small box wrapped in brown paper held together with twine, no return address. He opens the box. Inside, a tiny dog sculpted from wet sand. He touches the head of the dog. An eye opens and winks at him. Sand begins to dry and flake away. He gets a glass of water and pours some over the tiny sand creature. It reconfigures. He leaves the box by his bed, and each day puts more water over the shape as it slowly dissolves. Next morning he goes outside to get the newspaper before breakfast. A white fluffy dog comes out of nowhere, leaps into his arms, and begins licking his face. It sleeps with him and keeps him company when he descends into his place of darkness. He calls the dog Yaqui.

Rover's barking at the paper boy woke Tom that morning. He was still groggy and confused from the dream. *A box with a dog made of sand?* He had no idea where that dream came from, but at least the dream ended with a white fluffy companion. He went outside to get the morning paper, but instead he saw a small box wrapped just like the one in his dream. Afraid at first, he slowly reached down and touched the box to make sure he wasn't still dreaming. Then, he carefully took the small box to the kitchen table. *Should I open it? Maybe it's a bomb.* He looked to see who sent it, but there was no return address. He slowly unwrapped the brown paper, half-expecting to find a dog made of sand. He pulled open the cardboard and reached down between wadded-up sheets of newspaper until he felt something hard. He couldn't tell what it was, so he lifted it out and held it up to the light. It was a gold bracelet. Then he pulled out a piece of the crumpled newsprint and saw the word *Maui*. Breaking out in an instant sweat, he carefully unfolded the crinkled newsprint, smoothed it out, and placed it on the kitchen table. Scanning the articles, his eyes fixated on a headline: *"Molly Tanner, orchid maven, dies in fire."* The article was dated November 30, 2007. He continued reading. *"The morning of her yearly Garden Society of Maui fundraiser, Molly Tanner's body was found burnt beyond recognition among the charred palm branches and smoldering rubble* of what was once a thriving orchid estate. Built by her late husband Russ Tanner, who died a few years earlier during one of his orchid expeditions to the Amazon rainforest, the three greenhouses, along with the main house, burnt to the ground. Police are investigating the incident. They say the cause of the fire was arson. Molly Tanner is survived by her adopted son, Kyle O'Sullivan, who has graciously donated what is left of her estate to the Garden Society of Maui."

Tom stumbled to sit on the wooden chair by the table. Sweat dripped down his forehead. *My God. Who sent this?* He rummaged through the small box for a note, but there was nothing but more newsprint. Again he looked at the top of the box for a return address. None. *Was it Danny? Maybe it was the judge. Shit. The gold bracelet sure looks like the one the judge gave me.* Tom held the bracelet up to the light again, and examined the linking on the chain. The chain was much thinner and linked differently than the one the judge gave him. *Besides, I gave Danny the bracelet from the judge, and the cops must still have it as evidence from the fire. That psycho went out and bought a new one to send to me.* Tom's mind went through scenarios of how Danny could have found him in Tempe. The only connection would have been the Butterfly Lounge at Maui when he went there for his new identity documents. And the judge would never risk his reputation by walking into that place. *But Danny used to hang out there all the time. All he had to do was to ask if anyone knew what had happened to me.*

They all knew he and Danny had been in a relationship on and off, but no one knew he was the reason Kyle had left Maui. *It is definitely Danny. That shit. That fucked-up psychopath. He's found me.*

    Danny and Kyle smoke weed in their fort behind Molly's orchid houses. Danny has a white cast on one arm and a bruised eye. He finishes the joint and reaches into a bag, takes out a small garter snake, and with a Swiss Army knife, he begins to poke holes into the reptile, who writhes back and forth with each stab. Under his breath he chants, "Take that, you bastard. I hate you. Take that, and that." Kyle knows Danny is talking to his stepfather, who, in his drunken stupors, taunted and beat Danny. There was no one around to witness, since Danny's mother had died when he was ten. Danny finishes off the torture by cutting the head off the snake. He then gets up and walks a few yards to a makeshift graveyard where he's buried other animals he's killed. Kyle knows not to interfere when Danny goes into his Jack the Ripper mode. Then they fuck, like always, after Danny's gotten back at his stepfather.

Tom went into the bathroom to pee. There was a strange smell coming from the toilet area, but he was too distracted to pay it much attention. He looked into the toilet bowl at the dark brown ring near the water line. *Probably need to clean out the bowl with bleach.* He went into the kitchen to make coffee, but got sidetracked when he saw the gold bracelet on the table. He couldn't get Danny out of his mind.

The makeshift tombstone says, "For you poor suckers." Lilly is there now. She runs her index finger over the wet soil on the grave of the snake. They watch while Danny tallies up his kill, each grave marked with a pink and brown harp shell Danny picked up along the Maui shoreline. On each shell he's written in black marker the abbreviated name of the animal: TR for tarantula, SN for snake, PAR for parrot, STR for starfish, and the worst of all, CAT for cat. Lilly wipes a tear from her eye and heads toward the opening of the fort. She is the sentinel who watches over them while they fuck, in case someone is coming. The three fuckateers...except Lilly seems to get the raw end of the deal. Danny never looks directly into their eyes. Instead, his eyes dart back and forth like a crazy man's. But Lilly tells Kyle that Danny is in states of dissociation, like when Kyle's mother was murdered and he went catatonic. Lilly is smart like that. She understands human nature. So, Kyle figures Danny is doing what is necessary to survive his stepfather, just like Kyle had to when he found his mother lying in a pool of blood with her throat cut wide open.

The smell coming from the bathroom was worse. Tom knew he had to clean the toilet. He found a bottle of bleach and a toilet brush and cleaned the bowl, then flopped on the unmade bed, Rover at his side. Images swirled in his head in puddles of color. He knew it was a matter of time until Danny did something else even crazier, probably to torment him before the kill, just like he did to his stash of animals buried at Maui.

Loose cannon. Lilly had warned him. Tom lay awake for hours, trying to figure out what to do. *I'm a dead man. If I go to the cops they'll ask all kinds of questions about why Danny would want me dead. Then I'd have to tell the whole story about why I left Maui and changed my identity, and about how Danny set the fire and killed Aunt Molly instead of me, and about the gold bracelet left at the scene of the fire. Shit, then I'd have to tell the cops about the judge, who gave me the gold bracelet that I gave to Danny. The Tempe cops might even team up with the cops at Maui and reopen the arson case to try to prove Danny set the fire.*

In his state of half-consciousness, Tom tossed and turned in the bed while his mind ran more scenarios over and over like film in a projector. *And maybe even Mr. Leavenworth's murder would come out. Shit, Danny would have nothing to lose. If he's caught, he might even tell the cops that I came up with the plan to kill his stepfather. Then I would be an accomplice to murder. He doesn't give a shit. Just wants to make me suffer. Either way, I'm finished.*

Tom finally got up and went outside to get away from the smell in the bathroom, which hadn't gotten any better. Still in a dream-state, images formed more clearly in his mind with flashes of Danny's bizarre behavior. Kids used to tease Danny just liked they teased Kyle, calling Danny "Bucky Beaver," because of his two front teeth protruding forward when his permanent teeth came in. The two of them, "Reddylocks and

Bucky Beaver," became the brunt of class jokes throughout elementary school and into junior high. *I have to find Danny and stop him before he does anything else. Whatever it takes. What if I have to kill him? Oh my God.*

When Tom went back inside to lie down on the bed to get some sleep, the smell of bleach was so strong that he began to feel nauseated. Suddenly, he felt an uncontrollable urge to vomit. He ran toward the bathroom and barely made it to the toilet. Sweat seeped from his pores. His body felt clammy. Maybe he was getting the flu.

ೞ   ೞ   ೞ   ೞ

The next day Pen called, asking him to come to her place. It was Sunday, and Tom had promised to take her to a movie. Tom told her that he wasn't feeling well. He knew he needed to get out of that house, but being with Pen when he felt so crappy just wasn't going to work this time. Maybe he'd feel better if he went to Ixtlan to relax. Besides, he could see Dillon—the only person he was beginning to trust since he arrived in Tempe.

The drive to Ixtlan didn't seem as long this time, since Tom didn't stop to let Rover out to pee. When he pulled up to the house, Rover jumped over his lap to get out. Namaste and Zen ran out to greet them. Tom got out of the car and saw Dillon come out of the house. He asked, "What happened to the other dog?"

Dillon's face saddened. "Yogi passed yesterday. He was old. Got him from a shelter in Tempe when he was just a few months. The other two dogs really miss him. Glad you brought Rover today."

Tom couldn't help but fix his gaze on Dillon. He looked so different from the last time. Now he was dressed in tight black jeans and a white linen shirt. His shiny brown hair was braided with black and red ribbons intertwined and secured behind his head. He had on white flip-flops with a small red plastic flower at the juncture of his toes, which were painted with red nail polish. Tom took his canvas backpack with extra bottles of water and treats for Rover, and walked toward the house. On the way, he reached toward the bottom part of his canvas bag to make sure the cardboard box with the gold bracelet was there. He wasn't sure why he had brought it, but somehow he knew he had to. They entered the house and Dillon motioned for Tom to sit down at the wooden picnic table, still covered with the same red and white checked plastic tablecloth.

Jeffrey entered from the kitchen and offered them some mango iced tea. "Hi Tom. Good to see you again. Have something cold. You okay? You look a little piqued."

Tom took a sip of the iced tea, reached into his canvas bag, and took out the box. He set it on the table in front of Dillon. "I need to tell you something, well—private." Dillon motioned for Jeffrey to leave. Tom opened the box and took out the gold bracelet. He held it up to the light. Dillon's eyes widened as he looked at the piece of jewelry. "Is it real gold?"

"Not sure ."

"Where'd you get it?"

"That's a long story." Tom put the bracelet back into the box.

"Well, let's walk over to the commons and we can talk. It's a lot cooler there."

Tom felt huge relief to be talking to someone. His words spilled out like bursting flood gates of a dam. This time he didn't hesitate. His words came easily. The truth was not hard to tell to Dillon, just everyone else. Tom made sure not to mention any real names, especially Danny's. And he also made sure not to mention his relationship with the judge. Then, he paused to take a puff of his inhaler.

Dillon seemed confused. "So, how does this present of the gold bracelet you got in the mail relate to all of this?"

Tom continued. "It's the same kind of bracelet that was left at the scene of the fire on Maui. I think the person who wanted to kill me has found me in Tempe."

Dillon stood up. "My god. Have you gone to the police?"

Tom froze. "The police? No." Tom realized he was getting in too deep. Maybe he shouldn't have said anything to Dillon. He tried to compose himself. "Look, you're the only one who knows about all of this. Let's just leave it that way for now. I just told you because, well, I trust you." Tom's eruption of truth-telling was now more than he could handle. He needed to think before he said anything else to Dillon about Danny; otherwise he'd probably end up getting into his relationship with the judge, and how he got the gold bracelet, then gave it to Danny, and things would start spiraling out of control. Lilly's name would come up since she was his alibi for the night of the fire, and Tom didn't want to hurt her with the truth about her father. And he certainly didn't want his problems with Danny to ruin the judge's reputation. The judge had become like a father to him. He had figured it was better to make a clean break and not tell the judge where he was going, so no one would try to find him. But Danny did find him.

Dillon sat down and in an emphatic voice said, "Look Tom, we've had some pretty crazy things happen at Ixtlan. You're not the first person who's feared for his life. We're used to this shit."

Tom managed a smile. He took a long drink of the tea and decided to tell Dillon about the dream with the dog of sand in a small box, and how that same morning a box arrived at his doorstep with the gold bracelet. Dillon listened to Tom, then blurted out, "Yaqui? You named the dog Yaqui?" Dillon jumped up. "We're going on a little road trip." He called out to Jeffrey, who was in the kitchen, and told him they were going out for a while.

Tom grabbed the box on the table, put it into his canvas bag, followed Dillon out to the pick-up truck, and got in. "Where are we going?"

"There is someone I want you to meet. He can explain that dream better than I can."

Tom made himself comfortable on the front seat of the truck. Overhead, he watched as four white-necked ravens circled around them as they began to leave. Dillon pointed to the birds. "Good sign. The ravens are circling the right way."

Tom had no idea what Dillon was talking about, but he felt amazingly calm. He was so relieved that he had someone to talk to about his dreams, besides Pen. She said that dreams were just dreams, that they meant nothing. But Tom had always taken his dreams seriously, especially after his mother's murder. It was his dream life that had gotten him through the trauma. It was his dream life that let him escape into his world of imagination. And now his dreams seemed to be overlapping with his real world. He was glad he'd told Dillon his dream about the dog.

The dirt road out of Ixtlan was bumpy, but Tom was getting used to it. He took a drink from his water bottle. This time he wasn't nauseated. Dillon turned right, and headed toward the main highway. Tom opened his window and let the wind caress his face. He closed his eyes and basked in the heat of the sunlight. The sensuousness of that moment—endless vast desert ahead, miles of blue sky above, heading out into the unknown, sitting next to Dillon, pulled Tom into a state of calm he'd never experienced before. Dillon touched him on the shoulder and said, "Look over there."

Tom looked ahead and saw a small metal trailer surrounded by a clump of saguaro cactus, much like the one he'd lived in on Maui. Next to the trailer was a mound of dirt covered with a canvas tarp. There was a separate piece of canvas that looked like it was covering an entrance to the structure. They pulled up to the trailer and parked. In a few seconds a man opened the door and stepped onto the wooden porch. Dillon greeted the man by speaking in a louder-than-usual voice. "Felipe, sorry to come unannounced. There's someone you need to meet."

Felipe took off his sunglasses and motioned for them to come inside. Tom immediately saw that Felipe was Native American. He was wearing Levi's and a plain white tee-shirt. His long gray hair was braided in back and he wore a leather headband over his forehead. His face was weathered, probably from the dry Arizona climate. Tom couldn't tell how old he was. Tom entered a darkened room. His eyes needed to adjust. He smelled the sweet smell of something like incense. Felipe reached down and slid a pile of papers and magazines from the couch onto the floor. "Sorry about the mess. Wasn't expecting anyone. Have a seat." They both sat down on the couch.

While Tom's eyes began to adjust to the darkness, he

could see that the trailer was filled with all sorts of artifacts that he didn't recognize, but they reminded him of the native art from Hawaii.

Dillon spoke first. "Tom has visited us a couple of times, but today he told me about a dream he'd had, and I knew I had to bring him to you. Then, when we got into the pick-up truck there were four ravens circling above us."

"Four ravens. Yes, that's definitely a good sign. Now, tell me about your dream."

Tom recounted the events of the dream and how, that morning, a real box had arrived at his front door. He reached into his canvas bag and took out the box. Then he pulled out the gold bracelet and held it up to the light. But Felipe motioned for him to put the bracelet back into the box. He picked up a stick of what looked like weeds wrapped in twine, and lit a match. Then he held the flame to the end of the stick and it began to burn, sending the most wonderful smell throughout the trailer. "Smudge stick," Felipe said. "We need to clear out bad energy first."

Tom inhaled. This time he had no trouble with his asthma. "What is it?"

"Sage from New Mexico." Tom had never smelled burning sage before. The trailer was small and it didn't take long for the build-up of smoke to become too strong. Felipe stood up, opened the front door, then reached into a bucket of sand on the porch and snuffed out the burning stick. Tom went outside to get some fresh air.

Felipe turned toward him and said, "Yaqui? You named the dog Yaqui?"

Dillon laughed from inside the trailer. "Told you."

Felipe put his hand on Tom's shoulder. "Ever heard of the Yaqui Indians?"

Tom took a step back. "Not really."

"Well, you're looking at one now. There's a community of us living in Tempe. I chose to live out here alone."

Tom was speechless. Dillon came out onto the porch. The three of them stood for a moment in silence. Tom pointed over to the strange shaped structure covered with a canvas tarp. "What's that?"

Felipe answered. "A sweat lodge. We use it once in a while for cleansing ceremonies."

"Cleansing ceremonies?"

Dillon explained, "Felipe is a Yaqui medicine man. He supervises these ceremonies by administering peyote to help a person reach an altered state, like when you dream. This practice has been going on in the Native culture for many years. Amsted told me about it. He used to take LSD to reach an altered state. In the '60s, acid was a big deal."

Felipe nodded. "But we don't use it that way. Peyote is

used only for ceremonial purposes. It's part of our cultural practice."

Tom's adrenalin pumped full blast. He had so many more questions. Even though these words seemed strange to him, the concept of altered states seemed familiar. His dreams, his nightmares—maybe they actually meant something after all.

Felipe continued. "I'll tell you how we Natives explain it. We live in two worlds.

The world you see around you, the everyday world with cars and people and shopping malls, that's one world. That's what most people live in. But the world of dreams, of nightmares, of intuition, that's the spirit world, the one we access through peyote."

Tom felt a chill going up his spine. That was exactly how he lived, in two worlds. He'd never understood before. He took a deep breath of fresh air. The sweet smell of sage filled his lungs. Dillon stepped off the wooden porch and began to walk over to the sweat lodge. "I've done a couple of peyote ceremonies in here, but I've never gotten to the dream state that you have."

Tom followed him into the sweat lodge. There was a fire pit filled with large round rocks. An empty metal bucket sat next to the pit. Dillon explained how the rocks were heated with a roaring fire, then how water was poured over the hot rocks to create steam. The people in the lodge would take peyote and sweat, a form of cleansing the body. Eventually, they'd slip into an altered state of consciousness.

Tom began to feel claustrophobic. He walked outside and Dillon followed. Tom asked, "Ixtlan? Where'd that name come from? Is it a Yaqui word?"

Felipe answered. "Amsted took that name from one of the books written by Carlos Castaneda in the early '70s. It's a metaphorical place where the sorcerer, or man of knowledge, must go, because his elevated perspective leaves him little in common with ordinary people. He can never truly go home to his old lifestyle again."

Tom had never heard of the concept of man of knowledge. Warrior or sorcerer, yes, but that was in the context of comic books or movies. Yet, he somehow resonated with Felipe's words. He felt like he could never go home, back to his old lifestyle. In any case, both Dillon and Felipe seemed to feel his dream about the dog meant something special.

Felipe went back into his trailer and came out holding something wrapped in a small colorful blanket. He handed it to Tom. "This is the peace pipe I used when I first became a Yaqui medicine man." He took the pipe out of the blanket. It was made of wood, with carbon deposits on one end, and an inlay of turquoise held down by strips of rawhide in a crisscross pattern on the other. "It's made of cedar." He held the pipe to Tom's nose so he could smell it. "I'll teach you what you need to learn." He pulled out some tobacco from a pouch hanging from the pipe and stuffed a small amount in the metal bowl attached at the end. Then he lit it with a match, took a puff, and passed it to Dillon, who also took a puff. Dillon passed the pipe to Tom, who inhaled just enough to be sociable, but not to cough. Then Felipe held the pipe toward the sky and chanted something in a native tongue. Tom could see smoke still rising from the bowl of tobacco. He felt a chill run through his body.

Dillon took Tom's arm. "This is quite an honor, Tom. The last person to be given this peace pipe was my father. When he died it came back to Felipe, whose job was to keep it until he found the next guardian. This means he sees something special in you."

Felipe handed the pipe to Tom. "You are now the guardian of this pipe. It's now in your care."

Tom felt a surge of anxiety in his gut. "What am I supposed to do with it?"

You will know when the time comes. Meanwhile, keep it in a safe place. You told me about your Yaqui dream. That was my signal that I needed to pass the pipe on to you. Let me know about other dreams you've had, if you want. We will visit again the next time you come to Ixtlan. But before you go, I am giving you an Indian name." Felipe said something in Native tongue that Tom couldn't understand. Then Felipe said,

"Don't worry. It means 'shadow dreamer.' That's all you need to know."

Tom took the pipe and he and Dillon got into the truck and drove off. There was silence most of the way back to Ixtlan. Tom didn't notice that Dillon turned off the road and headed in a different direction. After a few minutes they came to a small building next to a gas station. The neon sign on the building was flashing on and off: *Blue Corn Diner*.

Dillon pulled up and parked in the dirt next to the gas station. "Thought we'd get a bite to eat before we return. I want you to meet the locals here."

Tom put the peace pipe and his canvas bag under the seat, and when he got out of the truck, he made sure his door was locked. They walked into the diner together. It took a moment for Tom's eyes to adjust to the dim light, but as he began to scan the room he was caught off-guard.

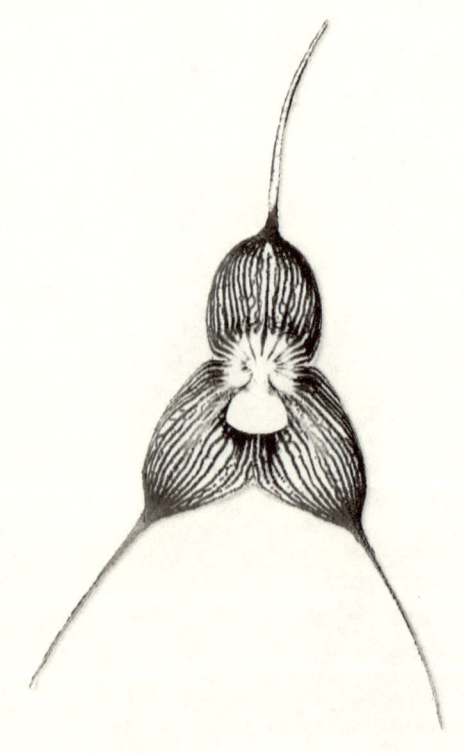

CHAPTER SIX

Blue Corn Diner

Men with scruffy beards, beer-bellies protruding over tight belted jeans. Men wearing skirts, painted toenails, hair in braids intertwined with colorful ribbons. Sexy young waitress in Hooters' garb serving iced pitchers of cold beer. Wooden picnic tables covered with red and white checkered plastic tablecloths. Sawdust on the floor, jukebox playing "Moon River." Two young men dancing in romantic embrace. Bartender, an older woman, weather-worn skin, bleached hair, designer jeans, and manicured nails, serving alcoholic drinks, mostly beer.

Dillon headed toward the bar and ordered beer for everyone. Tom was busy looking around at the unusual clientele. He felt like he was in some sort of altered reality, maybe a time warp out of a Star Trek movie. He noticed a display of flowering orchids at the back of the bar. The huge mirror behind them made it look like there were rows and rows of plants, reminding Tom of the greenhouse on Maui. He asked where they came from. Dillon told him there was a greenhouse in the back of the cafe where Danny grew them for the residents.

"*Danny?*" Tom's heart skipped a beat.

"Want to meet him? He's over there." Dillon pointed to a young boy who couldn't have been more than seventeen. He was talking to an older man who was wearing a skirt and silk blouse. He had dark-red lipstick on his lips and a colorful scarf on his head. The older man turned around and gave Dillon a hug. "Dillon. Great to see you. It's been a while."

Dillon returned the hug, then pointed toward Tom. "Red Wolf, this is Tom Tanner. He's visiting us at Ixtlan."

Danny turned around. "Hi. I'm Daniel, but everyone calls me Danny for short."

Tom breathed a sigh of relief. Daniel was definitely Native American. Tom hadn't thought about Danny and the gold bracelet for a few hours, but it didn't take much to remind him of what he had to face when he returned to Tempe. He felt like his world was now split into three separate parts: his life at Maui as Kyle, his life in Tempe as Tom, and his life at Ixtlan. He joined the three of them at a table and they sat down to talk. Red Wolf got into a conversation with Dillon while Daniel talked to Tom about orchids, and other things. He explained that he'd lived at Ixtlan since he was fourteen, after his father sent him to one of those religious summer camps in California where they "cured" men and boys of homosexuality. It was like an army boot camp where they tried to get the boys to "man-up." They even made him have underage sex with a woman. He managed to sneak out one night and hitch-hike across the country. He'd heard about a place in Arizona that was a sanctuary for gays.

When Felipe had learned that Daniel's mother owned a commercial greenhouse in Washington State, he asked Daniel if he could maintain one at the Blue Corn Diner. He explained how important flowers were in the Yaqui culture. According to Yaqui teachings, flowers sprang from the drops of blood that were shed at the Crucifixion. Flowers were viewed as the manifestation of souls. Occasionally, Yaqui men would greet a close male friend with the phrase "*Haisa swea*?" ("How is the flower?")

Tom was so engrossed in Daniel's story that he completely forgot about his own problems. He imagined what it must have been like for Daniel, hiding from who he was, being sent away to a religious camp to make him "straight." He thought his life on Maui was bad, but this was bad too. He told Daniel about his own love of orchids, and they began talking like he used to with his uncle at Maui. But after a while, Tom realized that Daniel was attracted to him, that the talk about orchids was probably more about getting into his pants. His gut clenched up —a warning sign to pull back. The last thing he needed was another kid with the name Danny, hanging around him. Besides, Tom had always liked older men, maybe because he never knew his own father.

Red Wolf reached over and touched Daniel on the shoulder. "Let's show Tom the greenhouse." They all walked through the back door of the cafe and across a few feet of dirt toward a structure made of clear Plexiglas. When they entered, Tom felt like he had been transported back to his home on Maui. Rows of orchids lined the aluminum shelves. A huge fan hung at each end of the greenhouse, and a misting system went off every few hours on a timer. There were an air conditioner and heater—perfect climate control for the middle of the desert. Tom walked from row to row, leaning down to look closely at the flowers and their tags. "You clone these yourself?"

Daniel smiled. "No, we send out seeds to a cloning plant in Taiwan. They grow them in sterile conditions and send them back when the seedlings are large enough to plant in bark or other media."

Tom looked up and saw rows of blooming orchids hanging in baskets. The roots, like tendrils, twisted out of the sphagnum moss. The fan-like leaves formed a symmetrical spray of greenery with a thick stem protruding from inside. Tom knew they were Vandas, and needed extra humidity. His uncle's Vandas were even more spectacular, but that was because they grew better in Hawaii. He felt like he was in a candy shop. Like when he was a kid on Maui, and his aunt used to take him to buy whatever he wanted when he got an A on his report card. Then at the far end of the greenhouse he noticed rows of hanging baskets, much smaller than the ones the Vandas were in. Daniel pointed toward the baskets. "Those are *Dracula vampira,* orchid of the night. Hard to grow in the desert."

Tom couldn't stop a tear from running down one side of his cheek. He stumbled backward. So many coincidences. So many new people, new ideas. He couldn't understand what was happening. Red Wolf came over to him and began waving his hands over Tom's head, then along his body. He told Tom that he was a Reiki master, a Navajo two-spirit person, or "nadleehi," trained in the healing arts. *Two-spirit person?* Tom was about to ask what that meant when Dillon opened the door to the greenhouse and motioned for them to go.

The Blue Corn Diner was teaming with activity by now. The lunch crowd had arrived. Dillon pulled out the menu—an array of soups, sandwiches, desserts, smoothies—all vegetarian, organic, and home-grown. Some of the produce had been grown in Tempe and some at Ixtlan. Dillon explained that Ixtlan residents based their lives on the concept of sustainable living and respect for Mother Earth. They also embraced many of the Native American values and spiritual practices, where the role of ritual could lead to altered states of consciousness.

Tom was beginning to understand. "So, who owns the Blue Corn Diner?"

Dillon answered. "It's a cooperative, owned by Ixtlan residents who live there full time, but it's open to the public. It took a few years for the locals to accept us, but as you see, now we're all one big happy family."

The buxom waitress came over to their table. She took their orders.

"Oh, how I wish Amsted could have seen this place." Dillon pointed to a picture hanging on the wall above the bar. "Dad, may you rest in peace. Hope you're watching now."

Tom looked up at the picture. Amsted was standing with his arm around another man, probably his partner, and he was holding a baby in his arms. The three of them were on a wharf next to a sailboat. Dillon pointed. "That's me when I was a few months old. Dad and Louie used to take me sailing on that boat." He took a sip of hot tea. The odor was strong, and Tom stopped to ask what kind of tea it was. Dillon told him was chaparral tea made from the creosote cactus that grew in the area. It was considered a medicinal herb by the Yaqui people and was often used as an antioxidant to help with upper respiratory infections.

"Are you sick?" Tom asked.

"Not yet. But I feel something coming on. Usually this tea stops it."

Tom realized that the smell was the same one that came from the cactus Rover brushed against the first time they came to Ixtlan. They finished eating and Dillon pulled out his wallet to pay the waitress, then motioned to Daniel and Red Wolf. "My treat." They all walked out to the pickup truck together. Daniel reached out to shake Tom's hand. "Come back soon."

℞ ℞ ℞ ℞

The drive back to Ixtlan took only half an hour. Dillon explained how the Yaqui dream was just the beginning of the connection he would have with Felipe Youngblood. Tom didn't go back inside the main house with Dillon. He knew if he did, he wouldn't want to leave. He needed to get home. Tomorrow was a work day, and anyway, Pen would be beside herself. He hadn't spent much time with her for the last few weekends.

It was still light when Tom returned to Tempe. Rover greeted him with a barking frenzy, wanting to be fed. The smell in the house was still there. Tom went back to the car to bring the peace pipe inside; then he went to the kitchen to grab some Oreo cookies and take a swig of buttermilk. But the stench was too much. *Emergency.* He picked up the phone and called the landlord, who said he'd send out his son to fix the leak in the morning.

There was only one room left that didn't smell yet. Tom grabbed the peace pipe, motioned for Rover to follow, and went into the room across from his bedroom to wait it out. The room where his precious Draculas hung from metal shelves, and where a few of the miniature orchids he'd ordered for the Phoenix Orchid Guild meetings sat on another shelf. The walls and ceiling were covered with plastic. Beads of water slid down the smooth surfaces from the last time the mister went off. Tom took a magnifying glass off the shelf and looked more closely at one of the miniature Cattleya plants with tiny lemon-colored flowers still blooming. The events of the weekend at Ixtlan faded into the microcosm-world of miniature flowers. Everything began to feel so unimportant, as he focused on the moment—on the orchids. He looked up toward the ceiling fan turning with an even hum, on schedule, misters beginning their cycle, on schedule, everything on schedule, predictable. His heart slowed down. He relaxed into his world of plants, where night dreams and day dreams merged into another dimension. A place where Kyle O'Sullivan and Tom Tanner could be one. Then he walked over to the shelves with the Draculas. The full-spectrum grow light reflected off of the ribbed surface of the dark-purple flowers snugly packed in sphagnum moss, reaching down through the basket—bat-like. *Dracula vampira. Orchid of the night. Safe and sound in your desert environment with your world in perfectly in balance.*

Shadow Dreamer. Tom said it out loud. "Shadow Dreamer." He walked into his bedroom and took out his uncle's journal from a dresser drawer. Then he went back into the room with the orchid plants and put the journal next to the peace pipe on a shelf in the closet. He carefully wrapped the colorful blanket over both of these precious possessions. The journal had survived the fire in Maui because Kyle kept it in his trailer. His aunt had given him Uncle Russ' journal for safekeeping. No one knew about the journal, now that Molly was dead. And Kyle had memorized all of the journal entries. His uncle never put his name in the journal, probably because some of the things he wrote about would have landed him in jail. But to Kyle, now Tom, the journal had become part of him. In his imagination, he could be Russ Tanner, orchid hunter, whenever he felt himself sinking into the depths of despair.

Then Tom grabbed a blanket and pillow from the same shelf and made himself a makeshift bed on the floor of the closet—just like when he was a child on Maui when he slept inside his closet to keep out the boogie man. He lay on his side, but felt something hard in his pocket. It was the gold bracelet that he'd stuffed into his jeans when he got out of the pickup truck to go into the Blue Corn Diner. He managed to pull out the bracelet and put it on the floor next to him. Then he drifted off to much-needed sleep. *Visions of raging fire, the smell of burnt flesh, fear, running, running for his life, the underbelly of Maui nightlife, floodgates open. Danny. It's just a matter of time.*

ભ ભ ભ ભ

The automatic timer clicked on at 6:00 a.m. and the grow light and mister started up. Rover, who lay next to him on the floor, nudged Tom with his nose, and Tom slowly got up to use the bathroom. The leaking pipe behind the toilet had burst and water was spewing all over, down the hall and onto the living room carpet. Thank God the small bedroom was a few inches higher than the rest of the house—probably an add-on for a baby's room or office. He walked barefoot on the linoleum floor, and when he got to the hallway his feet sloshed on the soggy carpet. Without even changing his clothes from the days before, he grabbed his shoes and dirty socks, grabbed Rover's bag of dog food, and went outside. The he poured some dog food in a bowl, shut the glass sliding door so Rover couldn't get back inside, and headed toward his car. He'd get breakfast at the Grille.

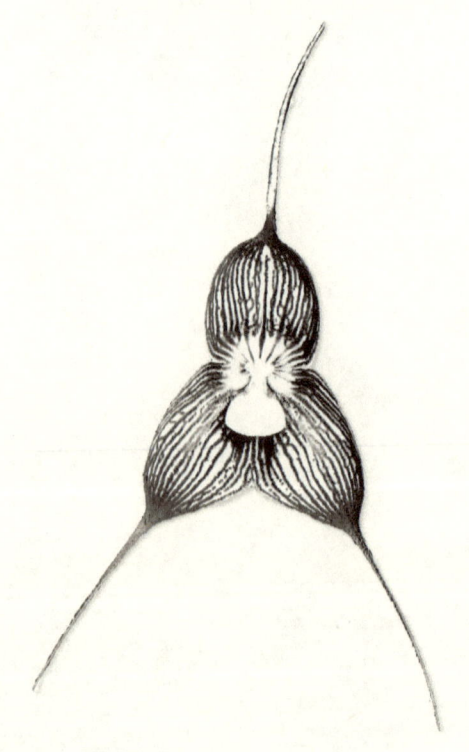

CHAPTER SEVEN

Road Trip

For the next few nights Tom stayed at Pen's place. The plumber's son had started to fix the broken pipe, but he needed to return with another part. Besides, the house had to air out before Tom could live there. Pen convinced Tom to take her on a road trip to Sedona over the weekend. He'd already taken Rover to a neighbor's house until his place was habitable.

Pen couldn't contain her excitement. "Shit. I finally get to see something outside of Phoenix." Between her work schedule and her car, which was always on the verge of some major crisis, her world had become insular and as she told Tom, "so boring." Tom's anxiety over the gold bracelet had been consuming him, but now that he'd told Felipe and Dillon the truth about who he really was, maybe this road trip would be a good time to tell Pen.

The drive from Tempe to Sedona was a little over two hours. Pen sat in the passenger's seat, staring out of the window, while Tom relaxed into the lilt of the car on the open road. They were heading toward Flagstaff—not the fastest route to Sedona, but a scenic one. Pen brought some water and sodas for the trip, along with a bag of fresh Oreo cookies, Tom's favorite. Tom was waiting for the right time to tell her about his real identity. Maybe he should wait until they get to Sedona and find a motel. They'd already been driving almost an hour and the only conversation was about the smelly house, Rover, and Pen's anger at not having more time with Tom.

Finally, Tom said, " So, why don't you finish your story about the time you broke your leg and had to go to Phoenix for a doctor?" Tom had been intrigued by her story which she started to tell him a few days before, but she'd stopped abruptly and changed the subject.

Pen squirmed in her seat. She popped open a can of Coke, took a gulp, and said, "Nothing to tell. I fell off my bike and broke my leg. They put a cast on too soon. My leg swelled up and then got infected. I had to go into the hospital for a week, so they sent me to Phoenix. That's all I remember."

"How long did it take for you to start walking again?"

"I don't remember. Maybe a month. I don't know." Tom wondered if this trip was such a good idea. They really had nothing to talk about. He decided he should just tell her about himself now. At least they'd be talking with each other. If she freaked out, they could always turn back.

"Pen, there's something I've been...." Just then, Pen started talking, oblivious to the fact that Tom had said anything. Her words tumbled out of her mouth like they'd been pent-up for years. Tom had never seen her like this. Almost like she was in a trance. Her story unfolded like one of his own nightmares where he was floating above the city in the cloak of shadows.

We live in a trailer park outside Tempe. I'm fifteen. My mother works the late shift at a local bar in Tempe, so when I come home from school, she's already left. I've been a latch key kid since I was in elementary school. Nothing bad ever happened until that day. There's a guy who lives in a trailer next to ours. He's weird, maybe even retarded. He lives there with his father after his mother leaves them. The other kids in the trailer park tease him and call him "silly Billy," because he always tries to make jokes, but they are terrible. He goes to a special school and when he turns eighteen stays home and helps with cleaning up the trailer park while his dad is at work. I feel sorry for him, and when I make chocolate chip cookies, I bring him some. One day I bring him a plate of fresh cookies and we sit down at his kitchen table to eat them. He goes to the refrigerator and takes out a carton of milk and pours a glass for me, then for him. He keeps looking at me in a weird way. When I get up to leave he grabs my arm, and throws me down on the couch and begins undressing me. I scream, but he puts a hand over my mouth. He's a big guy, maybe 260 pounds, kind of chunky, and he pins me down, and...well, rapes me.

Tom instinctively slowed the car down. He didn't expect Pen to open up like this. He wanted to stop her, to ask questions, but she just kept rambling on about how it hurt, how she bled, how she wasn't a virgin anymore, and how, a couple of months later, she found out that she was pregnant.

My mother reports Billy to the police and him and his dad are kicked out of the trailer park. But we don't press charges. We just get the hell out of there, and end up moving into a small apartment in Tempe, where my son is born. I drop out of high school during the pregnancy and most of the time I am alone in that apartment waiting, waiting.

"My God, Pen. I had no idea." He saw tears running down her face. "So, your son, he must be around eighteen now. Do you see him much?"

Pen put her head into her hands and began to sob. "He was hit by a car on his way home from school. Drunk driver. Broad daylight. Hit and run. Johnny was only seven." Tom's hands grasped the steering wheel. The same age as he was when his mother was murdered. *My God.* He wanted to blurt out his whole story to her. About his mother's murder, the fire, Danny—but he knew this wasn't the time. Besides, the truth about him would probably have crushed her. No. She was too fragile now. He'd wait until they got to Sedona.

They arrived in Flagstaff and pulled into a small diner to get some lunch. Both of them were silent. They ordered hamburgers and fries. Pen got up to go to the bathroom and Tom pulled out his inhaler. He'd needed it earlier, but was too engrossed in her story to pull it out. *Damaged goods.* That was how he saw her now. Kind of like Danny, only Danny ended up a psychopathic killer. Pen ended up being a survivor, trying to do her best with what she had. He put the inhaler away and pulled out a photo from his wallet. It was a picture of him with his mother at the beach on Maui when he was four years old. He felt a chill run through his spine. *Maybe I'm damaged goods too.* Pen returned from the bathroom. She sat down at the booth and reached for Tom's hand. "Thanks for listening. I never told anyone that story before."

Tom put the photo back into his wallet. "I'm so sorry, Pen. You must miss Johnny so much."

"I do. He wasn't at all like his father. Thank God. He had my blond hair and small thin body. Billy had black hair and was a stocky kid. And Johnny was so smart. He was the best reader in his first-grade class."

They finished eating and Tom asked her, "Do you feel like going to Sedona, or do you want to turn around and go back?"

No. Are you kidding? I'm fine now. I want to keep going."

He paid the bill and they got back into the car. Flagstaff's higher elevation brought an early October chill, and Pen put on a sweater. They got back onto the highway and drove a few miles to the Sedona turnoff. Pen had fallen asleep and Tom relished the silence. Time to think. To figure out what he would do about Danny when he got home. To enjoy the beauty of the October fall along the road to Sedona. He woke Pen. "You won't believe this." He pointed to huge red boulders that seemed to appear out of nowhere. Each curve of the road brought them deeper into a world of rock formations so surreal that Tom felt like he was in one of his dreams. Hues of red covered the landscape. Dimming sunlight reflected off the sides of towering red boulders, casting shimmering shadows as twilight approached. Red gravel paved the side of the road where rows of yucca cactus pointed their symmetrical spines toward the darkening sky. Tom was mesmerized by the beauty, by the peacefulness of the moment, by Pen's hushed voice repeating over and over, "Oh my God. Oh my God."

They came to the main town of Sedona and looked for a motel. They found one with a vacancy sign, and checked in. Pen flopped down onto the bed and Tom went into the bathroom to wash up. When he came out Pen had undressed. He closed the curtains, undressed, and lay down next to her. She reached over and began to stroke his shoulders, then moved her hand downward, and began to curl his red chest hairs in her fingers. He turned on his side and reached for her voluptuous breasts, caressing them in his hands, running his fingers over her nipples until they stood erect. She ran her hand down his thighs and began stroking his penis. They made love as the sun set, and in the now darkened motel room, they climbed under the covers and fell into a perfect sleep.

Early the next morning they packed up and got breakfast. It was too cold to go into the water at Slide Rock, so they walked around town and went into shops, not buying anything special. Finally, Tom said, "We need to get back before dark. I've got work on Monday." Pen seemed ready to return. She told Tom that Sedona was too "high scale" for her anyway. He knew exactly what she meant. She told him she wanted to drive for a while so he could tell her an orchid story. Tom got in the passenger's side of the car, put on his seatbelt, and while Pen pulled out onto the open highway he closed his eyes, and in his imagination he became Russ Tanner, world-renowned orchid hunter.

Bhutan Expedition, September 13, 1969.

We flew out of Bangkok just after a huge monsoon had turned half of Thailand into a huge lake, including some areas near the Bangkok International Airport. The taxi barely made it through the flood waters and we almost missed our flight. We got to Paro safely; then the next day we left on the expedition for the extreme western parts of Bhutan. Since there were no roads to speak of in that remote area, I had already set up porters and horses to be ready when we arrived. We loaded up with rice, chili peppers, instant coffee, chocolate, dried nuts and fruit, and water. The expedition consisted of myself, Aaron Hammer (a fellow orchid hunter from Hawaii), four Bhutanese guides, and two horses. We figured the monsoon season had already passed, but unfortunately we were wrong. The mountains flooded with cold rains while thousands of blood-sucking leeches managed to puddle in clusters around our boots while we tried to avoid direct contact with them. We hiked along a trail through muddy, leech-filled streams, slipping and sliding until we got our foothold.

The trail became steeper and steeper as nightfall approached. We had to constantly swat away hordes of those little suckers that attached to our boots and legs. I was close to passing out from fatigue, when we saw some lights on the far side of the valley, but we needed to cross a rickety bridge to get there. The rain made the bridge so slick, we barely got across alive. Unfortunately, one of our guides fell to his death below.

We finally reached the small village of Shebji, where we had a host already expecting us. We climbed a ladder to the living quarters and fell asleep. But the monsoons never let up. There was no point heading further up the precarious slopes toward higher elevations when mudslides and flooding were still going on. We waited two days until the rains subsided, and headed back to Ha, where we decided to explore orchids at the higher elevations where local farmers had cultivated crop fields on bunds and around farm houses. We were privy to a delicious meal at another one of our host's homes, in which he prepared *cymbidium pseudobulbs, or tubers, cooked like potatoes, with salt. We also had cymbidium "olachotho," where the flowers of the plant were separated, washed, then boiled in water for ten minutes until they got soft. The local cheese was then added with salt and chilies and simmered another five minutes. The dish went very well with local brown rice. It had a slightly bitter taste, but garlic, chopped onions and tomatoes, and turmeric powder, cooked in oil and added to the mix, took away the bitter taste.*

Pen interrupted Tom. "My God. That sounds unbelievable. He could have died on that trip. What an exciting life he had."

"Exciting, yes. Dangerous, yes." Then he paused. "He died on the Amazon River when the gators got him. At least that was the story."

"What do you mean?"

"Well, Uncle Russ was no saint. My aunt used to pray for him when he'd be on one of his adventures. Sometimes she'd pray for him not to get involved with the black market drug smugglers, or to avoid the orchid hunters with rifles."

"Rifles? Drugs?"

"Exotic orchids are worth millions. His orchid-hunting expeditions were private. Many people work for commercial orchid growers, but Russ collected for his own business, and that put him off the grid. Of course, that was before the CITES permits were enforced."

"What are those?"

"Convention on International Trade in Endangered Species. It didn't actually begin until 1975 and now it's the legal way to bring endangered plants and animals into the country."

Pen sat mesmerized while Tom continued.

"But, Uncle Russ always craved the unknown, the adventure. He wouldn't have had the patience to use the CITES permits anyway. Drove my aunt crazy. She knew it was a matter of time until he got caught—or worse, got killed."

"So you think he was murdered?"

"Your guess is as good as mine. At least I have his journal."

There was silence. Pen seemed confused. Then she said, "This happened a long time ago, right? Did you ever meet your uncle and aunt? Are they alive? You said you were from the Bay Area."

Tom's body stiffened. *Shit.* He took a moment to think. "Never met either of them, but my mother told me all about her sister in Hawaii and about my uncle and his orchid adventures."

"Hawaii?"

"Um, yes. Easier to grow orchids in a tropical climate." Tom realized he'd dropped a word of truth to Pen. *Hawaii.* But Pen wouldn't be able to connect the dots, since she'd never been out of Arizona. Her gaze never wavered. She seemed mesmerized by Tom's stories. "How did your aunt die?"

Tom continued. He was now back in the groove of the lie. "After my uncle died, my mother tried to get her sister to live with us in San Francisco, but my aunt hated cold weather. A few years later, she got breast cancer and died. I think I was around ten or so."

"How did you get the journal?"

"I remember one day when a package came for me. My mother left it on the kitchen table. When I opened it there was a handwritten letter from my aunt saying that she wanted me to have Uncle Russ' journal."

"Wow. Is that how you got all your smarts about orchids?"

Tom explained the lie about his mother's greenhouse business in San Francisco, and how he and his sister took it over after she died. He realized how close he'd come to a fuck-up. He couldn't let himself screw up again. Not with Pen, not with anyone. He was Tom Tanner now, and the only time he could talk about Kyle was when he was at Ixtlan. That shouldn't be too hard to do. He just needed to remember to compartmentalize his life.

They arrived in Tempe just as the sun was setting. Tom dropped Pen off at her place and told her he wanted to see how his house was doing after the flood. He picked up Rover from the neighbor and went home. The house still smelled, but it seemed better. He went into the bathroom and looked behind the toilet. No leak. He'd sleep at home tonight. In the morning he woke to the sound of Rover scratching around on the carpet. He'd torn the rug in the hallway outside of the bathroom. It was still wet and soggy, the perfect digging site, better than wet mud. Tom figured the landlord would need to replace the carpet anyway, so he let Rover have his fun.

୰ ୰ ୰ ୰

Over the next few weeks Tom saw a lot of Pen. They seemed to be getting closer and closer. Tom spent more time at her place after work. As long as he remembered he was Tom Tanner, he felt pretty good about continuing his relationship with Pen. He just couldn't ever tell her about his past. She definitely wouldn't be able to handle it. He knew that, after he heard her story about her rape, and her son's death. She was much too fragile to deal with the truth about who Tom Tanner really was.

Tom would recount adventures he'd memorized from his uncle's journal while Pen got ready for work, and when she left, he'd sleep at her place. But he noticed that he wasn't feeling himself. He had no energy. He had no appetite. Pen made him vegetable soup, and took care of him. He went home a few days a week, but spent the weekends with her. The smell at his house never completely went away even though the carpet was almost dry, and the landlord said he was going to replace it over

New Year's. He was just waiting for the insurance company to accept the claim.

Then one morning his doorbell rang. Tom answered it. The postman had left a small box on the front porch. *It's probably the miniature orchids I've ordered for the next Orchid Society meeting*, he thought. Tom took the box inside. There was no label from the orchid company, only his address written in sloppy handwriting—not unlike the handwriting on the box with the gold bracelet. *Shit. Not again.* He slowly unwrapped the box. This time there was no newsprint inside, only white paper towels wrapped around small objects and secured with masking tape. And just like the last box, there was no card inside, or return address on the outside. He got scissors from the kitchen drawer and cut the tape from one of the bundles. It was filled with a handful of shells, just like the ones Danny used at Maui for his grave markers. He unwrapped another bundle—more shells. And the last bundle, again shells. But on each of the last set of five shells were the words "Remember me." Tom dropped the box and the shells crashed to the floor below. *Danny.*

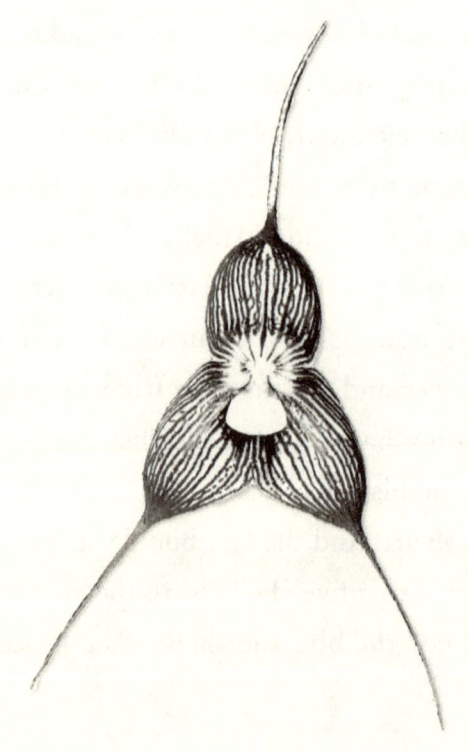

CHAPTER EIGHT

Return to Ixtlan

The desert holds him captive. Hands on steering wheel, slow vibrations from rubber on smooth road, spectrum of open sky dotted with white puffy clouds, Sierra Estrella's mountain chain like a cardboard cut-out against blue sky, hum of motor, soft breeze caressing his face, open vistas, straight ribbon-road leading to Ixtlan's turnoff.

Tom took in deep breaths of fresh desert air, but nausea set in as soon as he drove on the washboard road to Ixtlan. Even Rover crawled onto the floor of the passenger seat and began to moan. When they arrived, Dillon was waiting out front. He'd taken Tom's frantic call about needing to escape from the bowels of hell at his house in Tempe. They went inside and Rover ran through the house looking for the other two dogs. Tom immediately started talking to Dillon about the water leak, the smell in the house, and about his trip with Pen to Sedona. Dillon's comment was, "My God. You're a mess. And you don't look right. A bit pale, I'd say."

He told Tom to get into his truck—that they were going to see Felipe. Maybe he could help. When they got to Felipe's trailer, they saw another car parked in front. It was Daniel's. Dillon got out of the truck first, then walked up the steps to the porch and knocked on the door. When they entered, they saw Daniel sitting on the floor watching TV. Felipe took one look at Tom and said, "Shit. You look terrible." Tom began to feel dizzy, so he sat on a chair. Daniel jumped up and brought Tom a glass of water. By now, Tom was beginning to like all of the attention. But something was definitely wrong. He put the glass on a table and said, "Look, I just needed to get out of my place for a while. It still smells from the water leak, and the landlord needs to replace the carpet, and—well, Rover's started ripping it up himself."

Felipe broke out into a belly laugh, but Tom didn't see what was so funny. He still hadn't told them about the package of shells that he got that morning. Felipe saw how upset Tom was and said, "Maybe you need to sit in the sweat lodge for a while. That will cleanse you and you'll feel a lot better before you go back to your hell hole."

"I've never done a sweat before. What do I need to do?"

They went outside to the sweat lodge and Felipe began to explain. "First, we need to stoke the fire. After it's hot enough, we take a few of these dry rocks over to the fire and set them down until they get like hot embers. Then we take each rock and put it inside this here metal bucket and pour water over them until this place turns into one hot steam bath."

Tom smiled. "Steam bath? Used to do those in Maui with the guys at the Butterfly Lounge."

"We all did. In fact, I used to do them with Dillon's dad, Amsted, in San Francisco before I moved here. Those were the days—infamous bathhouses, Bette Midler."

Tom felt like he was getting an education about his own past—a past that went way beyond his small world on Maui. He was beginning to feel like he was a part of something much bigger than himself. And it felt good.

They all went back inside Felipe's trailer and hung out most of the day until the rocks were hot enough; then they walked over to the sweat lodge. Felipe motioned for Tom to strip down to his underpants. Then, Felipe checked on one of the rocks by poking it with a stick. "Took me a long time to find these rocks. Perfectly solid. Need to be solid. If there's even one crack in them, they could explode in the fire. Need to be perfectly dry each time or the moisture could cause a crack, too."

Once the steam started rising from the hot rocks, Felipe made sure the canvas flap covering the structure was sealed tight. "You can sit on the ground, or on those folding chairs if you're more comfortable."

Tom sat on the ground and crossed his legs. The hot steam filled his nostrils as he took in deep cleansing breaths. Felipe began to talk about the Native American traditions of sweat lodges and how he'd decided to build one on his property for the boys at Ixtlan, and anyone else who wanted to participate. He told the story about the first time he'd held a sweat lodge ceremony and kept everyone inside too long. Luckily they were all young, and recovered. He told them they were just dehydrated and that feeling faint was part of the ceremony. Luck was on his side that first time. From then on Felipe took the ritual more seriously and began a course of studies on how to become a medicine man, using the spiritual cleansing nature of the ceremony in the true Native tradition.

He reached under a blanket, pulled out a drum, and began a rhythmic beat, then chanted something in Yaqui. After a few minutes he put the drum down, reached for another pitcher of water, and poured the cool liquid over the hot rocks.

A hissing sound. More steam. Vapor fills the tiny space. They sit in darkness. Part of the ceremony. Darkness. Tom begins to feel like he is floating over the city lights of Maui, like in his dream. He peers down into the seething volcanic lava swirling around the crater, ready to pour over the edge onto the city below. His skin is burning, heartbeat racing, sweat beginning to ooze from his skin...light-headed, he slumps over on the dirt floor.

Tom was now lying face up on the ground outside the sweat lodge. Felipe poured cool water over his head and shoulders. Tom opened his eyes and saw that it was dark outside. Tiny stars flickered in the sky above. Dillon offered him a bottle of cold water and Tom took a drink, then another, and another.

"Dehydration. Sure got to you fast." Daniel bent down and wiped sweat from Tom's forehead. "I had the same problem when I started sweat lodges, because of my asthma. I still can't do them for more than fifteen minutes or so."

Tom tried to sit up. "What happened?"

"You're not cut out for sweat lodges." Felipe poured more water over Tom. "You might have been under the weather or something. Usually sweating helps with detox, but in your case, your body couldn't handle it. Happens sometimes. Don't worry."

Tom sat up slowly, with Felipe's help, and soon was in a standing position. All four of them were standing around in their underpants, steam still coming out of the flap covering the door to the sweat lodge. Dillon motioned for them to go back inside Felipe's trailer. "Tom, just to let you know, before you passed out you kept muttering something pretty weird about Danny."

"I did?"

Daniel put his hand on Tom's shoulder. "You were probably hallucinating, not even knowing what you were saying. Doesn't bother me."

Still confused, Tom managed to say, "Oh. I once knew this kid named Danny when we were in elementary school. He used to tease me all the time, called me Reddylocks because of my red hair."

Daniel laughed. "Wow. Reddylocks?"

Felipe motioned for them to follow him inside, where he offered some iced tea and homemade oatmeal cranberry muffins. "Here, this should give you back your strength."

Tom took a bite of the muffin and a sip of tea. The tea tasted bitter. He made a face. Dillon laughed. "It's chaparral tea made from the creosote cactus. Remember, you had some at the Blue Corn Diner?"

Tom tried another sip. Even more bitter. It seemed things weren't tasting right. His body began to shake with chills. Dillon told him to get dressed, that they were going back to Ixtlan and that Tom was to spend the night. Maybe he'd feel better in the morning.

Tom slept on the short trip back, and Dillon let him have one of the spare bedrooms in the main house. Tom crawled under the sheets and immediately fell asleep, Rover at his side. In the morning he woke to the sound of fresh coffee grinding in the kitchen. After he dressed and washed, up he joined Dillon for breakfast. "Where's Jeffrey?"

Dillon smiled. "Put it this way—he had a late night. Overslept. Hooked up with a new Ixtlan resident, young lad from Texas. Kind of took him under his wing, if you know what I mean."

Tom sat down on a chair by the stove. "Shit. What the hell happened yesterday? I've never felt that weak in my life. Thanks for taking care of me last night."

"You probably are fighting the flu. You shouldn't have gone in that sweat lodge."

"I don't know what's wrong with me. I've been feeling under the weather for almost a month."

"Maybe you should see a doctor when you get home."

"I will."

Dillon poured hot coffee for both of them. "Let's go into the dining room. There is something I want to talk to you about."

Tom was intrigued. He loved that Dillon took such an interest in him. For once in his life, he felt like somebody was watching out for him. Someone he could trust. Dillon reached out, took Tom's hand, and said, "Look, Tom. I've been thinking about your situation. It seems like maybe you need a break from all of that stuff at your house until the landlord gets the place livable. Maybe you could stay here for a while."

Tom's eyes fixated on Dillon's pools of deep brown. Every word felt like a soft blanket shielding him from the harsh reality of his world, from the shadows of his past. He remembered how the judge used to talk to him in the same reassuring soft voice. Dillon repeated his comment. "So, want to move to Ixtlan for a while?"

Tom tried to answer, but instead he began to sob.

"Here, take your time." He poured Tom more coffee.

Tom wiped his eyes with a napkin and blew his nose. Then he blurted out, "I know who's trying to kill me."

"What?"

"I got another box delivered yesterday morning. I was going to tell you about it, but then the sweat lodge thing happened. The box had a bunch of harp shells inside. They were wrapped in paper towels, and in one of the bunches the words 'remember me' were written in black marker on five of the shells."

"Harp shells? What are those?"

"Shells from Maui. Just believe me. It's the same person who sent the gold bracelet."

Dillon reached out and took Tom's hand. "You've got to tell the police."

"I can't. There's other things I still haven't told you about. My life as Tom Tanner would be ruined if the police got involved.

"Then that's all the more reason to use Ixtlan for sanctuary. Your life is in danger."

"You're right. I need to figure this out. It would mean I'd need to quit my job and leave Pen in the lurch. I'd have to disappear again, wouldn't I?"

"That's what most of us have done here at Ixtlan. We really didn't have a choice."

❧ ❧ ❧ ❧

The drive back to Tempe was a complete blur. Tom's mind went through various scenarios if he were to move to Ixtlan. Pen would be devastated if he left without a good reason. He'd just do what he was so good at, and tell her another lie. Say he needed to go back to San Francisco because of his cousin being sick. *What cousin?* He'd never talked about a cousin. *Didn't matter.* He could say it was only for a few months, and he'd be back. He could take a leave from his job, or quit. What about his precious Draculas? He could take them to Ixtlan and Daniel could put them in his greenhouse. What about Rover? He would tell Pen he'd leave the dog with a neighbor. What about his house? He'd leave the hell hole and find a new place when he returned. He pulled the car to the side of the road, got out to stretch, then began to feel light-headed, agitated, sweaty.

Suddenly, in the perfect stillness of Tempe's early November morning he let out a blood-curdling scream. *Danny, you shit. You fucked-up psychopath.*

Images of Danny's makeshift grave markers with harp shells initialed with each animal he's murdered. Images of Danny's brown eyes darting back and forth when he's in his manic mood. Of Lilly standing guard in front of their palm branch fort in Maui while he and Danny fuck. Of the fire, and the smell of his Aunt Molly's burnt flesh. Of the day he leaves Maui to start a new life.

By the time Tom got home he was exhausted, but he managed to change into his red concierge uniform and get to work a few minutes late. Luckily there were only a few guests checking into the Adobe Palms Hotel that day, so he had some down time. He sat on the chair in the cloakroom, hoping no one would find him for a while. After the Christmas party at the Grille, he'd start looking for Danny himself. Why should he just wait for Danny's next move, like a sitting duck? He'd tell Dillon that he wanted to hold out a bit longer before he uprooted his new life only to disappear again at Ixtlan. Until then, he'd just act like everything was normal.

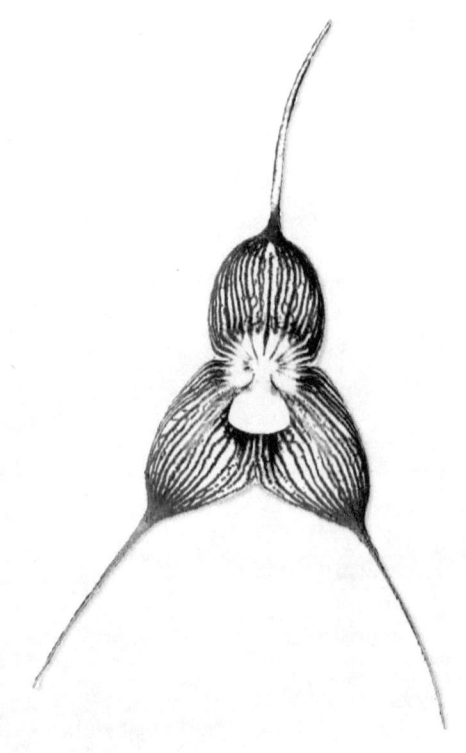

CHAPTER NINE

Christmas at the Adobe Palms Hotel

The Adobe Palms Hotel held its yearly Christmas party two weeks before Christmas. Tom really wasn't up to going, but Pen had been looking forward to it for months. After their incredible road trip, how could he refuse her? He'd never had a decent sexual relationship with anyone. Sex with boys and men was just for sex. But sex with Pen was tender and enjoyable beyond what he'd experienced. Mostly, it was her being tender, almost like when his mother used to rub coconut suntan lotion all over his body, and he would feel that tingly sensation. Pen had already bought him a red polyester dress shirt and a Santa Claus tie to wear with his black dress slacks. His hair had started to grow out, and she said he looked so handsome with his wavy red hair that she couldn't resist the red shirt and tie. Anyway, red was her favorite color.

The morning of the party Tom dressed, shaved, put mousse on his curly red locks, and sat down for a cup of coffee. He let his mind wander, as he often did when he was alone. He remembered when he was around four, and his mother had taken him to a specialty shop on Maui, where she bought him a tree ornament of blue dolphins swimming in a lagoon.

His mother tells him how each year since he was born, she's put another ornament on their tree. This year he's old enough to put his ornament on the tree all by himself. When they get home she has the tree all set up in a corner of the living room by the window. The tree looks real to Kyle, but he knows it isn't because it doesn't smell, and he knows how his mother puts the tree in a box after Christmas and stores it in her bedroom closet. She lets him take the ornament out of the box while she takes out four others. She tells him to watch, as she hangs the first glass ball, the one with a green sea turtle. "I bought this when you were born," she tells him. "You were my little turtle, my Christmas present." She smiles down at him and lifts the next ornament. "This one was for your first birthday." It's of a Maui sunset with two bending palm trees and a view of the ocean. The next glass ornament she hangs is of colorful tropical fish against a blue background. "This one was for your second birthday. You loved to visit the aquarium with me." Then she lifts a fourth ornament. "And this one was for your third birthday, last year." She holds it up to the light. A purple orchid outlined in black against white frosty glass.

"It reminds me of Aunt Molly's greenhouse and how much you love her orchid plants."

Kyle is mesmerized. He watches as she hangs each ornament on the branches of the tree, sunlight reflecting off each one like she has just hung four stars from the heavens. "Now can I hang mine?" He can't wait any longer. He lifts the fifth ornament from the box. She helps him put the metal hook in the tiny attachment; then he reaches as high as his arms will let him, and hangs the glass ball on a branch. The blue dolphins sparkle against the milky-white glass as light from the window pours over the tree. Kyle remembers his mother's piercing brown eyes looking down at him while she says, "Now, my little man, you will be four in a few days. You are old enough to hang your own ornaments, and one day you will see, the tree will be so full of ornaments that you will need to get a bigger tree." So many ornaments. He begins to imagine a tree so tall, with hundreds of glistening glass balls that it will reach the clouds, and in order to get to the top he'll need to climb to the heavens.

His mother has already cleaned up the empty boxes. She goes into her bedroom. The phone rings. He hears her talking quietly, then she lets out a huge sob. He walks over toward her bedroom and tries to listen through the closed door. He hears her scream at someone, then slam the phone down, then cry. She comes back into the living room, tears streaming down her pale face, walks right by him, grabs the tree, and throws it *to the floor. The five glass ornaments fly off the branches and onto the floor, shattering into hundreds of tiny pieces. At that moment, he knows he never wants another glass ornament, or another Christmas tree—or for that matter, another Christmas.*

Tom picked up Pen at 7:00. She answered the door with a lipstick in one hand. She was wearing a new dress of black shiny material. She had on red leather heels and a red dangly necklace made out of coral, or plastic that looked like coral. Her freshly dyed bleached-blonde hair was tied up in a bun at the back of her neck. Two red chopstick-like lacquered sticks crisscrossed along the back of her bun, holding it in place. He'd never seen her so dolled up. "Pen. You look really great tonight."

She kissed his cheek and left a light red lip impression. "You look pretty good yourself."

The Adobe Palms Hotel was lit up with colored lights outside and in. A huge six-foot-tall real Christmas tree covered with gold ribbons, white lights, and blue glass ornaments stood in the lobby. It was the most gorgeous tree Tom had ever seen. And the smell of the pine needles filled up the lobby, adding to the ambience. Pen looked at Tom and smiled. "This year's tree looks better than ever. I've been here since they started this tradition almost seventeen years ago."

Tom began to realize how limited her life had been. Seventeen years waitressing at the same restaurant. He was only four when she started working there. Pen led him to the main dining room where the buffet was. They filled their plates with food and found an empty table. Tom tried to eat the roast beef, but managed only a couple of swallows. Pen noticed how he was struggling to eat. "You don't look well to me. What's wrong?"

"I haven't been sleeping much, and I get stomach cramps when I eat. Maybe I'm getting the flu."

Pen took a bite of mashed potatoes. "Try these. Should help your stomach." She put some potatoes on her fork and lifted it to Tom's mouth. He took a bite. She rubbed her tongue over her red lips and stared into his eyes. "Tommy, I'm so glad we came together."

Tom swallowed the mashed potatoes. The jazz band began to play a romantic song. She stood up, reached out her hand, and asked him to dance. He took her hand and they walked over to the dance floor. The lights were low. They slow danced through the song, then went back to their seats. Tom was beginning to feel nauseated. He grabbed his stomach. The cramps were starting up. He told Pen he couldn't make it through the party and needed to go home. She asked if she could go with him and take care of him, but he was able to convince her to stay at the party. "I'll go to the clinic in the morning. You know almost everyone here. I'll call you when I come back from the doctor tomorrow."

The next day Tom called the hotel manager and told him he needed to take some time off. He said he was going to visit his cousin in San Francisco when he felt well enough, and that he wouldn't be back until after New Year's. He went to the clinic, where the doctor ran some lab work, and gave him some anti-nausea medicine and antibiotics. Tom figured with three weeks off he could lay low, maybe go back to Ixtlan, especially if he kept feeling so crappy. He could at least rest there without the smell of soggy carpet. Mostly, he needed to think of a way to find Danny. But he couldn't think about it now. He'd worry about it tomorrow. He undressed, then went into the kitchen for his nightly snack of buttermilk and Oreo cookies. But the minute he opened the buttermilk carton, the sour smell overtook him, and he felt nauseated. Weak in the knees, he stumbled to his bedroom and plopped down on the bed. He was having trouble breathing, so he took a puff from his inhaler and set it back on the table next to the bed. He was too nauseated to take the antibiotic the doctor had prescribed. There was a bitter taste in his mouth. *Must be time to throw out the buttermilk.* Rover jumped on the bed and sniffed Tom's mouth, then lay down next to him on the floor.

He's in his kitchen in Maui sitting at the metal table having his bedtime snack of Oreo cookies and milk. But this time he can't drink the milk. It's so sour it makes him throw up. His mother finally tosses the spoiled milk, replacing the whole milk with buttermilk. She says it's healthier for him, even if it tastes sour. He has no choice but to drink it. Eventually he gets used to it, and the sour taste doesn't make him sick. In fact, he starts to like it. She tells him that buttermilk is supposed to taste spoiled and that it lasts in the fridge for at least a month, unopened.

Now, darkness descends over his house. Tom can't tell if he is in Maui or Tempe. He's never experienced this kind of darkness. A vacuum of perfect calm. Then a flicker of light that gets brighter and brighter—like a train emerging from a dark tunnel. He tries to move, but he can't feel his body anymore. Suddenly, he feels himself floating above his body. He looks down and sees himself on the bed, Rover on the floor. He's in Tempe. But he's never felt so peaceful. He needs to remember this dream so he can tell Felipe when he goes to Ixtlan. Then, off in the distance he hears the drone of a train whistle. The train seems to be moving faster and faster. The light is getting closer to where he lies on the bed. For a split second he feels terror as he feels the swoosh of the train roaring past him. Then, perfect silence.

Part Two

"*The darkness restores what light cannot repair.*"
—Joseph Brodsky

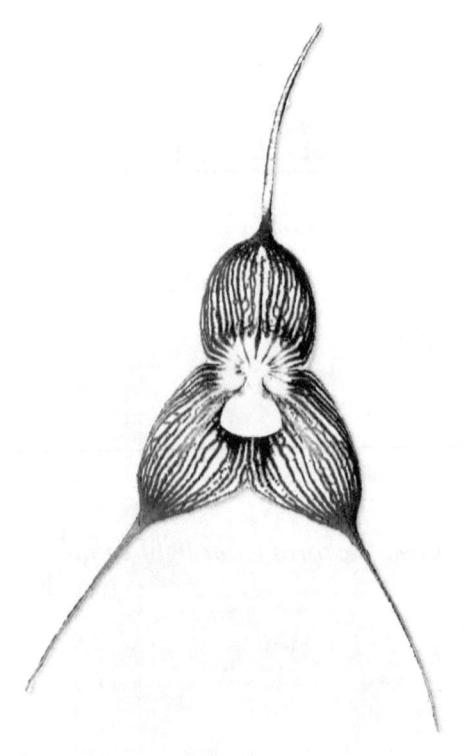

CHAPTER TEN

Officer Gomez

When he pulled up to the house everything seemed normal, unassuming, a typical Tempe suburb of run-down low-income homes separated by chain link fencing. Officer Gomez had grown up in a neighborhood just like this one. His father, a cop, had died when he was twelve, and his mother worked full time as a waitress to make ends meet. Andy Gomez was named after his father, who was shot in the line of duty. Andy Senior had always been his hero. It was assumed that Andy Junior would follow in his father's footsteps. A picture of Andy Junior, taken when he entered the police academy, sat on the bookshelf next to one of his father at the same age. You could hardly tell them apart. Andy Senior had the family sculpted nose, giving him the Clark Gable look that his son had inherited. But Andy Junior had also inherited his mother's thick black hair, which he kept braided and tied at the back of his head.

His Yaqui mother and Hispanic father raised him in Dolarosa, just outside of Tempe. The Yaqui Indians had lived in Arizona since the early 1960s when they received 202 acres from the federal government in Tucson, Arizona. Many Yaquis moved further north to Tempe, Arizona, settling in a neighborhood they named Dolarosa, meaning "Our Lady of Sorrows." The town incorporated in 1979 as Dolarosa, Arizona. Most of the town was Native American, many of them trilingual in Yaqui, English, and Spanish. Andy and his older brother had grown up speaking the three languages. He had become one of the favored patrol officers in his Tempe unit because of his street-smarts and his language ability.

The call came in around 9:00 a.m. Someone from the Adobe Palms Hotel had called to report one of their employees hadn't shown up for work in three weeks. It was the start of the new year and most of the hotel employees had used up their vacation over the Christmas holiday, but when Tom Tanner didn't show up for work in his punctual manner, they knew something had to be wrong. Officer Gomez parked in the driveway, made sure he had the right address, then got out of the car. He'd done welfare checks before, usually to find that the person had forgotten to call work if they were sick, or had gone on vacation and put in for the wrong return date, or were in the hospital and couldn't call, or maybe were elderly and had fallen in their home. The entire front yard looked like it hadn't been watered in months. There were pots of dead rosebushes along the ground by the chain link fence and the walkway. Weeds covered the rest of the yard. He had trouble opening the front gate. It jammed against the concrete below like it hadn't been used in years.

The front door to the house was locked. He knocked. No answer. He pounded a few times, then he called out, "Police, open the door." No answer. Gomez walked around toward the back of the property, hoping to find a way in. The back yard was small, and covered with weeds and dog poop. He saw a sliding glass door ajar, and pulled it open. The smell coming from inside the house caught him off-guard. He took out his Glock and cautiously proceeded into the darkened room. No one could have prepared him for this. The odor was so putrefying that he had to walk back outside and take a deep breath. He took out a handkerchief, covered his nose and mouth, and went inside. The house was dark, except for light coming from the sliding glass window. There was mold covering everything. He realized it could be toxic mold and that he should call the hazmat team, but he wanted to see if there was anyone in the house first. He saw water spewing from a broken pipe behind the toilet. It must have been flooding the place for days. He took a flashlight from his belt, bent down to find the metal valve against the wall, and managed to turn off the water. Then, out of the corner of his eye he saw someone lying naked, face down, on a moldy mattress in the bedroom.

By now, he could hardly breathe. He sloshed over the

moldy, soggy carpet and headed toward the sliding glass door. Once outside, he bent over and took deep breaths of fresh Tempe air, then called the precinct for backup and for a hazardous materials team. He knew he shouldn't go back inside until they arrived, but he remembered seeing something else lying by the side of the bed. Maybe a cat, or a dog. He took out his handkerchief, covered his face, and ventured back inside. This time he took the time to look more closely, noticing the powdery, moldy substance on everything, including the walls. Step by step, he felt like he was sinking into swamp mud. As his eyes adjusted to the dim light, he noticed the kitchen. There were piles of dirty dishes in the sink, and on the counter, empty buttermilk cartons. Then he went into the bedroom. Beside the bed was a small dog lying on its side. He put his hand on the animal's ribcage and felt a slight breathing motion.

Just as he was about to scoop up the dog to take it outside, his stomach tightened and he retched all over the carpet. He knew it wasn't over, but he managed to scoop up the dog, get him outside, and set him down on the cement, where he vomited again.

Someone called his name from the front of the house. Gomez answered, "Back yard. Front is locked up."

By then, he was sitting on the ground next to the half-dead dog. The other officer found him and stopped short. "My God, what happened?"

"You won't believe what's in that house." He stroked the dog and poured some water into an empty bowl that sat next to the sliding glass door. He put the bowl near the dog's mouth and sprinkled some water over its nose. The dog's tongue came out and Gomez put the bowl under the dog's head so it could drink. "Dog's half dead."

The other officer bent down to pet the dog. He saw the vomit. "This yours?"

Gomez nodded.

"Did you call hazmat?"

"They should be here any minute. I wouldn't go inside if I were you."

"No shit. Where's the body?"

"In the bedroom. Looks like it's been there awhile."

The other officer took out a handkerchief and put it over his nose. "What's that awful smell?"

"Not sure. Probably dog poop mixed into the wet carpet, and mold."

"Mold? From what?"

"I had to turn off the water behind the toilet. It's probably been flooding the house for days, maybe weeks."

"Could have caused the mold, I guess."

The dog raised its head. Gomez pet the dog's matted fur. "If only he could talk."

They heard sounds coming from the front of the house. The hazmat team had arrived. Four men walked toward them dressed in white bunny uniforms. Gomez felt like he was in a science fiction movie where the bad guys tried to kill the good guys with some chemical toxin. But this wasn't a movie. He told them to go toward the bedroom where there was a naked adult male lying on the bed face down. One of the men saw the vomit on the ground. "That yours?"

Gomez nodded. "There's dog poop all over the carpet— be careful. And there's some kind of mold covering everything."

"You're going to the hospital."

"What about the dog?"

"We'll take him to the vet. Don't worry."

Gomez heard the siren as the ambulance approached. He got up and began to walk toward the front of the house, but his legs were too weak and he stumbled. The other patrol officer grabbed him and said, "Wait here. They'll need to check you over first."

The paramedics came around back and began checking Gomez's vitals. One of the paramedics turned toward the house and said, "My God, what is that awful smell?"

Gomez told them what he found inside. They put him on

a stretcher and took him to the ambulance. The other officer stayed behind to watch over the dog.

☙ ☙ ☙ ☙

Gomez barely heard the soft voice of his mother singing a Yaqui lullaby. Her hand stroking his forehead while she sang, *"Huya aniwai, sea lihlihti heka, huya aniwai. Huya aniwai, sea lihlihti heka, huya aniwai. Wilderness world, flower freely is blowing, wilderness world. Wilderness world, flower freely is blowing, wilderness world."*

She used to sing that song to him when he was a baby to help him sleep. He hadn't heard it in years. He managed to open his eyes a slit. His mother's deep-brown eyes stared into his. "Son, wake up now."

Gomez felt like he had been drugged. He tried to sit up. His mother helped him by putting a pillow behind his head. He saw tears rolling down her cheeks. He knew why she cried. It had been only two years since his older brother, Jesús, had died. He was all that his mother had left. She made the sign of the cross over her chest. *"Gracias a Dios."*

"Madre, I'm going to be fine." Gomez reached for the buzzer by the bed and rang for the nurse. "I need to get out of here." The nurse came into the room and told him he'd been overcome by possible toxic mold. They'd had to give him oxygen to help him breathe, and steroids to reduce the inflammation in his lungs. He needed to remain in the hospital a few

more days for further tests to determine the kind of mold he'd inhaled.

Someone knocked on the door. "Gomez, you decent?"

It was Detective Palmer from his substation. He entered the room and walked over to Gomez. When Mrs. Gomez saw the detective, she ran over to him and gave him a big hug. "Tall one. Good to see you again."

The detective put his arm on her shoulder. He stood a good two feet above her. When he started as a rookie he'd worked under Andy Gomez Senior, who used to tease him because of his height.

Gomez turned toward his mother. "Water."

His mother reached for a cup of water and put the straw to his mouth. "You got sick from that smelly stuff in the house."

Gomez smiled. "Smelly stuff, yes."

Detective Palmer laughed. "That's a good way to describe it." He looked at Gomez and the two of them locked eyes in an acknowledgment of keeping the details of the horrific scene from Gomez's mother. Then he said, "You'll need to go off patrol duty for a few months. Maybe you can come to the precinct and help me with this case. I'm loaded down with paperwork on my other cases. I could use an extra hand."

Mrs. Gomez jumped in. "*Hijo*, that's a great idea. You need to get your strength back."

Gomez reached for his mother's hand. "*Madre*, why don't you go home now? I need to rest."

"Of course, *hijo*. I will be back tomorrow with your favorite—*tamales*."

By now, Gomez's eyes were half closed. The doctor walked in, and before Gomez fell asleep he heard Detective Palmer telling the doctor how the hazmat team had to upgrade to a Level A after the ambulance left the scene. The doctor's answer was simply, "Your friend needs to watch himself. We're not sure yet what was in that house. We'll keep an eye on him. Don't worry."

Gomez was released from the hospital after a week. Tests came back showing the mold had been at high enough levels of concentration that the doctors were concerned about Gomez's exposure. He was given respiratory therapy treatments, steroids, and antibiotics. Had he stayed inside the house any longer, he could have had a more difficult recovery. Doctor's orders were to keep him off patrol duty for at least six weeks. He needed to stay away from anything that might compromise his immune system, because he could end up with lung disease or pneumonia.

℃3   ℃3   ℃3   ℃3

The substation was teaming with activity. There had been a multiple shooting in the desert east of Papago. Phones were ringing off the hook. Detective Palmer motioned for Officer

Gomez to come inside his office. "Hope you're ready for this. Sit down at that desk. It's yours now." He pointed to a small metal desk in front of a window, opposite his own large oak desk that he used only when he left his office at City Hall to work on highprofile cases. "I'll clear that crap off and pull the files I have on the Tanner case. It's yours now. I'll supervise, but you can do what you want with it. Go at your own pace."

Gomez looked out of the window. January in Tempe was usually in the middle sixties, but today the temperature had already reached seventy-five. He wanted to be outside sitting in his mother's garden, in the shade of the large drooping branches of the Blue Palo Verde tree. He remembered how each spring the old tree would burst forth with brilliant bright-yellow flowers with red-orange spots in the middle. Then the seed pods would form, dangling from the branches like blue-green icicles. He and his older brother used to lie next to each other on the ground, looking up through the branches, counting the seed pods. Their mother told them that the seeds of the Palo Verde were used for food a long time ago, but they had a bitter taste. Some nights when the honeysuckle was in full bloom, he'd sit in the garden listening to Jesús practice guitar. Jesús was going to be the next José Feliciano. Gomez loved that garden.

Detective Palmer tapped Gomez on the shoulder. "Want a Coke? I need my morning caffeine fix."

Gomez looked up. "Sure." He knew he still wasn't feeling

himself, but maybe if he acted normal he would start feeling more normal. He was about to open the Tanner file when four officers walked into the office and yelled in unison, "Barf bag. How's it going?"

Gomez turned around. Four patrol officers who he'd worked with walked over to him and slapped him on the shoulders. One of the officers said, "Heard they found your vomit all over the scene." Another officer made a retching sound. Gomez tried to smile. Detective Palmer walked in with two cans of cold Coke and handed him one. Gomez opened the can and took a drink. He figured this was what "normal" was like.

Detective Palmer sat at his desk and motioned for the four officers to leave. "Officer Gomez has work to do. Leave him alone."

The case file was thin. Only a few pages. Gomez began with the report from the hazmat team. It all seemed like a blur. Words ran together in patterns of black and white like musical notes on a page. Once his eyes focused, he began to pick out certain words like soggy, dead body, animal feces, putrid, mold, Level A, and vomit. The entire scene flashed before him again. He'd never seen anything like this before. He'd been a cop for only two years, a rookie. No real blood and guts calls, only domestic violence, child neglect or abuse, and drug busts. But never a dead body. He shuffled through more papers, then came to a handwritten page by Detective Palmer. All it said was "Tanner Case: Interview the manager at Adobe Palms Hotel." Gomez picked up the file and walked over to Detective Palmer's desk. "You wrote this?"

"Yes. That's where to start. All we know so far is that someone from the Adobe Palms called our substation to find out why Tom Tanner hadn't shown up for work in three weeks." Andy felt relieved to be able to leave the tiny room. He felt claustrophobic in there anyway. He wasn't an indoors person. He headed toward the door then out of the building, got into his police car, and drove to the Adobe Palms Hotel. He'd been there a few times before. It had been where his senior prom was held and where his family celebrated his grandmother's eightieth birthday. But he never liked the place. Called it a gringo hangout. It was mostly for the tourists and out of town visitors, not for the locals. He parked his car near the front and went inside. The desk clerk was a young Hispanic girl. He asked her where he could find the manager and she pointed to a corridor where his office was. Gomez walked down the tile hallway and found the door with the manager's name on it. He knocked, and a young man in his thirties opened the door. Gomez held up the file and said, "I'm here about Tom Tanner. I was the officer dispatched the day someone from here called to say he hadn't been at work."

The manager motioned for Gomez to come in. "Yes. I heard about it. So, you were the one who found him?"

"Afraid so."

"Do they know how he died?"

Gomez took out his pencil and notepad. "I can't talk about that. I'm here to find out what you know about him. Do you have his paperwork from when he was hired?" The manager walked over to a metal file cabinet next to the window and opened a drawer. He fingered thorough a few files, found the one labeled "Tanner," and handed it to Gomez, who briefly scanned the pages. "Does he have any next of kin?"

"Not according to his paperwork. The only name on there is a Penelope Witherspoon. She's on the life insurance policy."

"Who is she?"

"She's a waitress at the Grille." He pointed toward the restaurant by the lobby. "I haven't told her yet about the life insurance."

"I need to talk to her."

"I'll check to see when her shift starts." He opened up a ledger book and scanned names of the Adobe Palms employees. "Penelope Witherspoon. Starts at six tonight."

Gomez thanked the manager and returned to the substation. When he arrived, he saw that Detective Palmer was busy talking on the phone, so he sat down at his desk and wrote up his notes from his conversation with the manager at the Adobe

Palms. Suddenly, Gomez began to feel dizzy. He hadn't eaten since early morning. Palmer got off the phone and saw Gomez slumping over his desk. "Kid, you okay?"

"Sir, I need to eat something."

"You're pushing it, son. Go on home and rest."

Gomez told Palmer that he would return to the Adobe Palms Hotel that evening to talk to one of the waitresses; then he left for home.

By 6:00, Gomez felt revived enough to drive the couple of miles from his home to the Adobe Palms Grille. Still in uniform, he parked the police car and walked into the restaurant. He asked to speak with Penelope Witherspoon, and the hostess pointed to a woman serving at one of the tables. He decided to sit down and order some coffee. When Pen came over to take his order he told her he needed to talk to her about Tom Tanner. Her body stiffened. Tears started to run down her face. She sat down across from Gomez and tried to compose herself. "I can't believe he's dead. Do you know what happened?"

Gomez took out his notepad. "May I ask you a few questions? How well did you know Tom Tanner?"

Pen looked over toward the fish tank where they used to sit together. "We met over there." She pointed to the tank. "I've only known him a year." She started to sob. Gomez took out a cloth hanky and handed it to her. "So he worked here too?"

"No, he was a concierge at the hotel. He used to come into the Grille for an early dinner sometimes after his shift."

"Miss Witherspoon, did you know you were the beneficiary of his life insurance policy?"

Pen wiped her eyes with the hanky. "Life insurance policy? I had no idea."

"The manager of the hotel will talk to you about that. I just need to ask a few more questions." Gomez asked Pen about their relationship and how much time they spent together. He wanted to know if she knew about the water leak in his house, and the mold. He asked if Tom had talked about where he was before he came to Tempe, and if he had any family he'd mentioned. Pen told him everything she knew. About his sister dying in a fire in San Francisco. About the leak in his toilet, the smell, and him staying at her place for a while. And how she loved to have him tell her stories about his uncle's orchid adventures. About him going to the Phoenix Orchid Guild on weekends. And about their recent trip to Sedona. She said she didn't know anything about any mold. Gomez didn't want to upset her by giving details of the scene when he found Tom, so he just told her that they were still looking into the cause of death.

Then Pen remembered one more detail. "Tom was sick around Christmas time. We went to the annual holiday party here at the Grille a couple of weeks before Christmas, and he could hardly eat. He had stomach cramps and felt nauseated. He said he was going to see a doctor."

Gomez wrote down what she said. "Thanks. I'll check into this. Do you know what doctor?"

"No. But he probably went to the clinic where most of the employees go from the Adobe Palms. We have medical insurance that covers us there."

"When was the last time you saw him?"

Pen wiped her eyes again. "The night of the Christmas party. He was supposed to leave in a few days for San Francisco to visit his cousin. He had three weeks' vacation due him. He said he'd call me when he got there, but I never heard from him."

"San Francisco. Is that where he was from?"

"Yes. Oh my God. I thought he just needed to get away for a while. He was like that. Said he needed his freedom, his privacy. I never thought something had happened to him."

Gomez thanked Pen and went home. He began to feel a certain excitement that he hadn't felt for a long time. As a patrol officer, most of his days were pretty boring, driving around waiting for something to happen. Then when it did, it would be something like a domestic violence call or a drug bust. He never knew from day to day what would happen. He'd either be bored, waiting for someone to commit a crime, or emotionally drained from having to deal with a crime scene. It was never intellectually challenging, like the detective work he was doing for the Tanner case. He liked this a lot.

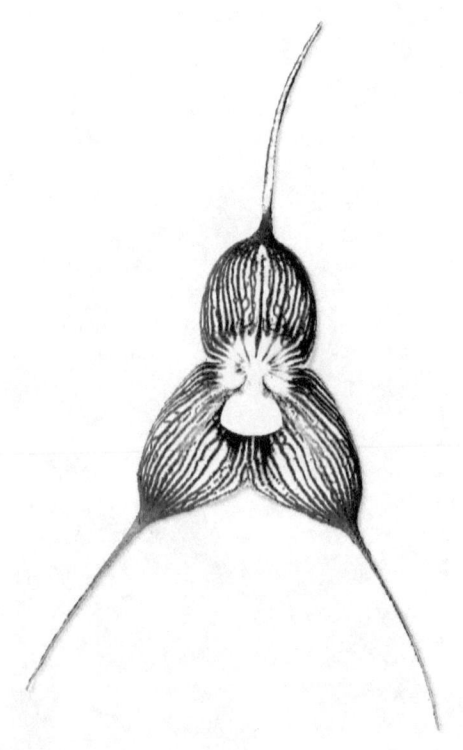

CHAPTER ELEVEN

Investigation

Gomez had just returned from the Phoenix Orchid Guild. He'd taken Pen's lead to see what they knew about Tom Tanner. What he found was not what he'd expected. Tom had been to meetings only a few times. Pen had told him he used to go almost every weekend. All they knew about Tom Tanner was that he'd recently moved to Tempe from San Francisco, and that his sister had died in a fire. They said he seemed to have an expertise in miniature orchids, and that he knew everything about orchid culture, orchid genre, orchid history. He was like a walking encyclopedia on orchids. They were even considering asking him to be on the board of the Phoenix Orchid Guild, but he hadn't returned their phone calls.

Gomez's notebook was beginning to fill up with information. When he returned to the substation, Detective Palmer told him that someone had to go back into the house to look for anything that might help the case. Gomez had already viewed the photos and videotape footage taken at the crime scene. He couldn't believe Palmer was asking him to go back there so soon. It had been only two weeks since he was released from the hospital, but since he was the first responder he knew he'd need to go back. He hardly remembered anything but the smell, the dead body, and the dog.

"Don't worry. I talked to the doctor. He said you'll be okay if you suit up. I know you've done it before. Went through your file. Pretty impressive. You'll be issued a Level A bunny suit. That should take care of you. Just remember Locard's Principle, will you? Don't screw up my crime scene."

Gomez gulped. "Sure. No problem." He knew about Locard's Exchange Principle. He'd learned about it in the police academy. *Anyone, or anything entering a crime scene both takes something of the scene with them, and leaves something of themselves behind when they leave.* He felt pretty good about how Detective Palmer was including him in the investigation. He could do this.

When he pulled up to the house, the yellow crime-scene tape had been replaced with red tape that read "Biohazard. Danger." His stomach clenched. He broke out in a cold sweat, grabbed a bottle of water, and gulped it down. He got out of the car, opened the trunk, and took out the bunny suit. He'd learned how to put those suits on when he worked on a couple of other cases that involved chemical spills. But never a Level A. He secured the hood over the collar of the suit and made sure to tape the booties over the white Mylar pants so there'd be no way for the toxins to get near his body. Then he made sure the tank of compressed air was working, and headed through the front gate toward the back of the house. A sign had been put on the front door that read "Warning. Biohazard. Entry Prohibited." He continued around toward the back of the house, trying to avoid the dog feces, opened the sliding glass door, and walked inside. This time it looked much brighter, since the curtains had been opened. Otherwise, nothing else had been touched. He walked toward the bedroom. The bed was still there, minus the body. Then he remembered the dog. *What happened to the dog?*

The rhythmic echoing of his breathing apparatus made him slightly disoriented. The bunny suit took some getting used to. He tried to navigate through the house systematically, looking around for anything that might be a clue to what happened to this poor bastard. This time the carpet was dry, but the place was still covered with mold. There were no pictures on the walls, no books or bookshelves. Not even a computer. There was a broken TV with old rabbit ears in the living room opposite the couch. The kitchen, with its linoleum flooring, apparently hadn't been affected by the mold as much. There were unwashed dishes in the sink, and a small fish tank sat on the counter half-filled with water and two dead koi fish, floating belly-up. He opened the refrigerator and saw a jar of peanut butter, some moldy bread, and two cartons of buttermilk, one unopened. There were soup bones in the freezer, probably for the dog, and three unopened cartons of Oreo cookies. *How could anyone live like this?* he wondered.

He walked back toward the bedroom and noticed an old dresser with a drawer slightly open. He opened the drawer and found it filled with underwear and socks. He noticed a small box in the corner. He opened it. Inside he saw a gold bracelet. He didn't touch it. Then he opened the other three drawers. Inside of one he saw a few issues of *Orchid Digest* next to a red tie with Santa Clauses on it. One of the drawers had a few pairs of folded slacks and jeans. Another drawer held folded dress shirts and a few T-shirts. He knew not to touch anything. He looked back toward the bed and noticed a small table with an electric clock, a small light, an inhaler, a bottle of antibiotics, and a bottle of anti-nausea medicine. He made a mental note of the inhaler—probably for asthma.

Then he noticed an unopened door opposite the bedroom. He didn't remember seeing it before. He opened the door, and to his amazement saw a tiny room, maybe large enough for a baby or small child. He started to walk into the room and tripped on a step. The bunny suit made his movements cumbersome. The room was at least two inches higher than the rest of the house. There was no mold in the room, probably because the water couldn't reach it, and like the kitchen it had a linoleum floor. The entire room was covered floor to ceiling with clear plastic. Along one wall he saw metal shelving holding smaller plants, some with tiny flowers. On the top shelf there was a fluorescent light. Then, hanging from the bottom shelves, was a group of plants in baskets filled with moss. He'd never seen plants like these before. They had strange-looking purple-black flowers protruding from the bottom of the basket below the moss. He pulled out one of the white plastic tags in the plants and read the *words "Dracula vampira." My God. What a name for a flower.*

He saw a fog machine that was hooked up to a timer. The ceiling fan was running, and there was an air conditioning unit in the window, also hooked up to a timer. There was a heater unplugged on the floor under the air conditioner. Suddenly, the timer clicked and the fogger went off. Mist quickly filled the room and Gomez's mask began to fog up. He started to leave the room, when he noticed a small closet door. He opened the door, and saw a crunched-up yellow blanket and a pillow on the floor, like someone had been sleeping there. Then, on the top shelf, he saw a colorful Pendleton blanket that looked like it was wrapped around an oblong object. He knew he wasn't supposed to move anything—Locard's Principle—but curiosity got the best of him. He carefully took down the blanket and unwrapped the object inside. It was a Native peace pipe made of wood. Gomez was taken aback. He looked more closely and realized that he'd seen this pipe before. Weak in the knees, he stumbled backwards and sat down on a folding chair next to the doorway. The turquoise stone, wrapped with strips of leather... those were the signature markings of Felipe Youngblood's peace pipe. He couldn't believe this was happening. The last time he'd seen that peace pipe was when he was twelve, right after his father was shot. *What would Tom Tanner be doing with this?*

He started to wrap the pipe up when he felt something hard at the other end of the blanket. He carefully unrolled the blanket until he saw a leather notebook held together with black duct tape. He opened the book and read the first page. It was clearly someone's private journal. The first entry was dated 1957. Gomez started to read, but couldn't understand most of the words since they sounded scientific. He did recognize the fact that it was something about an expedition to the Amazon rainforest, and that there was danger ahead. He flipped through the pages, each one written in perfect handwriting, almost like calligraphy. He looked for a name, or some reference so he could figure out the connection to Tom Tanner, but all he found were names of places, dates, descriptions of orchid expeditions to exotic places, and a few foreign names that he couldn't pronounce.

Gomez wrapped the blanket around the pipe, carefully putting the journal next to it. Then he put the bundle back into the closet exactly where he found it, closed the closet door, and left the house through the sliding-glass back door. As he passed the spot where evidence of his vomit still remained, he remembered the dog. He needed to find out about the dog. After all, he'd saved its life. Before he walked to his car, he removed the bunny suit and put it into a red bag marked "biohazard." Just then, an old beat-up car pulled in front of the house and parked behind Gomez's police car. The driver smoked a cigarette, looked agitated, and watched as Gomez put the bunny suit into the trunk of his car. The driver put out his cigarette, walked over to Gomez and said, "Excuse me, Officer. Do you know what happened here?"

Gomez asked who he was. The man said he was a friend of Tom Tanner. Gomez told the man he couldn't really talk about the case. The man asked, "Why is the place taped off? Did someone die?" The man began to pace back and forth.

"How did you know Tom Tanner?"

"Met him at the Phoenix Orchid Guild."

"I can't tell you much, but I am the one who found him."

"Oh, my God. How'd he die?"

"We're not sure of cause of death yet. How well did you know Tanner?"

"We were supposed to get together last week, but he never showed up. Now I know why."

"I may have a few questions for you later on. How can I find you?"

The man reached into his jeans pocket and pulled out a card that read "Phillip Marker, Tempe Botanical Gardens."

Gomez looked at the man's card. "What do you do there?"

"Well, I do lots of things. Mostly work with pesticide control, and watering plants." He took out a cigarette and lit up.

"So, where did you learn about orchids?"

"From my dad. He worked the botanical gardens in Florida. I helped him a lot."

Gomez put the card in the back pocket of his uniform. "I'll probably contact you after the crime scene is cleaned up. There's a room full of orchids that will need to go to someone who knows how to care for them."

"Crime scene?"

"That's what we call an unattended death."

The man smiled. "Let me know if I can be of any assistance."

Gomez took a drink of cold water and drove back to the precinct to make notes of everything he found in the house. He'd always been told that he had a photographic memory, so it wasn't hard for him to remember every last detail.

CB CB CB CB

The call came in about the dog a few minutes after Gomez had returned to City Hall. The vet said the dog was fine now, and ready to go to the pound unless someone wanted it. Gomez told him he would pick the dog up on his way home. When he got to the vet's they brought the dog out to him and he was shocked at how healthy the dog looked. It ran over to Gomez and jumped up on him like it had known him for a long time. Gomez thanked the vet and took the dog to his car. He took the dog to his small apartment, and that night both of them slept on the bed next to each other. From then on the two were inseparable. He named the dog Yaqui.

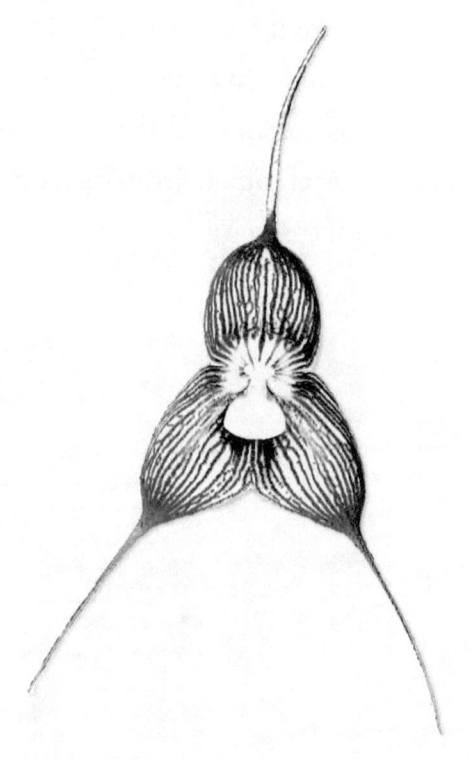

184   J. S. Bodin

CHAPTER TWELVE

The Wise Deer

The Wise Deer, so wise that when hunters search for him they can never find him. The hunters pass close to him, but never see him. After many years the deer becomes old. He asks the hunters to kill him, but they pay no attention to his plea. He follows the hunters' trails in hopes that he might encounter a trap in which he can put his head or feet, but he cannot find them. In his weariness, he speaks to the twilight, saying, "Now I render myself up." And he dies. (A Yaqui Folktale)

The office of the medical investigator was backed up, and it was taking forever to get the results of the autopsy on Tom Tanner. Detective Palmer was pulled onto another case. There'd been mumblings that it was more than a local shoot-out near Papago, and that it had international connections to a possible terrorist plot. Now the Department of Homeland Security was involved, and Detective Palmer would become swept up in a high-profile case that left him little time for anything else. Gomez was pretty much on his own with the Tanner case. He'd already interviewed everyone from the Adobe Palms Hotel who knew Tanner. He'd interviewed the people at the Phoenix Orchid Guild. He'd checked for social security numbers, old addresses, anything that would validate who this guy was, but everything turned up empty. Tanner was a fraud. A ghost in the system. The only tangible item he'd found was the journal written by an anonymous person who documented orchid expeditions, orchid sales, and from what Gomez deduced, illicit activities. At first he thought Tom Tanner had written the journal, but it dated back before he'd even been born. *How did he get the journal, anyway? Maybe the journal had something to do with why he died.* Gomez felt like he'd reached a dead end. The only place left to go was to find out how Tanner ended up with Felipe Youngblood's peace pipe. He needed to go to Ixtlan.

Memories of his trip to Ixtlan with his brother had blurred over the last ten years. All he knew was that if it hadn't been for Felipe Youngblood, his mother might have never recovered after her husband was shot. Mrs. Gomez had stopped eating, sleeping, talking. The parish priest tried to console her, but nothing was working. Even when Jesús showed up at the funeral after being gone for two years, Mrs. Gomez hardly acknowledged him. After a few days, Jesús told her they were going to talk to someone who could help. She absently allowed

Jesús to help her into his car. Andy got into the back seat. He was only twelve at the time and was also in shock. He was trying to deal with the murder of his father and also the fact that Jesús had been gone for two years and still hadn't told him why. Jesús was a changed person, and Andy didn't have any idea what had made him that way.

Jesús drove them to Ixtlan to meet a Yaqui medicine man who could help them. Andy had never even heard of Ixtlan. How did his brother know about it? He'd heard of Yaqui medicine men, but never met one. When they pulled up to Felipe Youngblood's trailer, Jesús helped his mother out of the car, up the wooden steps so they could go inside. Andy followed. Felipe immediately lit a stick of sage to cleanse the space; then he began a chant in Yaqui while waving the sage stick over Mrs. Gomez. At first, nothing happened—then all of a sudden she began to cry, then sob. She began talking to Felipe in Yaqui and by the time the ceremony had ended, she stood up and asked for a glass of water. From then on, she was on the road to recovery. Once Jesús felt she would be all right, he told Andy to take care of her like he used to, and he left. It was the last time Gomez saw his brother alive.

For the next few months, Andy did take care of his mother until she was back to herself. He'd leave for school after he made sure she had her breakfast, come home at lunch to make her a sandwich, and then make dinner. He'd learned to cook at an early age when his brother taught him how to make tortillas and refried beans, huevos, and other foods that they'd cook in quantities that would last a few days. Mrs. Gomez had taught Jesús what her mother had taught her about cooking. And there were always the special desserts like flan and *bisco-chitos*. But the worst part was that Gomez didn't have his older brother to help him, and he didn't know why. Gomez was devastated. He'd always looked up to his older brother. Wanted to be just like him. But something had happened the summer Jesús turned sixteen, and their father sent him off to a summer music camp where he could really learn how to play guitar. When he returned, Jesús seemed different. The day after he graduated from high school, he left.

Summertime in the garden. Long hot evenings where smells of honeysuckle fill the dark void of unknowing. Where beauty and terror exist simultaneously. Where dark clouds blur his vision so all he sees are the shapes between shadows. Then an image. Piercing eyes of a deer. Eyes that will guide him out of darkness. Mist surrounds the image, then begins to clear. The shapes take form. A deer standing alone. It speaks to him. "Be like me. Hide from them so they cannot find you. Then you will find truth."

The Estrella Mountains shimmered in the morning light. Gomez had already made it to the turnoff to Ixtlan, but had no memory of the short drive from Tempe. He hadn't thought about the wise deer since his brother's death. The Yaqui folktale about the Wise Deer had been Gomez's favorite. His mother used to tell him Yaqui folktales when he was little. But the Wise Deer remained stuck in his mind, perhaps because it was told to him when he was contagious with measles, and Jesús wasn't allowed in the bedroom. Gomez had his mother all to himself each night for almost a week. But now something very strange was going on. Gomez felt it in his bones, like the time he awakened from a nightmare at the exact moment his father had been shot. *His screams throughout the house. His mother trying to calm him. The police at the door in the morning. His mother's face turning white, then her body collapsing in slow motion onto the floor.* His memory of that event was etched in his mind because the image of the wise deer appeared to him at the moment his father had died.

When he parked the police car by the front porch, two dogs ran out to greet him. Then the screen door opened and Gomez saw a tall man with long brown hair, graying at the temples. The man wore a colorful skirt and a white linen blouse. He walked over to Gomez and reached out his hand. "Andy. You've grown into a handsome son of a bitch."

Gomez tipped his police hat. "I called ahead to let Dillon know I was coming. Is he around?"

"You don't recognize me?"

Gomez squinted his eyes from the glare of the sunlight. "Sorry."

"Guess you were around twelve last time you were here with your mother and brother, Jesús. I'm Dillon."

Gomez took a step back. It had been ten years, but he had no memory of Dillon looking that way. He remembered a man with long braided brown hair, who wore jeans and boots, sort of like a cowboy. Dillon motioned for Gomez to come inside and to sit down at the picnic table for some tea and biscuits. *The red and white checkered tablecloth*. He remembered that. He tried to compose himself. "Look, I'm here on official police business." He sat down, took a sip of tea, and pulled out his notepad. "Mind if I ask a few questions?"

Dillon motioned for him to proceed.

"Did a Tom Tanner ever come to Ixtlan?"

Dillon winced. "Yes. He visited us a couple of times. Why?"

"I'm afraid I have some bad news. Tom Tanner is dead, and we're questioning people who might have come into contact with him over the last few months."

Dillon's body stiffened. His faced turned pale. "Dead. Oh, my God. How? When?"

"A call came to the local substation from the Adobe Palms Hotel where Tanner worked. Said he hadn't shown up for work after New Year's. I was the patrol officer sent to check up on him."

"I had no idea something had happened to Tom. He told us he needed some time to figure things out…and that he didn't need our help."

"Figure things out? What things?"

Dillon tried to compose himself. "Tom came to Ixtlan a few months ago and told us that he thought someone was trying to kill him. He wouldn't tell us who. I advised him to go to the Tempe police, but he said it was complicated, and that he needed more time to figure out what to do. We offered him sanctuary here at Ixtlan, but he said he didn't need our help. I had no idea he was in such grave danger."

Gomez flipped through a few pages of his notepad, then found a clean sheet. He tried to do the drill like he'd been taught at the police academy, but words started coming out of his mouth that weren't expected. "I was the one who found him. He'd been dead almost three weeks."

"Oh, my God. How did he die?"

"Cause of death is still undetermined. However, there was toxic mold all over the house from a water leak behind the toilet."

Dillon stood up. "Yes, I knew about that leak. He said the landlord had been trying to fix it and that the house smelled like a cesspool. But he never said anything about mold."

Gomez realized that he'd probably already said too much.

No one knew about the mold yet. He began to write in his notebook. "How long had Tanner been coming to Ixtlan?"

"Only a couple of times in the last few months. He wasn't feeling well the last time he was here, and said he'd go to the clinic to see if he had the flu or something."

"So, when was he here last?"

"It would have been two weeks before Christmas. We expected to hear from him after New Year's."

"Why was that?"

"Well, that's the part of this investigation you need to take notes on. Let's go into my study where it's more private." Dillon led Gomez down a long hallway into another area of the main house. They entered a room with bookshelves floor to ceiling, along all four walls. Dillon sat in a large leather chair, and Gomez sat across from him on a smaller wooden chair. "So, what do you want to know, Officer Gomez?"

"I guess my first question is: How did Tom Tanner end up with Felipe Youngblood's peace pipe in his house?" Gomez began to feel like he was back on track. It was clear that Tanner had a connection to Ixtlan; it was clear that Dillon knew something. This Tanner case was twisting and turning like snakes in a fire pit, making no real sense, no concrete connections. First an unsolved, unattended death with toxic mold as a biohazard. Then no evidence that a Tom Tanner even existed.

The strange room filled with orchids. The orchid journal. And the peace pipe? It made no sense at all.

Dillon started at the beginning. He told Gomez how he'd received a call from someone he knew in Phoenix, at the Caveman Bar. That a guy named Tom wanted to get directions to Ixtlan and ended up driving there a few days later. When he got there, he said he'd left Maui and moved to Tempe to start over.

"Start over? From what?"

Dillon told Gomez about the fire and Tom's aunt's death. About Tom changing his name from Kyle O'Sullivan to Tom Tanner when he came to Tempe. About Penelope Witherspoon, about the gold bracelet, and that Felipe Youngblood gave Tom the peace pipe.

Gomez wrote all of this down on his notepad. "So he revealed his true identity to you. What was he hiding from?"

Dillon laughed. "What do you think?"

"I really don't have any idea."

Dillon spoke in a soft voice. "Andy, there are things you don't know about. And even though you are here on official police business, there is much more going on than just the Tanner case."

Gomez stood up. He knew Dillon was right. He'd sensed it the minute he found the peace pipe. But now he was so curious about this case that nothing could stop him. "Go on. I need to know."

"Tanner was like most of us here at Ixtlan—trying to live in two worlds."

"But he had a girlfriend, that Pen person."

"That didn't mean he wasn't gay."

"But why did he need to change his entire identity and lie about everything?"

"Well. That's the point. He was desperate after his aunt died in the fire. He felt he had no choice, because he thought the fire was really meant for him."

"You mean, someone tried to kill him before?"

"That's what he thought. And apparently he created a new identity to save his life."

Gomez wrote furiously. Now it was beginning to unravel. To make some sense. *Maui, not Northern California. Aunt died in fire, not Tom's sister. Kyle O'Sullivan, not Tom Tanner. Lied to Penelope Witherspoon. Was really gay. Lied to Phoenix Orchid Guild. Lied to Adobe Palms Hotel. Fake social security card. Fake driver's license. Fake passport. Fake bank account. No way to trace him until now. Tells truth to Dillon at Ixtlan. Felipe Youngblood hands over peace pipe to him for some reason.*

"Maybe it's time to talk to Felipe. You up for it?"

Gomez started coughing uncontrollably. Dillon brought him a glass of water. "You okay?"

"Yeah. Something caught in my throat."

"You said you were the one who found Tom. Right? Maybe that mold got to you."

"Actually, it did. I ended up in the hospital for a week. Still on meds and off patrol duty."

"Well, maybe Felipe can do something for you besides answer police questions."

Dillon motioned for them to leave. They both got into Gomez's police car and drove over to Felipe's. When they arrived there was a car parked in front of the trailer. They pulled up next to an old Chevy pickup truck and parked. Felipe came out of the trailer. "Police? My oh my. What did I do to deserve this?"

Dillon stepped out of the car first. "We're here because of Tom Tanner."

Felipe looked confused. "Tom Tanner—why?"

"We need to come in and talk. This is Officer Gomez. He needs to ask you a few questions. It's okay."

Gomez entered the small trailer and saw a man and woman sitting on the couch. The woman was holding a small child. Felipe introduced the family as friends of Ixtlan who lived a few miles outside of Papago and who came regularly to

Felipe because of their sick child. The baby couldn't have been more than a year old. The mother, clearly a Yaqui Indian, had tears in her eyes. She said something to Felipe in Yaqui, then stood up. Felipe handed her a bag of what looked like herbs, and the family walked out the door. Felipe went with them and Gomez could hear the father saying something in English that sounded like, "You've done all you can. We understand. Thank you."

When Felipe returned, he lit a sage stick and waved it over the walls and floor of the trailer. Gomez knew what that meant. He remembered when Felipe did the same thing when he and his mother and brother were there. Felipe sat down, composed himself, then said, "How can I help you, son?"

Gomez pulled out his notepad. "You remember who I am?"

"Of course. How could I forget? You've grown into a handsome man."

Gomez started to smile, but he also wanted to remain professional. "I'm afraid I have some bad news. Tom Tanner is dead. I was the one who found him at his home when the call came in from the Adobe Palms Hotel. He hadn't shown up for work after New Year's. I found your peace pipe the closet of one of the bedrooms. I want to know the connection he had with you."

Felipe's face turned white. He'd known how sick Tom had

felt before Christmas, but he never imagined how bad it was. "My God." His eyes filled up with tears. "Oh, my God. Do you know how he died?"

"Cause of death is still undetermined. But when I arrived at his place, it was covered with mold. It was so bad I ended up in the hospital with toxic mold exposure."

"Mold? I knew there was a water leak in the bathroom, and that the place smelled, but Tom never said anything about mold."

"That's because the leak had started up again. Water must have been running the entire three weeks over the holiday. We don't know if the mold killed him, or if he had an asthma attack, or what. So, Mr. Youngblood, could you please tell me how your peace pipe ended up in Tanner's closet?"

Felipe tried to compose himself. "Well, that's a long story. I don't know if you have enough paper in that notepad. Guess I can begin with the dream." Felipe told Gomez about Tom's dream of the dog of sand, in the box, and how he named the dog Yaqui.

He was about to continue when Gomez interrupted him. "Yaqui?"

"Yes. Yaqui. Why?"

Gomez's face drained of color. "Go on."

Felipe continued. He told Gomez about Tom's dreams,

and that he felt Tom had a connection to Ixtlan and to the Yaqui way of life that he hadn't experienced since Dillon's father lived there. Amsted had been the last guardian of the pipe, and when Dillon brought Tom to meet him, he knew who the next guardian would be. *Shadow Dreamer.* Tom was to be known as Shadow Dreamer from then on. Felipe told Gomez about the sweat lodge and that Tom was too weak, passed out, and had to go back to Ixtlan with Dillon.

Gomez hadn't blinked during Felipe's comments. He hadn't even written anything down on his notepad. When Felipe stopped talking, Gomez stood up and walked outside. He took some breaths of fresh air. The story about the dog kept pounding in his head. He walked back inside and said, "Well, I now have Tom's dog. He almost died from mold exposure and starvation. I found him on the floor next to Tanner's bed."

"You saved the dog's life?"

"Yes. But we never knew its name. So, when I got him from the vet a few days ago, I named him Yaqui."

Felipe grimaced. "Yaqui?"

Felipe motioned for Dillon and Gomez to go outside with him. He stopped by the rail of the porch and gave Gomez a long stare before he spoke. Then, in an almost fatherly voice he said, "Andy, I remember you very well, actually. When your brother Jesús brought you and your mother here after your father was shot in the line of duty, there were things that had happened in your family that you were too young to understand. If this Tanner case hadn't brought you to Ixtlan, you might never have met up with me again. We know things about your family that no one else knows."

"What things?"

"We know what really happened to your brother."

"My brother was beat up by some gang kids. A random act. They took his money and wallet. They never even caught the guys."

Dillon put his arm on Gomez's shoulder. "That's the story everyone was told. But that's not the true story."

"What do you mean, the true story?"

Dillon told Gomez about the first time Jesús came to Ixtlan. That he had just turned sixteen. That he'd come right after he returned from that terrible summer camp. He'd thought he was going for guitar lessons, but ended up in one of those Christian fundamentalist groups where they cure young man of being gay. "Said their motto was, 'Pray the gay away,'" Felipe told Andy. Jesús had explained to the men at Ixtlan that he'd ended up having electric shock therapy on his hands and genitals, and was forced to take nausea-inducing drugs while they showed him pictures of naked men. He'd had masturbatory reconditioning, visualizations, and prayer circles. "His words exactly. "

Felipe shook his head. "He said your dad told him no

cop's son was going to be a fag. Not in his house. When Jesús came to Ixtlan, he was almost suicidal, but we convinced him to graduate high from school then come live at Ixtlan. He'd agreed. After he graduated he left home, and did come to Ixtlan for a few months, then disappeared until he showed up for your father's funeral. Even your mother didn't know the truth about that awful camp. Conversion Therapy. That's what they called it."

Gomez's eyes glazed over, his mouth half open; beads of sweat clung to his forehead. He couldn't utter a sound. Dillon handed him a bottle of cold water. Gomez felt numb. That explained why Jesús never touched his guitar after music camp, why he never talked to his father unless he had to, why he became distant to his brother and his mother, and why he locked himself in his room most of the time he was home. Gomez was only nine when Jesús went to that camp. He couldn't have imagined anything so terrible happening to his beloved older brother, especially something that his own father had planned. He reached into his wallet and took out a picture of himself with Jesús, which had been taken in front of the hammock in their garden. He handed it to Felipe.

"This was taken by my father a few days before he sent Jesús off to camp. Jesús was so happy. He thought he was going to study guitar all summer."

Felipe took the picture to look at. "I'm so sorry about

all of this. But maybe there is a reason you're here. When we heard what really happened to Jesús, we couldn't believe the cover-up. There wasn't anything we could do. You were only nine and your mother would have been devastated if she'd found out the truth. Detective Palmer did it to protect both of you. At least that's what we found out later."

"Palmer? Was he on the case?"

"Said he knew your father well. That in all good conscience, he couldn't have Jesús' murder be a blight on your family name. He helped cover up what really happened."

"What really happened to Jesús? I need to know."

They sat down outside Felipe's trailer on a wooden bench. The sun had begun to set behind the Estrella Mountains, casting a light-orange hue over the desert. Gomez felt like he was in a time-lapse movie, freeze-frame, where this moment would be etched in his mind forever. Felipe's words echoed in his head, but he didn't feel like he was really present. He was hovering somewhere above the mountains, watching three tiny figures sitting around a trailer at sunset. And as he slowly soared higher into the salmon cloudbank, the landscape disappeared. He was now shrouded by a purple mist of darkness. The steady drone of Felipe's voice finally broke his trance-state with the words: "Jesús laying in a pool of his own blood."

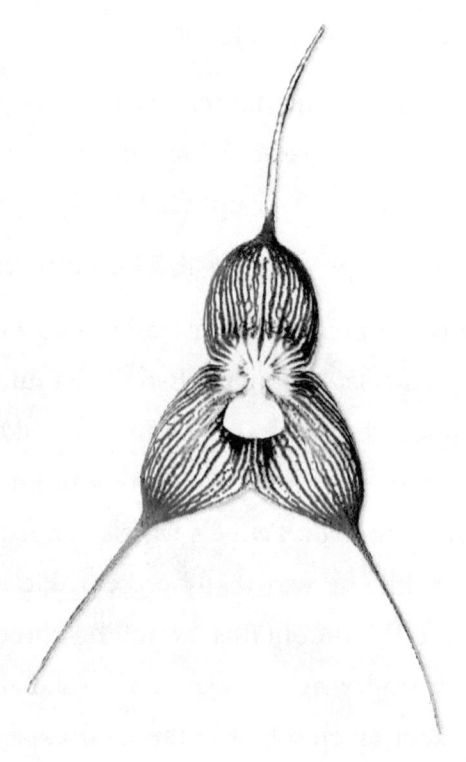

CHAPTER THIRTEEN

Two Spirits

Jesús walks out of the Caveman Bar. His long black hair flows below his shoulders. His tall thin body lilts along the warm pavement. Alone. A little high from pot and beer. He walks into the parking lot in the back. Some of the flood lights are busted out. In the shadows, two men approach him. They each wear a black sweatshirt with a hood, sunglasses, torn jeans, and leather cowboy boots. One man yells something, then unzips his jeans and pulls out his limp cock. Jesús tries to run toward his car, but the other man grabs him and forces him to his knees toward the now erect penis. They put his mouth over the warm cock and he begins to move up and down until it erupts. Then the other man unzips his jeans and Jesús does the same for him. No one is around to see anything. One man holds Jesús by his long black hair while the other goes to their car. He comes back with a wooden baseball bat, walks over to Jesús, and proceeds to hit him over the head, all the while yelling something in anger. Jesús crumples toward the pavement as each man takes turns pulverizing his skull with the bat. The two men take off. A couple of hours later, someone finds Jesús lying in a pool of his own blood and calls the police.

Palmer was about finished with his second cup of coffee when Gomez came into work the next morning. "How'd it go at that *fag* place yesterday?"

Gomez sat down at his desk, pulled out his paperwork, and excused himself to get a cup of coffee. He knew he'd have trouble relating to Palmer after what Felipe told him, but he had to find a way to get through this if he wanted to stay on the Tanner case. When he returned, Palmer had already left. Gomez had begun to document what Felipe and Dillon told him about Tom, but first he needed to clear his mind from what Felipe told him about his brother's murder. It was Palmer and another cop who had viewed the surveillance footage from the Caveman parking lot. According to Felipe, the other cop was a closeted gay who worked with Palmer and who knew Jesús. That's how Felipe found out what really happened that night.

Gomez couldn't focus on the Tanner case. He felt like his world was turned upside down. Just like he felt when he woke in the hospital after he'd found the dead body in the moldy house. He couldn't get the images out of his mind. He was still having nightmares about that crime scene, nightmares in which he saw the mold growing up the arm of the dead body where the fingers had touched the soggy carpet. He knew it was post-traumatic stress. He'd been warned by the doctors that this was a normal reaction, that he shouldn't be ashamed about vomiting at the crime scene, about passing out, about any of it. He'd been through a traumatic experience.

Now, the same thing was happening, only this time he was having flashes of his brother's murder. The same waves of nausea, the same sweats, the same rapid beating of his heart. How could he not have known about Jesús? How could he not have known about what his father put Jesús through, making him go to that Christian camp? He felt guilt that he couldn't have helped his brother. He felt his blood boil when he thought about his father, who had always been his hero. His entire world was crumbling. His poor mother. She had no idea about any of this, thanks to Detective Palmer. Gomez muttered under his breath, "The truth shall set you free." *Pile of crap. The truth shall screw up your life.*

The day wore on while Gomez tried to compile his notes from Ixtlan. He'd need to talk to Palmer sooner or later, but Palmer would be gone for the rest of the day. Gomez decided to leave work early to visit his mother. It had been over a week since he'd seen her. He didn't want to let on what he'd learned about Jesús, so he prepared himself to try to act normal. When he arrived the house was dark, except for the flickering light from the TV in his mother's bedroom. She lay asleep on her bed, one arm extended over the edge. Yaqui slept next to her. Yaqui had become her companion when Gomez was at work. It was barely 4:00 p.m. Why was she asleep?

"*Madre*, are you okay?" Gomez reached for her hand. Yaqui put his head on her stomach. She moved, then opened her eyes.

"*Hijo*. Get something to eat."

"*Madre*, are you sick?"

Mrs. Gomez made the sign of the cross over her chest. "Just tired, that's all."

But Gomez knew this had been going on since Jesús' murder. Sometimes his mother seemed fine; then suddenly she'd go into a depression, like now. He thought about the time Jesús took her to Felipe Youngblood after his father's murder. But he couldn't take his mother now. Not after he had learned the truth about what his father did to his brother. He tried to get his mother to take the antidepressants her doctor had prescribed, but the pill bottle remained unopened. He talked to her priest, but other than people coming from the church to check up on her and to bring her occasional meals, there was nothing else he could do. He couldn't ever tell her the truth about Jesús, especially the part about his father sending him to that Christian camp.

Restless. Unsettled. Nowhere to turn, he goes outside into the garden, lies in the hammock, and falls asleep. The gentle

*sound of water gurgling over the sides of a concrete fountain,
a recent memorial Gomez made for his brother, Jesús. The
fountain has a wooden cross at the top, with the words, "Jesús,
there is music in the stars." Along the sides of the fountain,
plastic flowers in bright colors. A picture of Jesús as a child sits
at the base of the cross. The scent of honeysuckle fills the air
while the gentle breeze rocks Gomez's body in the hammock.*

Gomez awakened to the smell of fresh tortillas and
beans. He went inside the house and saw his mother at the
stove, cooking. She offered him some coffee and told him to sit
down at the kitchen table. A tear rolled down Gomez's cheek
as he looked up at her. "*Madre,* you look better."

She put a warm tortilla on his plate, then spooned on
beans and sprinkled shredded cheese on top. "Don't worry
about me, *hijo.* I just get so tired sometimes. Eat." Then she sat
down next to him. "*Hijo*, you spend too much time worrying
about me. Now I worry about you."

"Me? I'm fine, *Madre*."

"No. All you do is work and take care of me and Yaqui.
You need a wife."

Gomez smiled. "A wife?"

"Yes. To take care of you and to give me a grandson. That
would make me happy."

"Okay, *Madre*, I'll look for one."

Mrs. Gomez glanced at him. "I am serious. Don't tease me."

CR CR CR CR

The next day at the substation, Gomez had a chance to give Palmer his report. He couldn't do anything else until Palmer gave him feedback. He'd hit a dead end with the Tanner case. He was still waiting for the autopsy report, but he felt he needed another case to work on to keep him busy.

Palmer held up the Tanner file and said, "Kid, you done good. You certainly have an eye for detail."

Gomez took a gulp of air. He'd started holding his breath when he saw Palmer take out the Tanner file from his briefcase. "Thank you, sir."

"You ever thought about becoming a full-time detective?"

"Actually, I have."

"Well, I think you are cut out for it. I don't remember ever reading such a detailed report. I'd suggest you take a look at a couple of books over there on my shelves." Palmer pointed to a shelf lined with books on police work. Gomez walked over and scanned the titles. Palmer pointed again. "That one. It's called, *Becoming a Detective: The How's and Whys.*" Gomez took the book off the shelf. Palmer told him to read it and if he really wanted to pursue this, to let him know. He told him there would be an opening at City Hall next year, and that he would recommend Gomez if he wanted it. For a moment, Gomez forgot what Felipe had told him about Palmer covering up his brother's murder. He forgot that he was angry with Palmer. He took the book and sat at his desk. Palmer handed him back the Tanner file and said, "I think you need to go back to that fag heaven again. There must be other fags that talked to Tanner besides the medicine man and that other character. What was his name? *Dildo?*"

Gomez felt his blood rush to his head. He wanted to say something to Palmer, who might as well have been referring to his brother, Jesús. He'd never thought about it before. Cops always talked about the fags at Ixtlan and joked about how airy-fairy they were. Once in a while there'd be an incident at Ixtlan and a patrol officer would come back to the substation impersonating the cross-dressers. In fact, Gomez himself had used the word "fag" many times. Never thought twice about it. But now everything was different.

He looked Palmer in the eyes and said, "Dillon. His name is Dillon."

ભ   ભ   ભ   ભ

Ixtlan had been the butt of jokes for years, not just because of the gay community, but its history as a POW camp had a particular story that the locals in Tempe loved to tell.

In the late hours of December 22nd, 1944, twenty-five Germans slip out of the hole of a tunnel built under the POW camp, and onto the banks of a canal, disappearing into the night. The plan is to escape to Mexico, possibly by stealing a boat and floating down the Salt River. It would have been a great plan—except there aren't any boats, and there is no water. Just because a map has something called a "river," there isn't necessarily any water in it. The POWs manage to escape and to take off in different directions. Back in camp the Christmas celebration ends and everybody goes to bed. The camp guards settle down for a quiet night until the base commander starts getting phone calls from residents and police in Tempe and Phoenix. People are complaining about Germans knocking on their doors asking to be returned to the Papago Park POW camp. It is a cold night, and some of the POWs miss their bunks and blankets. There are some POWs, however, who get as far as Gila Bend, and the German leader manages to hide out for over a month, probably staying in a cave near Camelback Mountain before being arrested in a hotel lobby in downtown Phoenix. Some say there were up to sixty fugitives. For decades after the war, there are stories of escaped POWs that either lived out in the boondocks or had assimilated into the local population

Gomez brought Yaqui to Ixtlan with him this time. When he arrived, Dillon opened the screen door to let them inside. "Great to see you doing so well, Rover."

Gomez corrected him. "Yaqui, remember?"

"Yaqui. Right. So, what brings you back so soon?"

"Detective Palmer wants me to talk to anyone else who might know anything about Tom Tanner. We're at a dead end with the case until the autopsy report comes back."

"Okay—I think I should take you to the Blue Corn Diner, then. Tom was there with me. I'm not sure who will be there now, but we can take our chances." They got into Gomez's police car and Dillon directed him to the restaurant. "So, Palmer is supervising you on the Tanner investigation?"

"Yes. Why?"

"No reason. Just a coincidence, that's all."

℘ ℘ ℘ ℘

The Blue Corn Diner was filled with people—some locals, and some from Ixtlan. The minute Gomez entered, all eyes turned toward him. One of the locals, a middle-aged man with a beer belly, scruffy graying beard, and missing front teeth came up to him and said, "Help you, Officer?" Gomez ignored him and followed Dillon to a table where they sat down and ordered ice water. The man followed them. "Hardly ever see uniformed police at the Blue Corn Diner. What's your business?"

Dillon waved his hand at the man. "Stubby, leave the officer alone. He's here on official police business. I'm handling it." The man winked at Dillon, went over to the bar, and ordered a beer. Gomez tried not to gawk, but he'd never seen a place like this. Many of the men wore skirts and blouses and had on make-up. Some looked so feminine that Gomez could hardly tell they were men. Then there were the beer-belly mountain-men types, like Stubby. They were sitting at the bar minding their own business. The waitress behind the bar could have been either male or female, but what poured out of her blouse certainly looked female to Gomez. He'd heard about cross-dressers before, even seen a few in Phoenix, but usually they were alone waiting for their next trick.

He turned toward Dillon. "Who did you want me to talk to?"

A young boy walked over to their table. He couldn't have been more than seventeen. He was followed by a woman who looked to be in her middle thirties. They sat down at the table across from Dillon and Gomez. Dillon introduced them. "Officer Gomez, I'd like you to meet Danny and Red Wolf. They live at Ixtlan year-round. They both knew Tom Tanner."

Danny motioned for the bartender to come over, and ordered a soda. "I can't believe Tom is dead. We're all still in shock."

Gomez pulled out his notebook. "How well did you know him?"

"Only really talked to him a couple of times. We shared a love of orchids. I take care of the greenhouse in back of the diner, and he knew all about the plants."

"Did he tell you about the fire in Maui?"

"Yes. I think he said his aunt died in that fire."

"Did he say anything about someone wanting to kill him?" Danny cringed. He reached over and grabbed Red Wolf's hand. "Kill him? No."

Dillon spoke. "I think Tom only shared that with Felipe and me."

Red Wolf pulled out a lipstick. "I worked a bit on his chakras when he was here. He was very agitated; I could see that."

The minute Red Wolf spoke, Gomez realized she was a man. The deep voice was a dead giveaway. He looked up and saw that she was fidgeting with her scarf, like she was afraid. "Don't worry, uh, ma'am. The only reason I'm here is because Felipe Youngblood's peace pipe was found at Tom Tanner's place. Do you happen to know anything about it?"

Danny answered. "Well, we heard that Felipe gave him that pipe for a special reason. The next time he came to Ixtlan everyone started calling him Shadow Dreamer."

Gomez wrote furiously. "Shadow Dreamer? What's that?"

"It's like Red Wolf's name. It is given to you by a Native medicine man to indicate a certain quality of who you are."

Red Wolf looked up. "My name was given to me when I was a baby. In the Navajo tradition if a baby is born male, but wants to live as a female, they are called 'nadleehi' or 'two sprits.' I was taught the healing arts, and was accepted in my culture for who I am."

Gomez tried to write this down, but his hand froze on the paper. He was losing focus. He kept imagining his brother hanging out at the Blue Corn Diner, maybe even talking to Red Wolf. The jukebox went on and a country tune started to play. A few men started to do a line dance in the middle of the room. He began to feel more and more comfortable, like there was something so right about this place. Yet, he could also understand the attitude of the cops at his substation. They'd never be able to accept the fact that a man would want to live like a woman, or that a man would love another man. He wondered if Jesús ever dressed up like a woman. He thought about his mother and how she would react. Maybe it was just as well that Palmer kept Jesús' murder under wraps. Maybe the lie made more sense than the truth.

Gomez was silent on the drive back to Ixtlan. When they arrived at the gate there was another car waiting to get in. Jeffrey came running out of the house with the three dogs following him. He unlocked the gate and the first car, a red Camry, drove up toward the house. Gomez followed, then parked the police car. Yaqui ran up to greet him. A tall handsome man, with short-cropped brown hair graying at the temples, got out of the car. "Officer, did I do anything wrong?"

Gomez noticed that the man was wearing a colorful Hawaiian shirt, light beige linen slacks, and leather sandals. "No. We just happened to arrive here at the same time."

The man looked relieved. "I'm looking for someone called Dillon. Where would I find him?"

Dillon got out of the police car. "I'm Dillon."

The man said, "I've come a long way to meet you. I'm Dean Salmon. Our fathers knew each other in San Francisco when we were kids."

Dillon walked toward the house and the two men followed. "Never heard of you. Have we ever met?"

"Very possibly."

Gomez figured he'd been there long enough, and turned to get into his police car when Dillon said, "Officer, come in for some tea and biscuits, please."

Gomez had a strange feeling in his gut. There was something about this man, but he couldn't put his finger on it yet, so he followed them inside. They all sat down at the picnic table and Jeffrey served tea and biscuits. Dean pulled out a picture from his wallet. "This is a picture of my father with the group of men he lived with in San Francisco."

He handed the photo to Dillon, who looked at it and exclaimed, "That's Amsted and Louie. They're in the picture. Which one is your father?"

Dean pointed to a handsome man with a handlebar moustache and long brown hair. "He died from AIDS when I was seven. My mother took me to a commune on Maui. Mom came from wealth. She was rebelling against her parents, who in her eyes represented the status quo. So she tried the counter-culture thing. But when they heard about me, their grandson, they insisted on raising me. They managed to get custody, and that was that. I never saw her again, and neither did they. If it wasn't for them I wouldn't have had the money to go to law school. Lilly was born before I even married, but I never hurt for money. I guess it was how my grandparents made up for their estrangement from my mother."

Dillon looked again at the picture. "I've never seen a picture of all of them together. Do you remember going to the marina on Louie's sailboat, by any chance?"

Dean smiled. "My God. Yes. I'd forgotten about that. I couldn't have been more than three."

Dillon looked up. "We must be around the same age then. Mid-forties?"

"Yes, and it looks like we did meet before."

Gomez stood up. "I think it's time for me to leave. I'll come back once I get the coroner's report. Dillon, thanks so much for all of your help. Nice to meet you, Mister Salmon."

He whistled for Yaqui to come, then walked to the police car. The drive back took no time at all. Gomez felt like he'd been transported from Ixtlan to the substation in one of those Star Trek devices, no memory of the trip, jumping from one reality to another. There was a thought that kept swirling around in his head. *Maybe Dean Salmon knew Tom Tanner. They both lived on Maui.* He walked over to his desk to look up Dean Salmon on the computer when he saw an envelope from the coroner's office. He opened it and saw the words "cyanide poisoning."

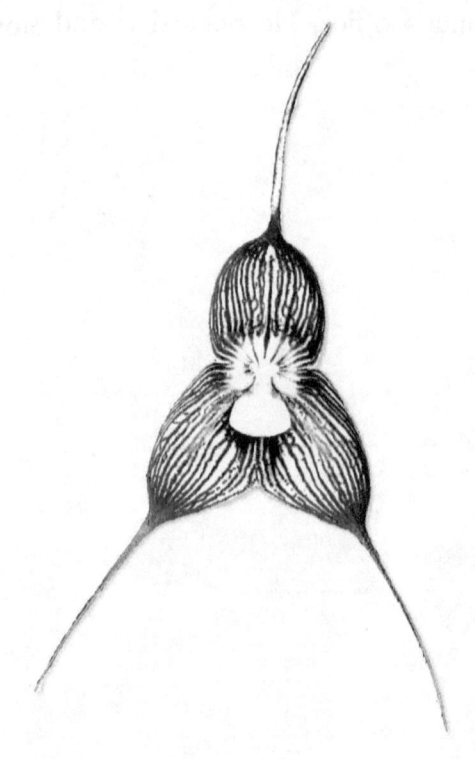

CHAPTER FOURTEEN

Cause of Death

This changed everything. Gomez called Palmer and told him about the coroner's report. Palmer was already on his way to the substation. Gomez handed him the file, and Palmer immediately called the CSI unit. They sent a team out to the residence and started an official homicide investigation. Palmer told Gomez to get the police car; he wanted to see the crime scene first hand. When they arrived, the crime scene investigators had already started dusting for fingerprints. Gomez took Palmer around the back of the house. Palmer wasn't one to mince words. He used to say that he could think better if he talked to himself. He began to reiterate Gomez's words almost verbatim as they came to the sliding glass door.

He pointed to a stain on the pavement. "Place where Gomez puked." As they entered the house, Gomez had to listen to Palmer talking to himself while reliving the crime scene, now a possible murder scene. Palmer came to the room with the orchids. The mister had just turned off and the air was thick with moisture. "This where you found that peace pipe?"

Gomez stood in the hallway outside the room and pointed. "There, in the closet."

Palmer opened the closet door. "Ever find out why that medicine man took to Tanner so much? Why he gave him that pipe?"

"It's in the report. Thought he was someone special. Maybe because of that dream about the dog. I don't know."

Palmer looked around the room, now cleared of the mist. "Strange case. That's all I can say. Here's a guy running from someone he thinks wants to kill him, manages to change his identity, and within almost a year to the day, ends up dead. Now, you tell me. Who would want to murder him with cyanide? It's a terrible death. Whoever it was must have really had it in for him."

Gomez flinched. He'd never thought about it that way. Palmer was right. They went back to the substation and Palmer said he wanted to go to Ixtlan with Gomez to talk to Felipe and Dillon. They seemed to be the only ones who Tom told the truth to. He also asked Gomez to talk to Penelope Witherspoon again to see if she got the life insurance, and if she remembered anything she hadn't told him. Gomez felt uncomfortable about going to Ixtlan with Palmer, but he realized he had no choice.

He was now in the middle of a possible murder investigation. He needed to stay focused, professional. Maybe he should call ahead to warn Dillon.

ᚩ ᚩ ᚩ ᚩ

The police car pulled up to the gate, and barking dogs brought Jeffrey out of the house. Gomez hadn't called ahead to warn Dillon. He figured things would play out better if he stayed out of it. He was not the lead detective. It was Palmer's case. Jeffrey motioned for them to come inside. Palmer introduced himself and asked to speak with Dillon, so Jeffrey escorted them to the library where Dillon was working. Gomez tried to stay calm. This was now a murder investigation, out of his league. Jeffrey knocked on the library door and a voice told them to come in. They could see Dillon sitting at his desk engrossed in reading. "Officer Gomez—back again?"

Gomez introduced Detective Palmer, who explained that he had some questions for Dillon. Gomez pulled out his notebook and waited. This was what he'd wanted, to learn how to become a detective. He had to keep his personal feelings out of this. He listened to Palmer ask Dillon detailed questions about Tom's visits to Ixtlan. When Dillon asked why there was so much interest in the case now, Palmer managed to evade the fact that it was now a murder investigation. Then they talked about the peace pipe and Felipe Youngblood. Palmer wanted to talk to him also, so they arranged another time for Palmer to come back to Ixtlan. When they returned to the substation Gomez typed up his notes, put them on Palmer's desk, and went home.

The next day at the substation was fairly calm until a phone call came in from Dillon requesting that Gomez come to Ixtlan again. He said it was something that was more of a private nature, and he didn't want anyone else involved from the police department yet. Palmer had taken a few days off to be with his family, so Gomez figured he'd just go alone. Gomez stopped by his mother's place to get Yaqui, and drove out to Ixtlan. When he arrived, the Camry was parked in front of the house. Dillon opened the screen door and Yaqui joined the other two dogs inside before Gomez made it to the front porch. Dillon motioned for him to sit at the picnic table and join him for a cup of coffee, and in a few minutes Dean Salmon joined them. His eyes were red, like he'd been crying.

The photo was worn, crinkled, like it had been in his wallet for years. There was a crease down the middle. The picture was of a red-haired teenage boy sitting on a chair next to a plumeria plant in full bloom.

Dean handed the photo to Gomez. "I knew him in Hawaii. Had no idea he was in Arizona, only that he disappeared after the fire. My God. I can't believe he's dead. Dillon told me what happened."

Gomez looked at the picture. It was clearly Tom Tanner. "How old was he here?"

"Fifteen."

Gomez tried not to show his surprise, but it was clear to him that the judge was somehow involved with Tanner. He tried not to show his curiosity. He needed to remain professional. Just then, Jeffrey brought some coffee out and set it on the table. Dillon poured cups for all three of them, then told Gomez that Judge Salmon was offering this information on his own. That he assumed there would be discretion on the part of the Tempe police for the information he was about to reveal. Gomez pulled out his notebook and began writing. "So, you are a judge?"

"Yes. This could ruin me if they find out about it in Hawaii."

Gomez looked up. "What could ruin you?"

"No one knows about my secret life there. I can't believe this about Kyle. He was my favorite."

Gomez tried to keep his cool. He wasn't used to hearing details about this sort of experience. "Your favorite what?"

"Look, we all have our secrets. I came to Ixtlan because of—well, it's a long story."

Gomez settled in the leather chair. "We just found out that the cause of death was cyanide poisoning. Tom was murdered."

The judge looked over at Dillon. "Did you know about this?"

Dillon cringed. "My God. Of course not. We were waiting for the coroner's report on cause of death. Tanner knew someone was out to kill him. When he told me, I told him to go to the police, but he said he wasn't ready. That he wanted to deal with it his own way."

Gomez waited until the judge had composed himself, and continued questioning him. The judge began telling Gomez how his life had fallen apart, how his wife had recently died, how his daughter Lilly was away at college, and how Kyle had suddenly left Maui after the fire—no note of goodbye, nothing. Gomez wrote everything down, all the while not looking up from his notepad. Then the judge said, "I used to give him presents. He loved presents. I guess I was his sugar-daddy. I knew that. But he was so loving and fragile. He especially loved the gold bracelet I gave him."

Gomez stopped writing and looked up. "Gold bracelet?"

"It was just something I'd had that he used to put on his wrist for fun."

Gomez wasn't sure where to go from here. Should he mention the gold bracelet that Tom had in his dresser drawer? Just then, Dillon spoke. "The second time Tom came to Ixtlan, he brought a small box with him. There was a gold bracelet inside. He said it was left at his doorstep with no note. When

I took him to see Felipe Youngblood, he told us that he was afraid the gold bracelet was sent by someone who wanted to kill him."

The judge's body stiffened. His face drained of color. No one spoke. Gomez broke the silence. "Look, no one is accusing you of anything. You volunteered to tell us that you knew Tom Tanner. Let's just go through this step by step." Gomez tried to imagine how Palmer would have acted. He had seen Palmer question a suspect once when he'd accompanied him on a case. Palmer was really good. Gomez remembered how smooth-talking Palmer was during the entire process, and how the suspect ended up admitting to a theft. Palmer had smooth-talked him into a confession. Gomez held his pen in one hand and pretended to write a checklist of items, then went through a series of questions that he made up on the spot. He asked the judge who would have sent a gold bracelet to Tom if it wasn't him. The judge had no idea. Gomez asked the judge if anyone could have known that he'd given Tom the gold bracelet. The judge said he and Kyle had an agreement that no one would ever know about their relationship, or about the presents he'd given Kyle. But then he remembered one day Kyle showed up half hysterical because he'd lost the bracelet. Said it fell off when he was cleaning out some of his things inside his aunt's house. The judge offered to buy him a new one, but Kyle said he didn't deserve another one. The judge never thought anything about the incident. He said that Kyle was always self-loathing like that. Then Gomez asked if Tom had any friends his own age that he hung out with. The judge mentioned that Kyle and his daughter Lilly were very close throughout junior high and high school.

Gomez looked up from his writing. "Your daughter Lilly? Did she know about you and Tom—uh, Kyle?"

"No. I was able to keep my two worlds separate. I hope she never finds out. Please."

Gomez went back to questioning the judge. "So, where is Lilly now?"

"Look, she's been at Caltech for the past year. She's studying to be a physicist. Her mother died a few months ago after living with MS for years. Please don't involve my daughter in this."

Gomez didn't respond. He kept asking questions and taking notes. Finally, the judge blurted out. "I didn't kill Kyle. I loved him. You have to believe me."

"Where were you on the night of the fire?"

"I already told the Maui police. I've been cleared. My alibi held. Check it out. I was at the hospital with my wife. She'd fallen and had broken her arm."

"Why did the police even question you if you if you kept your relationship with Tom a secret?

"Because of Lilly. They questioned her because she was

Kyle's alibi. They were together the night of the fire, and since I happened to be at home when the police came to verify Kyle's story, they decided to question me. Routine, they said. They knew Kyle spent a lot of time with Lilly."

Gomez asked about anyone else the judge might have known who would want to harm Tom. The judge's comment was, "Officer Gomez, I don't know how much you know about the kind of life Kyle lived in Maui. Until he met me, his life was always in jeopardy. He hung out on the streets. I'm ashamed to say that's where I met him. He was only fifteen. I convinced him to stop prostitution, that I would take care of him. I probably saved his life."

Gomez had one final question. It was a small detail, but he couldn't get it out of his mind. What were the odds of Tom ending up in Tempe, and then a few weeks after Tom's murder the judge coming to Ixtlan for the first time, and not even knowing that Tom had moved to Arizona? When he asked the judge that question his reply was, "I know how strange this looks, but I came to Ixtlan to find Dillon. I had no idea Kyle was in Arizona. But I remember mentioning to Kyle once that there was a place near Tempe where there was a sanctuary for gays, and that my father had told me about it. This is pure coincidence. That's all. I want to find Kyle's killer as much as you do."

Gomez said, "Judge, with all due respect, you should have

thought of that before you had Dillon contact me. You of all people should know that this investigation could compromise, as you call it, your secret life. I'm sorry."

"I know. But last night when Dillon and I were catching up, I was going down memory lane. And I missed Kyle so much. I took out a picture of him that I kept in my wallet and showed Dillon. I figured he'd understand. I was as shocked as anyone when Dillon recognized him as Tom Tanner. I had no idea Kyle came here after the fire. Then Dillon told me that Kyle had just died and that he had been afraid someone was out to kill him. I had to do something."

Gomez's head was spinning. *Kyle/Tom, at age fifteen, with the judge. Unbelievable. Illegal.* He wasn't sure what to write in his report, but he knew he'd need to tell the truth. Palmer would really have a field day when he heard about the judge's secret. But it sounded like most of what the judge had told him wouldn't help in the murder investigation. He wondered if maybe the judge should have just left things alone. He probably was so emotional when he heard about Tom's death that he wasn't thinking clearly. Well, now Gomez wasn't thinking clearly either. He needed to process what he'd just heard from the judge before he wrote the report for Palmer.

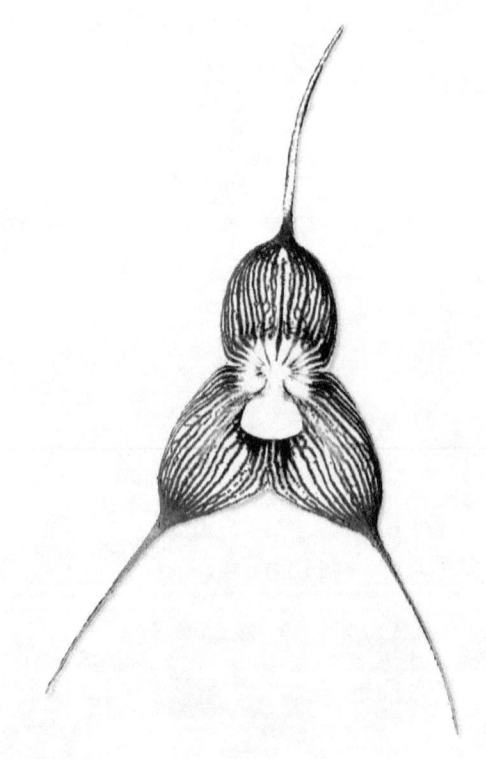

230   J. S. Bodin

CHAPTER FIFTEEN

Buttermilk

"The dying sun will glow on you without burning, as it has done today. The wind will be soft and mellow and your hilltop will tremble. As you reach the end of your dance you will look at the sun, for you will never see it again in waking or in dreaming, and then your death will point to the south. To the vastness." Carlos Castaneda, *Journey to Ixtlan*

Gomez's strength had returned. He noticed that he hardly got tired in the afternoons any more. The Tanner case was turning into a full-time investigation that kept him energized. He was beginning to imagine himself as a detective now. He knew he had to compartmentalize his life if he wanted this. He couldn't let himself think about his brother's murder, about Palmer's cover-up. He needed Palmer to put in a good word when the detective position came up next year. His father, Andy Senior, used to tell him that to be a good cop you couldn't let the bad guys get you down, no matter what you saw. "You need to remember you can't let them win." Gomez never expected the bad guys would end up being his own father and his boss. It wasn't so much what he'd seen, it was what he didn't see—the cover-ups, the lies, the truth. He could either stay a patrol cop or work hard to become a detective. Then he could deal with his brother's murder. Maybe reopen the case, find new evidence that Palmer hadn't destroyed.

The effects of cyanide ingestion are similar to the effects of suffocation because cyanide stops the cells of the body from being able to use oxygen. A person may have general weakness, confusion, excessive sleepiness, headache, dizziness, and seizures. Chronic poisoning over a long period of time will have a more gradual onset. The skin of a cyanide-poisoned person can sometimes turn pink or cherry-red. Sometimes the person's breath can smell like bitter almonds. Cyanide can come as a gas or in a solid powder that looks like white sugar.

Cyanide poisoning was determined as the official cause of death for Tanner. Mold was a second complication. The coroner's report stated that Tanner had died well before the mold had reached toxic levels. Gomez realized that the water leak behind the toilet probably started around the time Tanner died, and by the time the call came in from the Adobe Palms Hotel, the mold had over two weeks to build up to toxic levels. Most likely, Tanner's loss of appetite and flu-like symptoms were from small doses of cyanide ingestion over a period of a few weeks or months. The contents of Tanner's stomach included significant traces of cyanide, along with traces of buttermilk and other absorbed food matter. Tanner's body had a cherry color, as expected with cyanide poisoning. However, Tanner's naturally ruddy complexion, along with the fact that carbon monoxide poisoning also produces a level of redness on the body, obscured the actual cause of death at first. It was not until a forensic pathologist did more testing that they were able to rule out carbon monoxide poisoning and determine the cause of death was cyanide poisoning. The toxicology analysis of Tanner's blood also revealed significant levels of cyanide.

Palmer instructed Gomez to go back to the Phoenix Orchid Guild while they waited for a match on the fingerprints. Maybe one of the members knew something they hadn't thought of the last time Gomez was there questioning them. The next monthly meeting was coming up in two days. Gomez dropped Yaqui off at his mother's house and drove to Phoenix. When he arrived, he parked the squad car and walked into the meeting just before the show and tell portion. All eyes turned to him. He said he had an announcement, that Tom Tanner had been murdered, and that he needed to ask a few more questions of anyone who had spoken to Tom. Five people raised their hands, so Gomez questioned them in another room of the church, took notes, and drove back to Tempe. The whole thing took only three hours. He didn't want to return to the substation too early, so he decided to drive by the crime scene to see if the tape had been removed yet. When he arrived, the house looked like all of the other houses on the block. No evidence of a crime at all. There was a sign on the front gate that said "Do not enter." He figured the landlord put it there to keep people out until the property was ready to be rented again.

Gomez parked the car in front of the house and just sat there to collect his thoughts. *Poor bastard. Who would want to poison you?* He reached across to the passenger's seat, picked up one of the detective books he'd borrowed from Palmer, and began to read. He needed to slow down, focus, set goals. What had happened to his brother was in the past. He couldn't change anything. He needed to think about himself now. He needed to make up for his brother's murder by becoming someone his brother would be proud of. Maybe he'd try to learn guitar. Jesús always told him he had a good ear for music. Gomez felt his entire body begin to relax. He hadn't felt that way since before that terrible day when he was called out to the Tanner residence.

The Arizona sky filled with colors of the sunset, this time a deeper salmon and brighter yellow than Gomez had ever seen. He was about to turn his key in the ignition to go back to the substation when he heard someone call out his name. In his rearview mirror, he saw a man walking toward his car. It was Phillip Marker. Gomez waited until he approached, then turned toward the window. Marker took a deep puff on a cigarette, threw the butt on the pavement, and said, "Officer Gomez, I see the place is almost back to normal."

Gomez nodded. "Sorry about your friend." Then he remembered he hadn't interviewed Marker yet. He should have been at the monthly meeting of the Phoenix Orchid Guild. But he hadn't been there. "Mister Marker, do you have some time for a few questions? I didn't see you this morning at the Phoenix Orchid Guild meeting."

"Oh. No. Well, I didn't go this month. I had to work."

"Perhaps you'd like to sit here in the front seat with me. It shouldn't take more than a few minutes."

Marker walked around to the curb, opened the passenger's door of the patrol car, and got in. Gomez pulled out his notepad and said, "We have some information you might want to hear before I ask you any questions."

Marker reached in his jeans pocket and pulled out a pack of Marlboros. "Mind if I smoke?"

"Actually, I do. I'm not supposed to be around any irritants. My lungs."

"Sorry. I understand." He put the cigarette back in the box.

"I might as well just come out with it. We now know that Tom Tanner was murdered. Poisoned with cyanide. Know of anyone who might want him dead?"

Marker reached for the door handle and got out of the car. "I need a cigarette. Sorry." He pulled out the pack of cigarettes again, and as he struck the match he took a deep cleansing breath, then answered in a calm voice. "As I told you before, Officer, I had just met Tom at the orchid meetings. I didn't know him well at all."

Gomez stayed in the car while Marker talked. He couldn't help notice the lack of emotion on Marker's face—a face that looked worn for its years. He couldn't have been much older than Tanner. Marker's disheveled black curly hair covered his ears, and stubble from his dark beard covered his chin. He was dressed in old jeans and an old work shirt, and had on dirty tennis shoes. His teeth were slightly stained, probably from cigarette smoking, and Gomez couldn't help noticing how the two front teeth protruded outward. *Buck teeth.* Gomez asked Marker if Tom had said anything about a fire. He didn't say which fire—the real one in Maui, or the made-up one in San Francisco.

Marker nervously managed to evade the question by having a coughing fit, saying he needed to get some water. He walked back to his car, then over to Gomez and said, "I need to drive to the convenience store around the corner to get something to drink." Gomez knew what it felt like to be unable to catch his breath, so he offered to drive Marker to the convenience store.

"No. That's all right, Officer. I just need a minute. I'll be fine."

Gomez watched while Marker suddenly stopped coughing and reluctantly got back into the police car. "So, are you up for a couple of more questions?"

Marker's entire body stiffened; then he began fidgeting in the passenger's seat. Gomez wondered if there was something wrong with him, or if he was on drugs. He asked how many times he'd talked to Tom Tanner, and what they talked about. Marker gave one- or two-word answers, like "A couple," or "Not much." Gomez wasn't getting much information out of him, so he told him he was finished for now. Marker quickly opened the car door, got into his own car, and sped off without another word. Gomez knew something was off with this guy, but he figured Marker had other problems that he didn't want Gomez to find out about. Problems that didn't have anything to do with the Tanner case. Then Gomez remembered the orchids that were probably still inside the house. He'd go back to the substation, finish his report for Palmer, put a note to ask Palmer about the plants, then contact Marker again. He'd know what to do with the orchids.

ભ   ભ   ભ   ભ

When Gomez got to the substation the next morning, Palmer was already there. Gomez handed him a copy of the notes he'd taken from Judge Salmon and from Marker. Palmer read them, looked up, and said, "Wow. Amazing stuff. What those fags won't do for a piece of ass. My God."

Gomez tried not to wince. "Sorry I didn't clear it with you first, but you were taking time off, and the phone message said they wanted me to come alone."

Palmer smiled. "Kid, you've done great investigating on this case. No problem. What about this Dean Salmon character—the judge? I think maybe I should go back to fag heaven and question him more. Seems he knew Tanner pretty well, if you get my drift."

"Not much more to ask him. He was in love with Tom, when he was Kyle O'Sullivan. It's all in the report. I know he didn't kill him. In fact, he didn't arrive in Arizona until a few days ago. Tom was already dead."

"Maybe yes. Maybe no. He could have tracked Tom to Ixtlan. Who knows? Don't rule him out as a suspect yet. Make sure he doesn't go anywhere. And, also, what about his daughter Lilly?"

"I guess if we have to, we could track her down at college. But, it's sensitive. She and Kyle were best friends when they were teenagers, and all the while her father was—well, Kyle's sugar daddy."

"That sicko judge was a predator. You said he was a circuit court judge in charge of family court? My God. No wonder he's afraid. He could go to jail for a very long time. You need to keep an eye on that weirdo."

Gomez kept his eyes on his notebook. He knew Palmer was right. The judge was picking up underage boys for sex. But the fact that he risked his reputation to tell Gomez he knew Tanner must count for something. It seemed that the judge really wanted to find Tanner's killer.

Palmer put his hand on Gomez's shoulder. "Well, let's follow up and see how things develop. Just remember, you're new at this. You have no idea some of the things I've seen people do. In fact, it's often the ones who seem the most innocent who end up guilty. But hey, you've done a great job. You're a natural at detective work. Thanks again."

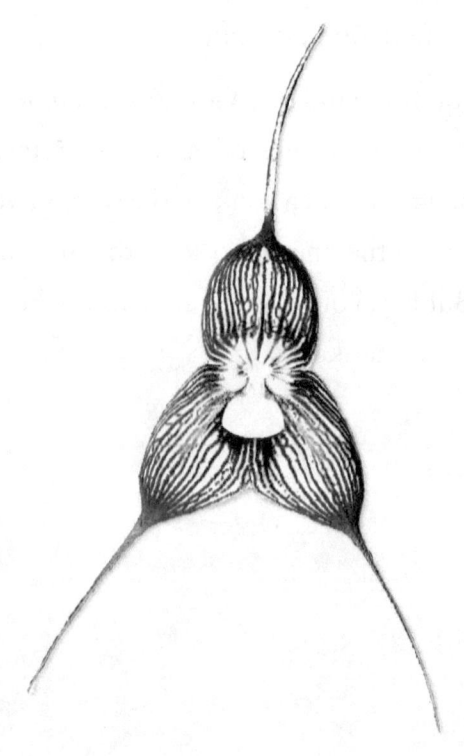

Chapter Sixteen

Dracula Vampira
Orchid of the Night

The Psychopathic Mind. Gomez was immersed in the book that he'd pulled off Palmer's shelf. If Tanner's killer was caught, Gomez wanted to learn more about what kind of person would go to such lengths to kill him—first the attempt in Maui with the fire, then in Tempe with cyanide poisoning. *The true psychopath has little facility for empathy. They may seem your ordinary person, friendly, smart, personable, but they have no remorse for their behavior. They also show very little affect, often remaining unruffled, calm, in the face of adversity.*

Palmer came into the office and pulled out two tickets from his briefcase. "Here, Gomez —for you."

Gomez reached out his hand. "For me? Why?"

"For being a damn good investigator. Your eye for detail

is impeccable. Now we just need a match on those fingerprints. Thought you might like to go to the Arizona State Sun Devil football game. Got these for you. Pricey—but hey, you deserve it. Take along a girlfriend." He winked at Gomez.

Gomez hated Palmer for being such a bigot, and for covering up his brother's murder. But Palmer was good to him, and he definitely wanted to go for the detective opening, and needed Palmer's recommendation. He took the tickets and thanked Palmer.

Palmer saw what Gomez was reading. "See you've found the book on psychopaths. Think Tanner's killer was one?"

"Don't know. Could be."

"Why don't you take a few days off? I'll let you know if we get a match on those fingerprints."

Gomez needed a few days off. Even though his energy had returned, his mental state was not great. He needed time to process what he'd learned at Ixtlan about his brother's murder. He grabbed his briefcase, put the two tickets inside, and walked out of the building to his police car. On his way home, Gomez decided to drive by the Adobe Grille to tell Penelope Witherspoon about the murder investigation, and to ask her a few more questions. When he arrived, she was on break, smoking a cigarette out front. "Officer Gomez, good to see you again. What brings you back here?"

Gomez cleared his throat. "Miss Witherspoon, we just

learned that Tom Tanner did not die of natural causes. We think someone murdered him."

Pen's body instantly stiffened and her face drained of color. "What? Who would want to murder him?"

"Well, that's what we're working on now. We're waiting for a fingerprint match."

Pen's knees buckled. She edged up to the wall of the Adobe Palms Hotel and leaned against it for support. "This can't be true. I thought he died from an asthma attack from all that mold."

Gomez explained to her that the mold had formed after Tom's death because of a water leak from the toilet, and the autopsy showed only minute amounts of mold spores in his lungs. He told her that Tom died of cyanide poisoning. Pen looked like she was about to be sick, so Gomez suggested they go inside the hotel and sit down. He ordered water for her and waited until she looked better. Then she blurted out, "Oh, Tommy. Who would do this to you?"

Gomez needed to ask her some more questions, so he took a chance and said, "Ms. Witherspoon, there are some things you need to hear about Tom Tanner that he might not have shared with you."

Pen looked up. "What things?"

"Well, during the course of our investigation we found out that Tom Tanner was not his real name."

"Not his real name? My God."

"I'm so sorry. His real name was Kyle O'Sullivan. He took on a false identity when he left Hawaii."

"Hawaii? He said he'd never been to Hawaii. He came from San Francisco. That's what he told me."

"I'm sorry. Did he mention a fire?"

"Yes. He said there was a fire in the greenhouse in San Francisco. It burnt down and his sister was killed."

"Yes. There was a fire, but it was his aunt who died, and it happened in Maui."

Pen's eyes glazed over. "His aunt?"

Gomez tried to stay calm, to keep his voice even and soft. "I know how difficult this must be for you, but I need to ask you a couple more questions. Did he ever mention a place called Ixtlan?"

Pen gulped. "Never. What is it, anyway?"

Gomez wasn't sure if he should explain Ixtlan to Pen just yet, but he took a deep breath and said, "It's a place out near Papago. A place where gays can seek sanctuary. Tom spent quite a bit of time there over the last year on his days off."

Pen's face froze. "A place for gays? He went there on his days off?"

"Yes, ma'am."

"No—he told me he was going to the Phoenix Orchid Guild on his days off."

"I hate to bring this up, but may I ask if you and Mr. Tanner were ever…intimate?"

"Intimate? You mean, did we ever have sex?"

Gomez paused. "Yes."

"Yes, we did."

"I'm so sorry, but Tom Tanner was a fraud. Everything we found out about him since he came to Tempe turned out to be a lie."

Pen looked up at Gomez. She started to say something, then blurted out, "So are you saying that Tommy was really gay?"

Gomez cleared his throat. "Well, it's not for me to say, but he definitely had an entirely different life in Maui. We know that for sure."

"How did you find out?"

"As I said, we learned all of this during the course of the investigation. I can't really go into details. I came here to tell you about the murder, and to ask you if you've received any of the life insurance money yet."

Pen started to mumble to herself. All Gomez could make out was something about "…a lie, all a lie, how could I not have known?" Gomez ordered two coffees, then repeated, "The life insurance policy. Have you heard anything yet?"

Pen looked up. Tears were running down her cheeks, smearing her make-up so her face looked like a raccoon's. Gomez definitely felt sorry for her, but he was exhausted and ready to go home. Then, Pen responded to the question. "Officer, I'm sorry. Yes. I have heard from the life insurance company. I should be receiving a check for $25,000 in a few weeks." She started to sob. "Why did he leave the money to me if he didn't love me? I thought we actually had something. How could it all have been a lie?"

Gomez asked, "Do you know what you will do with the money when it comes?"

Pen wiped her eyes with a napkin, and black make-up smudged all over it. "I've got to get out of here. I'll leave Tempe. Never been anywhere in my life, except when Tommy came along and took me to Sedona before Christmas. I have a cousin in California. She lives in Laguna Beach. Waitressing there is better than in Tempe. Higher-end clientele." Gomez was about to get up when Pen said, "Gay? He was gay? My God. No wonder."

Gomez smiled to himself. He was pretty sure he knew what she was thinking, but he managed to stay calm. "I think it's a good idea to leave Tempe. Start somewhere new. Look, it's clear that Tom felt something for you. Otherwise he wouldn't have taken out the life insurance policy in your name. You shouldn't beat yourself up. You have to admit, he was in a tight spot."

The waitress brought coffee and Pen took a sip from her cup. She looked over toward the table by the fish tank where she first met Tom a little over a year ago. "I know he felt something for me. I thought we had a chance. First guy who ever treated me like a lady."

ରେ   ରେ   ରେ   ରେ

Wildflowers painted the landscape along Arizona's vast stretches of desert. It was now early March, an early spring ushered in by a series of late-winter storms transforming miles of arid landscapes into a patchwork quilt of oranges, whites, purples, yellows, reds, and greens. Gomez was deep into his studies, learning everything he could about becoming a detective. Gomez had just finished making a call to Phillip Marker to tell him to pick up the orchids from the Tanner residence, now that the crime scene had been cleaned up and was ready for the landlord to re-carpet and paint for a new tenant. But Marker's number had been disconnected. *Shit. Just my luck. Guess I could take the orchids over to that Daniel kid at the Blue Corn Diner.* But that could wait until tomorrow.

He left work early and decided to stop by the Tanner house to see if the orchid plants were still there. He'd arranged with the landlord to pick them up and take them to Daniel at the Blue Corn Diner in the next few days. When he arrived, a truck was parked in the driveway with "Carpet Services" painted on the side. Gomez figured the landlord had already contracted with a biohazard crew to clear out the mold, and now he was getting the place ready for a new renter. Gomez parked the patrol car in front of the house. He half expected to see Marker in his rearview mirror sauntering toward him, buck teeth and all. But no one was around. He got out of the car, opened the chain-link gate, and went inside the front yard. The dead rose bushes had been removed, and so had all of the weeds. Everything was dirt, probably ready for some sort of cheap landscaping. Maybe kitty litter gravel. It would do the job and keep the dirt from blowing during Tempe's windy season. He walked around toward the back and saw the same dirt—no dog poop, no weeds. The sliding glass door was ajar and he walked inside the house. He could hear sounds of workmen in the back rooms. The concrete floor in the living room was obviously being prepared for new carpet. He walked toward the bedroom, encountered one of the workmen, and said, "I'm here to see about the plants in that other bedroom. Are they still there?"

The workman got up from a kneeling position. "Some. Don't know yet whether to put new carpet in there. Waiting for the landlord to tell us."

Gomez opened the door to the other bedroom. The hanging plants were gone, but the miniature plants still sat on top of the metal shelf. His photographic memory kicked in. *What were those plants called again? Funny-looking plants hanging upside down in moss from the bottom of the basket. Strange heart-shaped flowers, purple-black color. Dracula vampira.* Gomez walked over to one of the workmen and said, "Do you know if anyone came here to take out some of these orchid plants?"

One of the workmen answered. "Yeah. Yesterday. Some guy said the landlord told him he could take the plants if he wanted. We need to clean out that room anyway."

"Do you remember what the guy looked like?"

"Yeah. Sort of scruffy, dark curly hair."

Gomez smiled to himself. *That son of a bitch Marker. Took the Dracula plants and left the rest. Then vamoosed. In the wind. Who the hell was that guy? And what made him think he could just show up and take those orchid plants?* Gomez made a mental note to check on him in the criminal database to see if he could find anything on him when he got back to the substation.

Gomez walked out of the house back to his car and got

inside. He sat in the driver's seat for a few minutes to collect his thoughts. He opened the windows. A cool breeze blew, bringing the sweet smell of honeysuckle. He felt amazingly calm. He closed his eyes and let himself feel the warm sun on his face. He imagined the wise deer standing in the garden next to his brother's memorial fountain. The deer's deep-brown eyes seemed to be smiling at him, and he heard the deer whisper something. At first he couldn't make it out; then the deer repeated the words. *"Be like me. Hide from them so they cannot find you. Then you will find truth."* Gomez opened his eyes and gasped. He felt adrenalin surge throughout his entire body.

He started up the car and drove to his mother's house for dinner. She insisted that he take home the leftovers, so he walked out with Yaqui on his heels, waiting for a taste of scraps when they got in the car. Now Gomez was thinking more clearly. *The peace pipe.* He'd go back to City Center in a few days and ask Palmer if he could have Tanner's peace pipe. He'd return it himself, to Felipe Youngblood. If it hadn't been for that pipe, he never would have figured out Tanner's Ixtlan connection, and he might never have known the truth about his brother's murder.

When he arrived home it was already dark. Gomez went into the kitchen and opened his refrigerator. The carton of buttermilk sat unopened on the top shelf next to a carton of orange juice and a bowl of grapes. He opened the buttermilk, poured some into a glass, opened a cupboard above the sink, and took out a tray of his mother's *biscochitos* cookies. All through the investigation, Gomez kept it a secret. What were the odds of both him and Tanner drinking buttermilk and eating cookies before they went to bed at night? The sour taste of the milk mixed with the sweet taste of the cookies had become a family tradition for Gomez. It was his father, Andy Senior, who started it, saying that buttermilk was much healthier than regular milk because it helped with digestion. Eventually there was only buttermilk in the family refrigerator. Mrs. Gomez didn't drink it, but she used it in her cooking, especially her *biscochitos*.

Gomez closed the blinds to his bedroom, undressed, and rolled into bed. Yaqui jumped on the bed and settled on top of the covers next to Gomez's feet. The gentle motion of the ceiling fan lulled him into the serenity of perfect calm, something he hadn't felt for months. Just as he was about to fall asleep, he had an image of Tom Tanner lying on his bed with mold growing up his fingers, and Yaqui lying half-dead at the foot of the bed. Goose bumps formed on Gomez's arms and chest. Images bounced back and forth in his subconscious, ping-ponging from one disjointed thought to another.

Tanner in Hawaii roaming the gay bars. Tanner with the judge. The gold bracelet in a heap of rubble from the fire at Maui. Jesús strumming the guitar in the garden. His father sending Jesús away to music camp. Jesús lying in a pool of his own blood. The peace pipe. Felipe Youngblood. The name Shadow Dreamer. The Dracula vampira orchid. The Wise Deer. Phillip Marker.

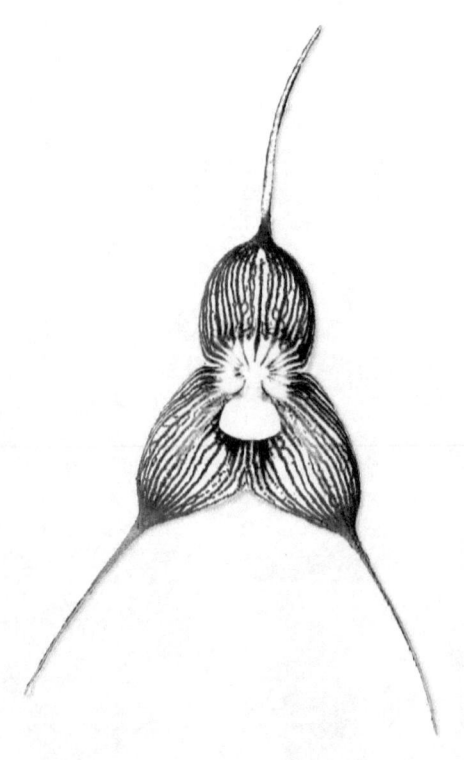

CHAPTER SEVENTEEN

Four Years Later

A blue and red Spider Man piñata hangs from the palo verde tree. Lucas lifts the wooden bat toward the prize. Eyes covered a with black cloth napkin, he sees only into darkness. His tiny body, three today, cannot hold the weight of the bat, so Gomez reaches down to help his son. Screams of joy from the children waiting to collect the prize as the piñata bursts its content in projectiles of sweet butterscotch, chocolate, caramel, and mint candies. Scramble of tiny feet around the palo verde tree. Sounds of water running down rocks from the memorial fountain for Jesús. Abuelita Gomez sits in a chair watching her grandson, eyes glazed over from a recent stroke, Yaqui at her side. Always the dog at her side. Gomez motions for his wife to sit next to him at the picnic table, the one covered with a red and white checkered plastic tablecloth. He tells her that he is happy. Her deep-blue eyes, pools into her soul, say it all. And in that moment there is only perfect calm.

୪ ୪ ୪ ୪

The garden looked pristine for the party. Andy Gomez had decided to spend more time working in the garden with Lucas, who was now old enough to plant his own carrot, radish, and squash seeds. The newly constructed raised beds made it not only ornamental, but practical, since Lucas was just tall enough to reach into the moist dirt with his pudgy fingers, and stuff a seed down deep enough, then cover it with soil. The raised beds had been built so Abuelita Gomez wouldn't have to kneel on her knees to do the gardening. But that was before her stroke. Now all she could do was sit in her wheelchair and gaze out at the garden while her son and grandson tended to the summer's yield. It had been three years since her stroke and no matter how much therapy she'd been given she seemed to plateau, confined to her wheelchair, barely able to utter intelligible words. Andy moved into her house with his new wife, who was pregnant at the time, and who agreed to take care of both the new baby and her mother-in-law. The garden had become the family gathering place for most meals, since Tempe's climate afforded almost year-round outdoor living. The memorial fountain for Jesús had turned into a shrine, with tin crucifixes placed among the marigolds and snapdragons, and with Jesús' picture strategically placed at the top, embedded in a large carved-out stone. Mrs. Gomez's favorite spot was under the shade of the palo verde tree, where she could keep an eye on Lucas while he played in the garden. He'd bring her little presents of the seed pods that had fallen from the tree. Since she hardly uttered a word, little Lucas had figured out a way to communicate with her by conversing for both of them. He'd ask her a question and then answer it in a deeper voice, as if she were the one speaking. Lucas, like his father, was already almost fluent in three languages: Yaqui, English, and Spanish.

It had been four years since Gomez had wrapped up the Tanner case, and still no killer had been found. The case was turning cold, and Gomez had moved on. He was now Detective Gomez, working at City Hall. Palmer had been transferred to the Phoenix Police Department after Gomez exposed the truth about Jesús' murder, proving that it was really a hate crime. Gomez found the surveillance footage from the Caveman Bar in Phoenix, which proved that the perpetrators attacked Jesús because he was gay. Gomez's determination to vindicate his brother's murder made him a sort of folk hero in the gay community, especially at Ixtlan. As far as his reputation at City Hall, it was mixed. Some old-guard cops felt he should have let sleeping dogs lie. They still felt loyalty to their buddy, Sergeant Andy Gomez Senior, and supported Palmer's cover-up. But the younger cops applauded what Gomez had done.

What Gomez hadn't planned on was that the press would

get wind of the hate crime cover-up before he'd told his mother the truth about Jesús' murder. He knew the truth would be disturbing to her, so he'd planned on telling her bits and pieces at a time. Unfortunately, one night when Mrs. Gomez sat on her couch watching TV, the news headline caught her attention when she heard the words "Son of late police Sergeant Andy Gomez, Sr. hate-crime murder cover-up." A few days later she had her stroke, but not before she'd heard about the summer camp Jesús had been sent to where he'd undergone conversion therapy, and not before she learned about his stay at Ixtlan and his attempted suicide. Gomez's guilt consumed him for over a year. He knew it was his fault that his mother had the stroke, that the truth about Jesús was more than she could bear. The press had leaked the story before he could prepare her for the truth.

But something in him had changed after the Tanner case. He started to feel an uneasiness, an energy that kept him moving forward. At first it almost consumed him. All he wanted to do was to find Tanner's killer. The fingerprints were never conclusive. There was never a match that pointed to anyone. He knew this happened sometimes, that the Tanner case could remain cold for a long time, maybe never be solved. But after a year, his focus shifted to proving that his brother's murder was a hate crime. He'd never felt so energized before. Finding out the truth about his brother's murder, then risking his job by exposing Palmer's cover-up, had empowered him to the point of almost feeling invincible. But his mother's stroke brought him back to reality. Luckily he had Mary at his side to console him, and when she told him she was pregnant, he realized he needed to focus on his family now.

❧ ❧ ❧ ❧

After the birthday celebration ended and Lucas and Mrs. Gomez had gone to bed, Gomez and Mary sat out in the garden downing a bottle of red zinfandel wine. Bursts of jasmine and honeysuckle snaked through the night air, filling their senses as the wine began to lull them into drowsiness. They went inside and made love, moonlight flowing through the bedroom window, casting shadows from the palo verde tree along their naked bodies. Andy watched as Mary fell asleep, tracing her perfect features with his eyes. Her long blonde hair surrounded her head on the pillow, making a halo around her youthful face. Milky white skin glowed in the moonlight, eyelids closed, covering her best feature: her ocean-blue eyes with flakes of gold dust. It had been her eyes that attracted Andy the first time he'd met Mary. They met when Gomez had been on a murder case. Mary was the neighbor of the murder victim, and had been brought to the police station in Tempe for questioning. He watched through the one-way mirror, hardly hearing her testimony, only gazing into her blue eyes. He asked her out after a few months, and after a few dates she found out she was pregnant. He asked her to marry him, and had the wedding at the Adobe Palms Hotel. Mrs. Gomez was ecstatic. She would have preferred her son marry a Yaqui or Hispanic woman, but when she saw how happy Gomez was, she accepted Mary into her life.

The wine should have made Gomez sleepy, but instead he felt a surge of adrenalin. His son had just turned three. Mary was already talking about wanting another child. He was almost thirty. Life was moving so fast now. He went outside and walked into the garden. The full moon made it so bright; he could almost see into every corner of the garden as if it had been daylight. He sat next to the memorial fountain and talked to Jesús, as he had done many times before, when he knew he'd be alone. How could he sleep? He'd never felt so happy.

ભ ભ ભ ભ

It was Sunday, church day. Sundays had become a family routine, with Mary getting Mrs. Gomez up first for her shower, then dressing her for church. Gomez would get Lucas up, then get him ready. They'd sit down for a quick breakfast of cereal and fruit so they would have time to wheel Mrs. Gomez the four long blocks to church, Our Lady of the Cross, the same Catholic church Gomez had been attending since he was a baby. Church had always been special for Gomez, but now that Lucas was getting older, it was even more important. Lucas was beginning to ask questions, to engage in conversations that dealt with topics far beyond the experiences of a three-year-old.

Gomez remembered how he had been the same way as a child. He'd constantly ask questions, until his mother would say, "*Hijo*, go ask your older brother."

So, Gomez would ask Jesús, "How many stars are in the heavens?" Jesús would take him outside when it got dark, and they'd sit in the garden while Jesús played his guitar and sang a made-up answer. After the service, Gomez liked to take his family to the park across the street so Lucas could play with the neighborhood children. Mrs. Gomez would sit in her wheelchair watching her grandson, so Mary and Gomez could have some time together strolling hand in hand along the dirt path that went around the park.

When Gomez got to work the next day he paused for a moment, as he did every day, to admire the brass name tag on his door that read "Detective Andy Gomez." He needed to remind himself each time he walked into his office that he was now a real detective, and that his life had changed so drastically since the Tanner case. It was one of those unbearable scorching Arizona summers. Gomez was having trouble breathing through the medical mask that he had to wear when it was haboob season. The notorious dust storms had gotten worse over the last few years, and since Gomez had developed severe asthma since his mold exposure, he was at risk for lung infections. As a child, he used to like watching the storms from his bedroom window. He'd watch as the downdraft of colder air reached the ground, then started to blow the loose silt and clay up from the desert floor, creating a wall of sediment that preceded the storm cloud. His brother Jesús told him the wall of dust was almost a hundred miles wide, with winds up to seventy miles per hour. Once after a haboob, there was a mud storm where it rained and all of the dust turned to mud. That was the time his mother gave them special masks to wear because it was almost impossible to get any clean air to breathe.

Gomez was about to go to the Coke machine to get a can to drink when his phone rang. The voice at the other end sounded familiar, but he wasn't sure he was hearing it correctly. "Who is this?"

"It's been a few years, Andy. This is Felipe Youngblood. How are you doing?"

Gomez stopped walking. "Felipe."

"Have you made any progress on the Tanner case?"

"None. Couldn't get a fingerprint match."

"Well, I'm calling because I think you need to come to Ixtlan to meet someone."

Gomez felt his heart begin to race. He knew Felipe wouldn't have called him if he didn't have something important to share. "When would you like me to come?"

"How about tomorrow around noon. Would that work?"

Gomez looked at his calendar on the desk and said, "Yes. I'll be there."

"It will be good to see you again. By the way—brave thing you did when you exposed Palmer for covering up your brother's murder."

"Thanks."

"I heard about your mother's stroke. I'm so sorry."

Gomez realized that Felipe had probably been keeping tabs on him over the last four years, or he wouldn't have known about his mother. But it didn't make him angry—in fact, he felt like Felipe was watching out for him. He was anxious to go back to Ixtlan anyway. He had become a friend of Ixtlan, especially when he returned the peace pipe to Felipe.

By the next day, the dust from the haboob had mostly cleared, and Gomez didn't need to wear the mask. The drive to Ixtlan had become very familiar. He drove straight to Felipe's place, and when he pulled up his police car he saw Dillon's truck parked in front of the trailer. Felipe came out to greet him. He used the Yaqui greeting *"Haisa swea?* How is the flower?"

Gomez felt honored that Felipe would use such an intimate greeting, reserved for family or good friends. *"Haisa swea?"* he said in return.

Felipe offered him coffee. Dillon came from another room in the trailer, and greeted Felipe with a big hug. "It's been awhile. Heard you're now a full-fledged detective at City Hall. Congratulations."

Gomez sat down at the table. He didn't mind that Felipe and Dillon were being friendly. He liked visiting with them. He kept waiting for one of them to tell him why they had called him, but Felipe kept asking questions. He wanted to know what he'd been up to for the last four years. So, Gomez told them about his three-year-old son, about his wonderful wife, and about his mother's stroke.

Dillon spoke. "Yes. I'm so sorry. We heard about her stroke after the media coverage of Palmer's cover-up of Jesús' murder."

Gomez smiled. "And how did you hear about the stroke? It wasn't in the news."

Felipe smiled back. "We're keeping tabs on you, that's all. Actually, we knew when Lucas was born—almost sent you a box of cigars, but Dillon said no."

Gomez took a sip of the hot coffee. "It's okay. If it hadn't been for you two I never would have learned the truth about my father, and my brother's murder, and about Palmer. I feel like you've changed my life forever."

Felipe commented, "It wasn't us that changed your life. It was Tom Tanner. Think about it."

Gomez realized Felipe was right. If he hadn't been the patrol officer who was sent to the Tanner house, he might never have been involved with the Tanner case at all. "So who do you want me to meet?"

Felipe's eyes lit up. "We think we can help you. There might be a break in finding Tanner's killer."

Gomez almost choked on the last sip of coffee. "You're serious?"

Felipe told him to drive back to Ixtlan's main house. That he and Dillon would meet him there. Gomez walked out of the trailer, got into his police car, and headed toward the Ixtlan complex. He got there before Felipe and Dillon, so he waited outside the gate. His heart was pounding with anticipation. *A break in the Tanner case. Four years later. My God. This can't be happening.*

Dillon pulled his truck up to the gate, and Jeffrey and the two dogs came out to greet them. Gomez got out of his car and followed them inside. They all sat at the picnic table with the red and white checkered plastic tablecloth, and Jeffrey brought out some iced tea and scones. Felipe began to tell Gomez why he had called him out to Ixtlan.

"A few days after you came here to interview the judge about the Tanner case, the judge went back to Hawaii and there was a huge scandal. Apparently, an underage prostitute, a boy age thirteen, told his parents that the judge solicited him for sex in front of the Butterfly Lounge in Maui. The boy's family went to the police. But because the judge had connections, he agreed to pay the family off in exchange for leaving Hawaii for good. So the judge returned to Ixtlan three years ago for sanctuary."

Gomez listened to Felipe. Part of him felt like he was listening to a story out of a crime thriller—the kind where the perpetrator is often hidden in plain sight: the priest from a local parish, the trusted therapist, the friendly next-door neighbor. *And now, a judge? My God.*

Felipe continued. "The judge had been helping us here with any legal matters that might come up, and he was teaching some of our members paralegal courses. But it was all hush-hush. Then, a few months ago he had a massive heart attack that required quadruple bypass surgery. He's here recovering."

Gomez sat frozen. He didn't know where this was going. What did this have to do with the Tanner case? "He's here? Where?"

"In one of the bedrooms in the main house."

"So...what does this have to do with the Tanner case?"

Felipe told Gomez that Lilly, the judge's daughter, was also at Ixtlan helping take care of her father. He and Dillon decided to call her when the judge went into surgery. She hadn't known anything about the judge's secret life in Maui or about the scandal. She'd been in grad school at Caltech and hadn't even seen her father in a couple of years— just talked to him on the phone. When they called her about his heart surgery, she came immediately. Once she got to the hospital in Tempe, they had time to talk while they were in the hospital waiting room. Dillon decided he'd better tell Lilly about her father's connection to Ixtlan, and why he was now living there. He told Lilly about the scandal in Maui, and that the judge was seeking sanctuary at Ixtlan.

She was in shock at first, but then she wanted to know more, so they told her about the Tom Tanner murder and her father's connection to Kyle O'Sullivan in Maui. After she recovered a bit, she dropped a bombshell. She told them about a phone call she'd gotten from a Danny Leavenworth who had been friends with her and Kyle in Maui. She told them Danny had called her to find out if she knew what had happened to Kyle. That he'd left Maui after Kyle disappeared and ended up in Florida working at a plant nursery. But Lilly knew better. She wasn't even sure he'd called her from Florida. She knew he was a psychopath and a liar. She told Dillon and Felipe that Danny was the one who set the fire in Maui—the one who tried to kill Tom Tanner—that he probably had tracked Tanner to Tempe and poisoned him.

Gomez's heart was racing. The adrenaline was surging throughout his body. He felt like he was on a roller coaster, on the upswing almost ready to reach the top and take the plunge down toward the bottom. "So how can I find this Danny Leavenworth?"

Felipe hesitated for a moment. "That's why you need to talk to Lilly."

Gomez felt like electrical circuits were going off inside his head. He felt the same in his gut. It was the ride of a lifetime. Felipe and Dillon motioned for him to follow them. They went down a hallway, and Dillon knocked on a door to one of the bedrooms. "Lilly, Detective Gomez is here to talk to you."

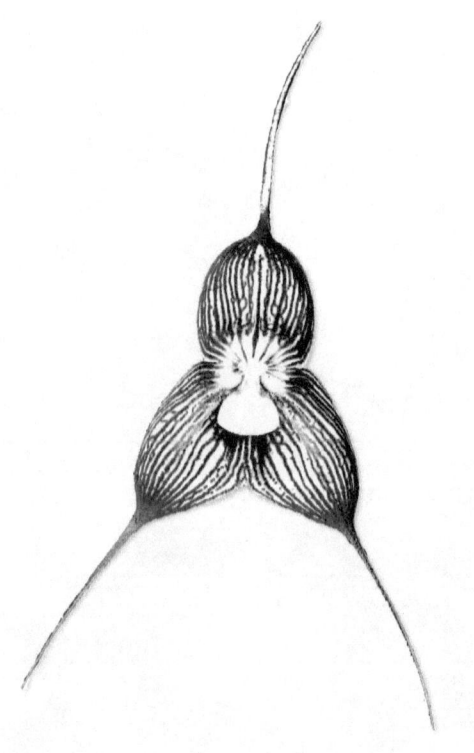

CHAPTER EIGHTEEN

Revelations

The room was darkened. A tiny night light stood on a stand next to the bed where the judge lay asleep. Lilly motioned for them to sit at a round table not far from the bed. She put her fingers to her lips to keep things at a whisper. Felipe introduced Detective Gomez to Lilly. Gomez was overcome by her simple beauty. He had assumed if she was at Caltech she'd have more of the nerd look, with short-cropped hair and horn-rimmed glasses. But instead, she looked like a Hollywood model. In fact, she looked a little like his own wife, Mary. Her long blonde hair was tied back in a ponytail, and she wore a simple blue cotton T-shirt and blue jeans. But even in such casual attire she definitely looked beautiful. Lilly opened the curtains near the round table to give them some light. Gomez took out his notepad and tried to act professional. He was dying to know what she had to say.

Felipe started talking first. "Officer Gomez knows all about your father and his connection to Tom Tanner. He was the first responder when the call came from the Adobe Palms hotel where Tom worked. They said he hadn't shown up for work after New Year's."

Lilly looked up. "You found him?"

Gomez winced. "I'm afraid so."

"Oh, my God. Poor Kyle. I should have known Danny would go this far."

"What do you mean?"

"To chase Kyle down like that. He obviously found him in Tempe. That was just like Danny. Once he got an idea in his head, you couldn't stop him."

"But you said Danny called you from Florida. He could have taken off to Florida after he poisoned Tom—uh, Kyle."

"That shit. He said he'd been living in Florida the last four years. He always lied. You could never believe anything he said."

"Don't worry. We can check the phone records to see where the call came from."

Gomez wrote down some of the things Lilly said, but his hand couldn't keep up. It was like the floodgates had opened, and Lilly told him about things in her relationship with Kyle O'Sullivan that went as far back as their childhood. She had tears in her eyes when she said, "We used to call ourselves the three fuckateers. It might sound deranged, but those days were actually some of the best memories from my childhood."

Gomez wrote down *the three fuckateers*. "May I ask what exactly that means?"

"Oh, it's a long story. Kyle and Danny were in what they called a 'fuck buddy' relationship at that time. I would stand outside this fort we'd built behind one of Molly's greenhouses. We made it out of dry palm branches. It was our little hideout, away from the teasing and taunting that all three of us experienced in junior high. We looked out for each other that way. And of course, it was a place to get high."

Gomez wrote furiously. "So, why do you think Danny called you the other day?"

"I have no idea why he called me. He's like that. Erratic, unpredictable. I think he's freaking out. If he did poison Kyle—uh, Tom—then he probably needed someone to talk to, someone who knew him. He never was any good at making friends, and now that Kyle is gone, well...I'm probably his only friend., or so he thinks. I can't believe I felt sorry for him after his father died. I even visited him in the foster home."

"When did his father die?"

"Danny must have been around fourteen. His dad fell from the top of Haleakala during one of his Sunday hikes."

"What happened after that? How did Danny do in the foster home?"

"How do you think? He ran away and they put him in a different one. Eventually he dropped out of high school and ended up doing tricks on the streets."

Gomez wanted to know more, but Dillon stood up and interrupted them. "I need to get back to the commons. We're preparing one of our big meals for tonight's harvest festival." He reached out and shook Gomez's hand. "See you later for lunch?"

"I'd love to, but I need to get back to City Hall."

Felipe stayed while Lilly told them more about her childhood with Kyle and Danny. Then Lilly broke down and began to sob. "I had no idea my father was leading a double life. He seemed to be so devoted to my mother. And he was so well respected. How could he have done this to us?"

Felipe calmed her down. "Lilly, your father is a good man. He is just messed up, like most of us. Did he ever tell you what happened to him after his father died?"

Lilly looked up. "No. I knew his father died very young of a heart attack. Guess it's in my dad's genes."

Felipe continued. "Yes. But did you know that your father actually knew Dillon when they lived in the same house in San Francisco?"

"San Francisco? I thought he grew up in Providence, Rhode Island with his grandparents."

"He was adopted by his grandparents when he was around ten years old. But he was born in San Francisco. His father was a gay man who lived in a house with Dillon and two other gay men. They had formed a family and were raising two children, your father and Dillon. Their mothers didn't want the responsibility of a child. They were living their own version of counterculture by being fag hags, living as hippies, doing drugs etc. It was a wild time, as you know."

Lilly hadn't moved. Her eyes were fixed on Felipe's. "So, did he ever know his real mother?"

"After his father died, his mother took him with her to Maui where she lived in a commune for a while. Then, when her parents heard that they had a grandson, they were able to get full custody of your father and adopt him. They brought him to Providence and raised him as their own. He never saw his mother again."

"My God. He never told me that story. He said he lived in Hawaii, and that his mother died before I was born."

"I don't know why he didn't tell you. Perhaps because the Maui experience is what probably started his interest in young boys."

"What do you mean?"

"The judge told us that he was raped repeatedly by one of the commune members, an older man. At that time there wasn't much supervision, and according to your father, his mother was sleeping around and doing drugs, so she wasn't aware of the rapes. When his grandparents adopted him and his life turned around, he never looked back. But he told us he couldn't get the trauma out of his mind. He thinks that's why he became a family court judge. To protect children from abusive environments."

Lilly slumped on her arms and put her head on the table. "Protect children? My God. He was doing the same thing to them that was done to him."

"Not the way he saw it. Besides, the boys he picked up might have been underage, but it was consensual. Illegal, yes, but consensual."

A groaning sound coming from the bed stopped the conversation. Lilly jumped up and ran over to her father, who was now awake. "Dad, would you like some water?"

The judge tried to sit up. Lilly helped prop him up in a sitting position, and gave him a cup with a straw. Gomez hardly recognized him. He'd lost so much weight and looked so pale. Lilly took the glass from her father's hands after he finished a few sips of water, and pointed to Officer Gomez. "Dad, you remember Officer Gomez, don't you?"

The judge turned toward Gomez, but the light from the

open curtains made it difficult for him to see. "I can't make out your face. Who are you?"

Lilly realized the light was too bright for her father, so she closed the curtains and turned on the light at the small table next to the bed. The judge squinted and reached for his glasses. "Of course. I remember you." Then a tear slid down his right cheek. "Did you ever find Kyle's killer?"

Lilly pulled up a chair and sat next to the bed. "Dad, Felipe called Officer Gomez to tell him to come to Ixtlan to talk to me. I think you should also hear what I have to say. I think I know who poisoned Kyle."

The judge motioned for Lilly to help him lie back down. He was clearly in pain from the open heart surgery. "Lilly, what are you saying? How could you possibly know? You've been at Caltech since before Kyle left Maui."

"I got a call the other day from Danny Leavenworth. Remember him from Maui? Kyle and I used to hang out together when we were kids?"

"Danny Leavenworth? All I remember is that he was always getting into trouble. Even had a juvenile record. Didn't his stepfather die in a hiking accident at Haleakala?"

"Yeah. Well, you don't know the whole story of why Kyle left Maui. It was because of Danny Leavenworth. He's the one who set the fire that killed Kyle's Aunt Molly. The police found a gold bracelet in the burnt rubble. A bracelet that Kyle had given Danny. Kyle called me when he knew the police were going to talk to him, and even though he knew he would be cleared, for some reason he needed me to cover for him. I agreed to say he and I were together that night."

The judge's face drained of what little color he had. "A gold bracelet?" Then he composed himself. "That was the night your mother ended up in emergency for a broken leg. Remember? You called me and said you were on the Big Island with a friend, and I said I'd go to the hospital."

"Yes, Dad. I was on the Big Island."

"I always wondered why you lied to the police when they came to the house. I knew you were covering for Kyle, but it wasn't any of my business." Then the judge paused, and in a slow, steady monotone he said, "Did you ever find out where Kyle was that night?"

"Yes. He told me he was doing tricks that night in front of the Butterfly Lounge."

The judge didn't say anything more. His eyes closed. He seemed like he couldn't handle any more information. Lilly motioned for all of them to leave the room. They went back into the kitchen and continued talking. Officer Gomez took out his notepad and wrote down everything that Lilly told him about her conversation with Danny Leavenworth. That Danny had called her out of the blue to ask how she was doing, and if she'd heard from Kyle. That she told him she hadn't heard from Kyle, but that before he disappeared, Kyle told her about recognizing the gold bracelet the police found at the scene of the fire. That Kyle knew Danny had set the fire, and meant to kill him. That Kyle was going to leave Maui and start a new life somewhere, to get away from Danny.

Gomez wrote furiously. He asked her if Danny knew she and the judge were at Ixtlan. Lilly took a breath and paused. "No. Definitely not. He said he missed the old days of the three fuckateers, then hung up the phone."

Gomez looked up from his notepad. "Did he say where he was living now, and what he was doing?"

"He said he'd been living in Miami, working at some plant nursery for the last four years."

"Miami. Can I see your cell phone? Which one is his number?"

Lilly read out the number Danny had called from. Gomez told her he'd get back to her after he talked to the Miami police. He wanted to know if she would be willing to fly to Miami with him to set up a meeting with Danny. It would be an undercover operation with her wearing a wire. She would try to get Danny to admit to setting the fire in Maui. That would be enough to arrest him. In any case, there would be undercover police nearby.

Lilly didn't say a word. Her deep-blue eyes darted back and forth like she was weighing her next few words. Then she blurted out. "I want to nail that bastard. I always knew he was a loose cannon, but now he's out of control. I'll help in any way I can."

Gomez stood up. "You'll have to call him back and tell him that you will be in Miami and want to see him. Do you think he'd go for that?"

"The sooner we nail that bastard, the better. For all I know, he's scheming up a way to intimidate me, maybe even kill me. He finished off Kyle, so maybe he figures I know too much and I'm his next victim. I could say I have a conference in Miami and that I could meet him for coffee somewhere."

"That would be perfect. I'll get back to you when I know more details. Meanwhile, take care of your father. It seems like the older we get, the more important family becomes, no matter what has gone on in the past."

Felipe smiled when he heard Gomez's comment. "Words well spoken."

Gomez was ready to leave. He was about to walk out of the bedroom when he thought of something else. He turned toward Lilly and said, "One last thing. Could you tell me what Danny Leavenworth looks like?"

Lilly looked up from her chair. "Danny? Sure. He has black curly hair, an unshaven look with black stubble, uh, and buck teeth." She laughed. "Kids used to tease him and Kyle. Called them Bucky Beaver and Reddylocks."

Gomez's body stiffened. *My God. It was Phillip Marker all the time. Right in front of my nose.* Gomez stumbled toward the door. Lilly asked him if he was all right, but he kept walking until he got to his car. He had to get back to City Hall. He needed to run the fingerprints again with Leavenworth's name. He needed to contact the Miami police ASAP. He needed to find out about jurisdiction. Leavenworth could be charged with arson, and with the murder of Molly Tanner in Maui. And he could be charged with murdering Tom Tanner in Tempe, if they got a match on the fingerprints. *And who knows what else he'd done?*

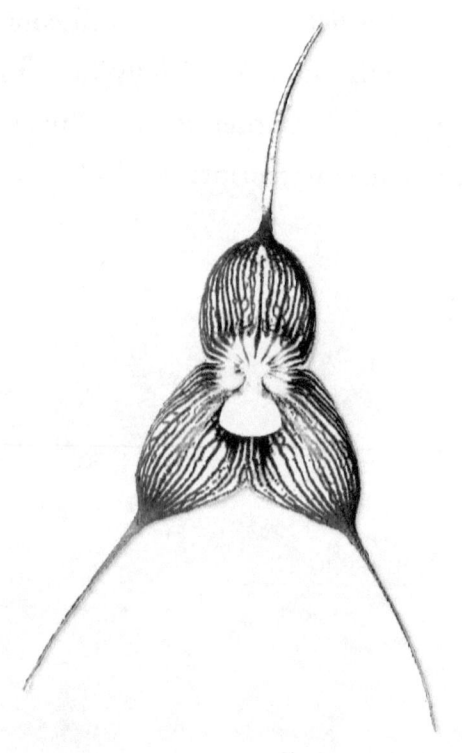

Chapter Nineteen

Undercover

They looked like an ordinary couple—Gomez, wearing a tan sport jacket and black slacks; Lilly, with a cotton summer dress and sandals. Gomez felt strange, as the plane took off. He hadn't been on a plane since he was in the police academy, when he took a trip to Las Vegas with a few buddies. And he'd never been away from Mary for more than a night, if he was working late on a case. He told Lucas that he had to go away for a few days on business. That he'd bring back a present from Florida. Lucas' comment was, "What's Florida?" Gomez tried to explain about there being different states besides Arizona, and that one day he would take Lucas to Disneyworld in Florida. Lucas had heard of Disneyworld. He seemed satisfied with his father's explanation and went off to play in the garden.

Lilly sat in the aisle seat, and after the plane took off she closed her eyes and fell asleep. Gomez, in the window seat, looked out as the plane ascended through the brown haze, still visible from the haboob. *Toward the heavens. Toward Jesús, toward Tom Tanner, and toward his father.* Gomez wondered if they were all watching him. If they knew what was about to happen.

The stewardess interrupted his thoughts when she asked him what he wanted to drink. Then, Lilly woke up and asked for black coffee. Gomez turned to Lilly and asked, "Are you sure you're up for this?"

"I'm fine. I always fall asleep on planes. The coffee will help."

Lilly started asking questions about the undercover operation. She had already called Danny, persuading him to meet her at a shopping mall in Miami, where undercover police from the Dade County Sheriff's Office could hide in plain sight while she wore a wire. She told Danny that she had a conference in Miami and could take a few hours off to meet him. Danny fell right into the trap. Said he couldn't wait to see Lilly again.

Gomez reassured her that she would be surrounded by undercover officers who would be able to hear her conversation with Danny. They could move in at any time and arrest him, but they wanted her to try to get him to talk about the Tanner murder.

Lilly sighed. "You said you got a fingerprint match this time. Right?"

"Yes. Under the name Danny Leavenworth, thanks to you."

Lilly hesitated. "So, can we have some kind of code word in case I start to feel scared? I haven't seen Danny in so long. I have no idea how crazy he's gotten. For all I know, he carries a weapon, or something."

"Yes. When we get to Miami, they will brief you on what to do. I'll need to stay out of sight, since he could recognize me."

Lilly closed her eyes again. "I think I need to sleep some more."

Gomez turned toward the window and gazed out at the cloudless blue sky. He tried to relax. The next few days would be crucial for him. He was already thinking about how this Tanner case had changed his life. Maybe one day he would tell Lucas about it, like his own father used to tell him about special cases. But first he needed to see how the undercover operation played out. Anything could happen.

ԳՑ ԳՑ ԳՑ ԳՑ

The plane landed, and an officer from the Dade County Sheriff's Office was standing at the baggage claim, holding a sign that read "Dade County Sheriff." He was wearing a uniform with a tan shirt and brown pants, unlike Gomez's uniform in Tempe, which was navy. The officer escorted them to his police car and drove them to a hotel near the International Mall. The meeting was to take place the next day at the food court. Danny had agreed to meet Lilly at 2:00 p.m., enough time for the officers to set Lilly up with a mic and wire and to test it.

Lilly wore a flowered cotton summer dress and carried a white cotton sweater in case the air-conditioning got too cold in the mall. She had a microphone and radio recording device taped to her chest. The device was so small that it was undetectable. Gomez watched as five plainclothes undercover officers tested the equipment. When Lilly felt secure, knowing that the police could hear her and she could hear them, they told her to order something to eat. Then one of the officers guided her to an empty table outside the food court, where she could be easily watched. Gomez waited inside one of the stores. Lilly sat at the table alone, waiting for Danny to show up. It was five past two when she noticed a handsome young man walking toward her. She didn't recognize him, but she whispered into the mic that someone was approaching her. The man was wearing a slick yellow blazer that looked like it was made of silk. He had on black slacks and a black shirt with a black-and-yellow striped tie. He wore dark sunglasses so Lilly couldn't make out his face. His blond hair was cropped on the sides and curly on top. He was clean-shaven. *This couldn't be Danny.*

The man approached Lilly, took off his sunglasses, and smiled. Lilly gulped. She hardly recognized him, except for the buck teeth. "Danny?"

"Yes. It's me. Didn't recognize me, did you?"

"My God, you look great."

Danny sat down at the table across from Lilly, with his back to the police. Lilly quickly scanned the area around her to make sure she could see the undercover officers from her vantage point. One police officer was sitting on a bench reading a paper, not far from the food court. One was sitting at a table nearby, reading a book and eating a hamburger. And one was standing by a popcorn stand ordering popcorn. Lilly started to relax. She asked Danny if he wanted to order any food. He said he would in a few minutes—that he wanted to sit for a while. Lilly started the conversation. "Danny, you dyed your hair. It looks great. What have you been up to?"

Danny fidgeted in his chair, then took out an electronic cigarette and blew out water vapor. Lilly couldn't contain herself. "I've never seen one of those. Do they work?"

Danny inhaled. "Better than nothing. Can't smoke anywhere these days. So far, no one's bothered me."

Lilly didn't know what else to ask Danny. She couldn't mention the Tanner murder yet. So, she said, "You obviously are making some money. You said you worked at a plant nursery. That can't pay much."

"Shit, no. It's minimum wage. I found another job, kind of like a consultant. That's where I make money."

"Wow. That's great. Consultant?"

"It's hard to explain. But, you know how I am good with chemicals and pesticides and all?"

Lilly remembered when Danny worked at the botanical gardens with his stepfather, and how he had access to chemicals and knew all about pest control. She realized this was the perfect time to mention the Maui fire. "Sure. I remember how you and Kyle and I talked behind Molly's greenhouses in our fort. You knew shitloads about chemicals."

Danny smiled and his buck teeth protruded, like when he was a kid. Lilly started to feel move relaxed. Memories of their childhood flooded her thoughts. She decided to take a risk, and mention Kyle again. "I miss Kyle. Why did he have to disappear after the fire? How could he do that to us?"

Danny's back stiffened. "So, have you heard from him?"

"Nothing. It's like he's disappeared from the face of the earth."

Danny adjusted his tie. "Well, I'm so glad you could meet me here. I miss the old days."

Lilly wondered what Danny was really into with his consulting job. He looked like he was dressed for the Italian mafia, or maybe as a pimp. Or maybe he changed his look to evade the police after he murdered Kyle. Then she said, "Look, Danny. I need to tell you something. I wasn't completely honest with you."

"What do you mean?"

"I saw Kyle just before he left Maui. He called me because he needed me as an alibi for the night of the fire." "Needed you for an alibi? Why?"

"Remember how we three used to cover for each other when we cut school or got in trouble?"

"Sure."

"Well, Kyle didn't want the cops to know he was on the streets in front of the Butterfly Lounge, doing tricks that night. So, I agreed to meet him to say we were together at my house. The Maui cops fell for it. They thought we were fucking."

Danny inhaled from the electronic cigarette. "You and Kyle? That's a joke."

"I know. But, he also told me that the cops found a gold bracelet left at the scene of the fire. He said it was the one he'd given you."

Danny's expression froze. Lilly noticed that familiar look of dissociation, like Danny had disappeared. Then she said, "Kyle left Maui because of you. He knew you were the one who started the fire. He knew you meant to kill him."

Danny slid his chair back. Lilly looked around to make

sure the undercover police were still there. Danny stood up and said, "Think I'll get something to eat. Want anything?"

Lilly realized that Danny was probably going to try to disappear. She quickly said the code word, "sweater," and four undercover cops walked over to Danny and without incident cuffed him and took him out of the mall. Danny didn't have time to make a scene. Gomez came out of one of the stores and escorted Lilly back to the hotel. It was over.

℞ ℞ ℞ ℞

Gomez had done his homework. He had already secured an arrest warrant, issued by a court in Arizona. He'd need to stay in Miami a few more days so he could testify before a magistrate judge, and persuade the magistrate that there was sufficient evidence to issue an order to extradite Leavenworth to Arizona. Gomez had already contacted the attorney general's office in Arizona to request extradition from Florida to Arizona. But it could take up to thirty days to complete the request and get it approved by the governor's office of Florida. Gomez knew the process was now out of his hands. Leavenworth would remain in jail in Florida until his appearance before a magistrate. At that point, he would hopefully agree to be extradited, rather than fighting extradition. Gomez knew this all could take time, so he sent Lilly back to Ixtlan to be with her father, and he made plans to return to Tempe as soon as his appearance before the Florida magistrate was finished.

At the airport in Miami, Gomez remembered to buy Lucas a present—a Miami Dolphins hat. He found some pearl earrings for Mary. The flight home was uneventful. In fact, the whole ordeal at the International Mall seemed uneventful. There was no huge arrest scene, no outbursts from Leavenworth, nothing. What did he expect? This wasn't some action movie. This was the Miami police doing a great job, following procedure.

When Gomez got home, it was well past midnight. Lucas was asleep, so he left the present by the bed on a nightstand, and went into his bedroom. Mary was asleep, but she woke up when she heard Gomez come in. She turned on the light and Gomez came over to kiss her. Mary told him how much she missed him and that she never wanted him to leave her again. Gomez gave her the earrings and crawled into bed. He was exhausted and told her they'd talk more in the morning.

ལ ལ ལ ལ

Over two months passed. Leavenworth fought extradition, which held things up even longer. But when a call came to Gomez's office that four police officers were needed to help transport Leavenworth back to Arizona, Gomez felt that surge of adrenalin again. He called the sheriff of Maricopa County and asked him to send four experienced deputies to Miami. Because Leavenworth fought extradition, he was considered dangerous, and since they would fly back to Tempe on a commercial airliner, the officers needed to be in plain clothes.

Leavenworth couldn't be handcuffed either, because of federal safety regulations, so this required four experienced men who had worked with extradition cases before. Gomez knew he couldn't go because Leavenworth would recognize him and could make a scene on the plane. But as soon as the Maricopa County deputies put Leavenworth into a Tempe jail cell, things would be different. He'd have Leavenworth all to himself. He'd nail that bastard for Tanner's murder, and hopefully for the fire at Maui and for Tanner's aunt's death. *And who knows what else he might confess to?*

The day had finally arrived. Gomez woke up extra early so he could dress, shave, and eat breakfast, ready to face Leavenworth. He had been preparing for this moment since his days with Palmer at the substation. He'd read so many books on psychopathic killers, and on ways of interrogating murder suspects, and on how to get inside the criminal mind. He'd use a technique called "suspect interrogation" where he could be free to use his own imagination, limited only by the laws and courts. And he certainly had a vivid imagination. When he was a kid, Jesús and he would sit in the garden and make up stories about their favorite super heroes. Jesús would start the story, then stop in mid-sentence so Gomez could continue. They'd use the names of the super heroes, but the story had to veer from the one they'd read in a comic book or seen in a movie. This led to outrageous plots with twists and turns, usually revealing their own internal struggles. But because no one ever heard their stories but them, they considered it their secret.

When Gomez got to the jail and headed toward the interrogation room where Leavenworth would be waiting, he felt another surge of adrenalin. He wondered if he was turning into an adrenalin junkie, like so many of his colleagues who seemed to live from murder to murder—the more gruesome, the better. When he arrived and saw Leavenworth through the one-way mirror, he hardly recognized him. It seemed that Leavenworth was like a chameleon, ever-changing. His peroxide, short-cropped hair was now shaven off completely. Stubble of dark roots had begun to pop out of the shiny surface of his scalp. He had on a jail uniform— a pink shirt and black-and-white striped pants, a brainchild of a past Maricopa County sheriff. Only the signature buck teeth gave him away. Gomez motioned for the officer who stood outside of the room. He opened the door and both of them went inside. The room was narrow, maybe six feet wide, with a one-way mirror.

Gomez sat down with his back to the mirror, so the prosecutor and police officers in the observation room would be able to observe Leavenworth's facial expressions as he responded to the questions. The other officer turned on the video recording equipment, and Gomez said, "Date, September 13, 2012. Time, 1:30 p.m. Place. Tempe Police Department jail, 235 E. 27th Street. Interview room four." Then Gomez looked directly at Leavenworth, took a deep breath, and began the interrogation.

"Mister Leavenworth, as you already know, I am Detective Gomez from the Tempe Police Department." He pointed to the other officer and said, "This is Officer White, also from the Tempe Police Department. I am here to ask you a few questions. Before I begin, I want you to state your full name, and date and place of birth."

Leavenworth kept his eyes focused on the metal table in front of him. Gomez repeated the question. Then, in a whisper, eyes still focused on the metal table, Leavenworth answered. Gomez took out a paper and put in front of Leavenworth. "Here is a signed statement that you already were read your Miranda Rights when the Dade County Sheriff arrested you at the International Mall in Miami. Is this your signature?"

Leavenworth nodded.

"We need you to speak your answer."

Leavenworth mumbled, "Yes."

"Do you understand why you have been arrested and extradited to Tempe?"

Suddenly, Leavenworth looked up and in a loud voice he said, "Not really. I don't know why the fuck I'm here, or why I've been held in that shit-hole of a jail in Miami. Who the fuck do you think you are? "

Gomez shoved another paper in front of Leavenworth, who started to tap his left foot on the floor while he fidgeted in his chair. The photo was of Tom Tanner. It showed him covered with a white sheet at the morgue, only his face visible, cherry-colored, like he'd been sunburned.

Gomez said, "Recognize him? It's your old buddy, Kyle O'Sullivan from Maui. Or Tom Tanner, as he was called here in Tempe."

Leavenworth didn't move. His eyes glazed over; the foot-tapping stopped.

"We now have a fingerprint match. We know that you were in Tom Tanner's house. We found your prints on the buttermilk carton in the refrigerator and on the handle of the refrigerator. Tom Tanner died because of cyanide poisoning. Cyanide was found in the buttermilk, and in his stomach contents."

Leavenworth sat motionless, eyes fixed on Gomez.

"Look, we know you and Kyle were once friends, back in junior high on Maui. According to Lilly Salmon, you were—well, fuck buddies. Right?"

Leavenworth looked up and began to glare into Gomez's eyes.

Gomez continued. "We also know that you were the one who set the fire on Tanner's aunt's property, and that the fire was meant to kill Kyle, not his aunt. Lilly told us that the gold bracelet, found at the scene of the fire, was the bracelet Kyle had given you. She also told us that the reason Kyle left

Maui was because he knew it was only a matter of time until you would try again. He left because of you, for God's sake. And you followed him all the way to Tempe, and then you put cyanide in the buttermilk and killed him. My God, what kind of a person would do that?"

By now, Gomez was screaming at Leavenworth. Maybe it was the years of pent-up emotion, or perhaps part of his interrogation technique. He wasn't ever sure why, but by the time he'd finished, Leavenworth had a look of terror on his face. Gomez sat down and composed himself. "Look, it's over. You'll get thirty to life for the Tanner murder, and then some, if they prosecute you for the fire at Maui, and Molly Tanner's death."

Leavenworth slumped onto the table and began to sway his upper body back and forth, as if wiping up a spill on the table top. Then he mumbled something incoherent under his breath. Suddenly, Leavenworth stood up, and with superhuman strength he lifted the metal table with both hands, still handcuffed, and pushed it toward Gomez. Officer White grabbed Leavenworth and put him in a choke-hold until help arrived. Gomez left the interrogation room while they tried to subdue Leavenworth.

☙ ☙ ☙ ☙

Fifteen minutes passed. Leavenworth calmed down, and Gomez started the interview again. This time Officer White was standing directly behind Leavenworth, and there were three more policemen in the room with them. Gomez sat across from Leavenworth and started the video again, stating the time the interview had stopped, and why, and the new time it began. He was about to say something when Leavenworth started muttering again. This time it was less incoherent. "How could she do this to me? I thought she was my friend. The three fuckateers. Bonded for life. I loved him. Why did you tell me about Haleakala? I can't trust you anymore. You deserve to die. To die...to die...to die."

Gomez watched as Leavenworth began to unravel. Was this a confession? He interrupted Leavenworth's muttering and said, "Who deserved to die?"

"He knew too much. They knew too much."

"Who knew too much?"

"The fort, Haleakala. I loved him. He had to die."

"Who had to die? Tanner? Kyle?" Just then Gomez realized that Lilly was watching from the observation room. "Lilly?"

"She visited me after I pushed him. She was my only friend besides Kyle. She came to the foster home. Why did she turn on me?"

"Pushed who? What do you mean?"

Leavenworth was now muttering under his breath. Gomez left the room and asked that a doctor be brought in to sedate him. There was nothing he could do until Leavenworth was able to resume the interrogation. He went into the observation room and motioned for Lilly to come out. She was in tears. He asked her if she knew what Leavenworth meant when he referred to Haleakala. Her face was already drained of color. She said she needed to sit somewhere, so Gomez took her to the lounge and got her a coffee. Lilly tried to speak, but the words got stuck in her throat. Then she said, "He killed him. My God. It wasn't an accident. He pushed him off Haleakala."

Gomez took out his notepad. "Haleakala? What is it?"

"It's one of the highest mountains on Maui. Danny's stepfather used to hike it on Sundays to watch the sunrise. It was an accident. He slipped and plunged to his death. Danny was a mess afterward. He was sent to a foster home. He was only fourteen or so."

"You don't think it was an accident, do you?"

"No. I guess Danny got away with murder. He must have pushed his stepdad off the cliff."

"So, do you think Kyle had anything to do with it?"

"I don't know. Maybe. After that, Kyle and I hardly saw each other. He changed somehow. And he and Danny never saw each other much either. Then after the fire, Kyle called me to be his alibi. I always covered for him. We were the three fuckateers. We always helped each other."

"How would Kyle have been involved?"

Lilly wiped her tears and blew her nose into a tissue. "Maybe he knew about it and promised Danny he'd never tell. Maybe he even gave Danny the idea. Danny was always saying his stepfather said the reason he hiked up Haleakala was to keep Danny in line. After Danny's mother died, his stepfather turned into an alcoholic who abused Danny all the time. Who knows? Danny and Kyle were both screwed-up teenagers then. Anything is possible."

Gomez stopped writing and looked up. "So, Danny killed his own stepfather, Tom Tanner, Tom's Aunt Molly, and God knows who else."

☙ ☙ ☙ ☙

The next day, Leavenworth was brought back into the same interrogation room. Gomez planned to continue where he left off. Leavenworth seemed much calmer now, maybe on medication, but in any case he was deemed able to continue with the interrogation. Gomez pulled out his notepad and began. "Mister Leavenworth, I hope you are feeling better today. I have just a few more questions to ask you. Yesterday you said, and I quote, 'He knew too much. He had to die.' Who were you referring to?"

This time Leavenworth wasn't looking down at the metal table. He was looking directly into Gomez's eyes. "He's inside you. I see his blue eyes looking at me. He's come back to haunt me."

Gomez was taken aback. "Who is inside me? Tanner?"

In an eerie voice, Leavenworth started to rant, "His blue eyes are looking at me right now. He's in there. He's in there. Oh my God." Leavenworth started choking and gasping for air. "He's come for me. Help! I deserve to die. Deserve to die. I didn't mean to kill you, but you know I had to. You knew too much, too much." Then he stopped screaming and began to hum a melody that sounded like a nursery rhyme. Gomez knew that Leavenworth was either having a psychotic breakdown or was damn good at making it look like one. Either way, he knew he couldn't continue the interrogation. He motioned for help, and the medics took Leavenworth out of the room. He'd most likely be given a psych-eval, and returned to jail, probably on suicide watch.

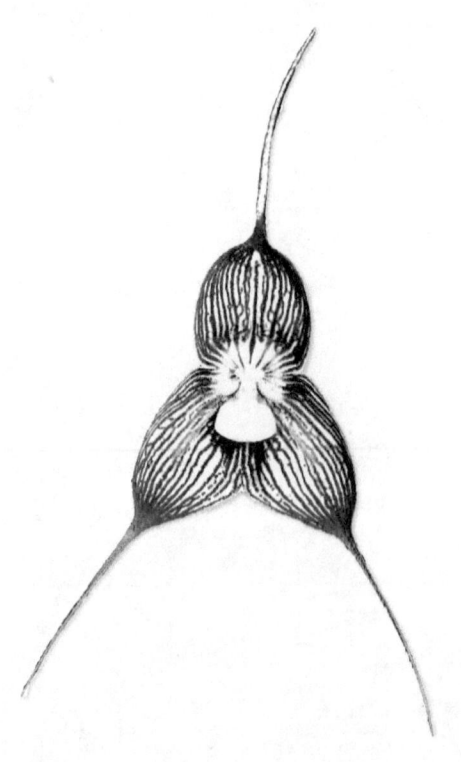

EPILOGUE

The wise deer stands directly in front of Lucas, who reaches out to touch the deer's black nose. Two deep blue eyes peer into Lucas' brown ovals. Soul to soul, the two greet each other. Out of the black of night, the deer's body begins to shimmer with yellow light. Lucas tells the deer that he thought deer had brown eyes. The deer smiles and says, "The truth has set us free."

Gomez woke from the dream. It was still dark outside. He walked into the garden and sat on a bench in front of Jesús' memorial fountain. There was no light from the moon because of a thick cloud cover. The sound of water trickling over the rocks always comforted Gomez. He reflected on his strange dream. Blue eyes. The deer had blue eyes. Lucas saw blue eyes. Leavenworth saw blue eyes, Tanner's eyes. Somehow, Gomez knew that Tanner and he were connected, maybe soul to soul. Just like the dream. After a few minutes, he got up and went to check on Lucas, who was sleeping peacefully in bed. The next morning he was at the kitchen table reading over some of his notes when the phone rang. It was Sergeant Bailer. He told Gomez the good news on the phone, but he wanted him to come to City Hall to help process Leavenworth's paperwork. Leavenworth's confessions to three murders were considered legal. After a thorough psychological evaluation, Leavenworth was considered psychologically fit. His antics in the interrogation room were fake. Good acting. Lots of practice lying, no doubt. He would be able to receive legal counsel. He would receive a plea agreement between the prosecution and the defense attorney. Since Leavenworth didn't have sufficient funds to hire an attorney, a public defender would be appointed for him. He'd probably receive thirty years to life for the Tanner murder. If he were to be convicted for the fire, Molly Tanner's death, and his stepfather's death on Maui, he could end up with concurrent sentencing. Either way, Leavenworth would be off the streets for good. After an exhausting day at City Hall, Gomez left for home, knowing that soon, he'd never have to deal with the Tanner case again. It was over.

He walked into his house well after midnight. His body was exhausted but his mind was still racing. The house was dark, except for the nightlight coming from Lucas' bedroom. Gomez tiptoed down the hallway and entered his son's room. He reached down and gave Lucas a kiss on the forehead, then sat in a chair next to the bed. Moonlight cascaded through the sheer curtains covering the window, and as Gomez watched his son sleep he remembered the lullaby his mother used to sing to him. He wanted to sing it to his son, but he didn't want to wake him. He looked down at Yaqui, sleeping on the floor next to the bed, and began humming. Somehow, he couldn't stop himself. Then he began singing the words. It was the same lullaby that his mother sang in the hospital, when he'd had the exposure to the toxic mold.

Yaqui came over and curled up next to Gomez, and for a few moments the two of them sat in silence as the moonlight flooded the room. Then, Gomez got up and walked outside into the garden with Yaqui following. Gomez reached to take off Yaqui's collar. He looked at the dog tag that still read "Rover." *I need to change this.* He put the tag on top of one of the stones on the fountain, next to the picture of Jesús. Then, he turned toward Yaqui, who was lying at the base of the fountain. "I think it's time for you to get another dog tag with your new name, Yaqui."

Yaqui looked up at Gomez and yawned. Gomez continued. "Without your master, I never would have found out the truth about my own family. You have the honor of representing Tom Tanner alongside my brother." Then Gomez walked over to the hammock under the palo verde tree and lay down. The pungent odor of honeysuckle burst into the night air, blurring his senses. Gomez closed his eyes, and a kaleidoscope of images danced around in his head as he began to relax for the first time in days.

A dog made of sand, that Tanner named Yaqui. A gold

bracelet. Jesús strumming the guitar next to him in the garden. His brother lying in a pool of his own blood. Tom Tanner lying face down on his bed. Mold from the carpet crawling up Tanner's arm. The dog, half-dead at the foot of the bed. The peace pipe in Tanner's closet. Felipe Youngblood. The judge. Lilly. Lucas sleeping peacefully. The wise deer. The Dracula vampira orchid. The word Shadowdreamer scrolling in front of his eyes, like ribbons of bright yellow sunlight against the contrasting purple-black of night.

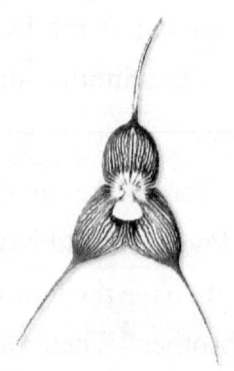

ABOUT THE AUTHOR

J.S.Bodin, a retired educator and award winning author and poet, received her Ph.D. in Multicultural Teacher Education from the University of New Mexico. Her novel, *Walking Fish*, won the New Mexico Book Award and the International Book Award in gay/lesbian fiction. Her book of poems, *Piggybacked*, was a finalist in the New Mexico/Arizona Book Awards. Her poems have appeared in various anthologies and literary publications. She plays jazz piano and is a watercolor hobbyist.

See her websites at: www.walkingfishnovel.com. and www.joannebodin.com. Email at: jbodinauthor@gmail.com.